Praise for
Carolyn Wall's debut
SWEEPING UP GLASS

Winner of the Oklahoma Book Award

"This extraordinary debut novel, both a 'what happened' and a 'whodunit,' explores survival and the guilt that can accompany it. The writing is filled with arresting images, bitter humor, and characters with palpable physical presence. The fresh voice of that clear-eyed narrator reminded me of Scout in Harper Lee's *To Kill a Mockingbird*. I literally could not put it down."
—*The Boston Globe*

"By the end this rich literary portrait of a woman and a place unexpectedly transforms into a surprise-filled thriller."
—*The New York Times*

"If it seems implausible for reviewers to compare the almost-unknown writer Carolyn Wall of Oklahoma City with Harper Lee, Flannery O'Connor, and Charles Portis, you haven't read her debut novel."
—*The Courier-Journal*

"This is a perfect little book, like a head-on collision between Flannery O'Connor and Harper Lee, with a bit of Faulkner on a mystery binge. I loved every page of it. Just my kind of book."
—JOE R. LANSDALE, Edgar Award winner

PLAYING WITH MATCHES

PLAYING

A Novel

WITH MATCHES

Carolyn Wall

BANTAM BOOKS TRADE PAPERBACKS

NEW YORK

A Bantam Books Trade Paperback Original

Copyright © 2012 by Carolyn D. Wall

Published in the United States by Bantam Books, an imprint of The Random House Publishing Group, a division of Random House, Inc., New York.

BANTAM BOOKS and the rooster colophon are registered trademarks of Random House, Inc.

Library of Congress Cataloging-in-Publication Data
Wall, Carolyn D.
Playing with matches : a novel / Carolyn Wall.
p. cm.
ISBN 978-0-345-52569-7—ISBN 978-0-345-53439-2 (eBook)
1. Mute persons—Fiction. 2. Prisons—Fiction. 3. Mississippi—Fiction. I. Title.
PS3623.A35963P53 2012
813'.6—dc22   2011032703

Printed in the United States of America

www.bantamdell.com

2 4 6 8 9 7 5 3 1

Text design by Virginia Norey

This book is for
Darrell, Bill, Melvin, Harold, Ron,
Charles, Jack, Lloyd, and Doug, with love.
All these years, I don't know what
I would have done without you.

Thy people shall be my people.
—*Ruth 1:16*

PLAYING WITH MATCHES

1

If there's help for the little guy—for my Harry, who won't talk—it'll be north on a green elbow of the slow-moving Pearl River. But that's the one place in the world I cannot go. It would mean the chicken circus, the boy who lived in the tree. The burning bed. Hell's Farm and the curse of Millicent Poole.

Wherever we go, Thomas Ryder will come after us—won't he? I hope he's frantic and sorry, and that he never finds us. But I'm waffling in my thinking. In this tiny motel room with the worn-thin rug and the rusty washbasin, it's been a long night. The storm has played out. I leave one candle burning.

But oh, God, Harry's neediness points me upriver. It steers me home.

The candle sputters out. In the stifling dark of after-storm, I kiss my children's damp foreheads, and I pray for three things:

Jerusha will remember me.

She'll do for my Harry.

And she'll care for them both while I'm locked away.

2

"Upriver" is Potato Shed Road—dusty shotgun houses and run-down duplexes, folks backed up to False River and poor as Job's aunt. Miss Jerusha Lovemore's place was a good ways along, a clapboard house with two floors, a small attic, and a crooked turret.

It was widely known that Jerusha once worked for a chicken circus up in Haynesville. What exactly she did there seems a subject best left for adult conversation. In the end, though, she took up a riding crop and thwacked the ringmaster, in the name of the Lord.

Then she bought an old car and putted down through the long green state of Mississippi, heading for the town of False River, where her sister lived. She used a chunk of her circus-earned money to buy the big house, and she settled in. Rapidly, she grew to know her neighbors. Her years under the big top had done her no harm because she beat her rugs regular and went to church on Sunday. She put up bread-and-butter pickles and was a right hand at turning out sweet-potato pie and jalapeño corn bread.

Past Auntie's place was a narrow field of weedy grass, and then the bony old house that belonged to my mama.

I, Clea Shine, was born in Mama's kitchen—on the table, so as not to ruin the sheets upstairs—and I lived there for one hour and ten minutes. It took Mama that long to get down off the table, clean herself up, and step into her high heels. Then she carried me, in a wicker laundry basket, over to Jerusha's.

I picture Mama wobbling off through the brown grass, wrapped in a sweater, for it was coming on winter.

Poor Auntie, as I came quickly to call Jerusha. I was chicken-legged skinny and already howling for my dinner. She couldn't have known beans about foundlings and such. And I was a handful.

But her sister, the broad-in-the-beam Miss Shookie Lovemore, was herself raising up a fat daughter called Bitsy, and Miss Shookie knew all there was to know about everything.

For a long time, in those days, I had not a tooth in my mouth nor a hair on my head and according to Miss Shookie, I cried all the time. I must have given Aunt Jerusha one everlasting headache. Still, she held fast to my hard little body, and rocked me long, and hummed slow, quiet streams of things like *We. Shall. Not. Be. Moved.*

At nine months I came near strangling with the whooping cough, and while I crouped and hawked up phlegm and sucked air, Auntie dangled me by the heels over the kitchen sink. For three weeks, she fed me with an eyedropper, slapped mustard plasters on my chest, and whomped my back with the pink palm of her hand. At least once each night, she pinched my nose and blew in my mouth just to keep my lungs going.

And all that time, Mama was across the field. Auntie couldn't help but hear the piano music pouring from there, and I wonder if that noisome key-plunking helped or hindered her in laying this white child down to sleep. It was my lullaby, but maybe Auntie cursed the racket and hated my mama and all the men who came there—prison guards, mostly, but others too, looking for a fine time. Mama obliged them. She was a tireless thing and could drink and dance and laugh all night. For a few dollars, she laid the men down.

My earliest memory could be nothing but a trick that my brain played on itself. I seem to recall Auntie's front window being propped up in the hope of a breeze. Inside, I rested my chin on the sill—and thrust out my tongue to receive a drop of whiskey, amber in the moonlight and tasting like butterscotch. It could not have happened, of course, because Auntie kept screens on her windows. Still . . .

Sometimes she and I sat on the upstairs gallery, cracking beans into plastic bowls, *snap snap*. From there, we could see Mama drifting out into the yard, lithe as a willow and throwing slops, her yellow hair backed by the sun glinting off the wires of the Mississippi state penitentiary, another quarter-mile on, at the end of the road.

In the heat of the day, Auntie draped a sheet over our upstairs gallery rail, and there we sat, her in her slip and me in my undies, overseeing the dirt road and the prisoners working the far fields in their orange suits, while even the dust shimmered in the heat. Toward the end of the day, we watched guards in gray uniforms park in Mama's yard. Sometimes she'd greet them at the door—the river wind lifting her pink feather boa. Her silver-heeled slippers winked like glass in the twilight.

The weeds grew tall around Mama's place, and the upstairs

windows cracked and fell out. I suppose the place looked spook-
ier than all get-out, because teenagers drove by and threw rotten
fruit. They chanted things I could not understand, and spray-
painted words on the peeling clapboard.

I determined I would learn to read those things. They might
tell me something about my mother. Maybe in my heart I already
knew what those words said, because, while I grew lankier and
clumsier with my long legs and feet, the worst of me was a wide,
smart mouth. It spewed chatter and backtalk. Lying was neither
harder nor easier than telling the truth. In fact, all my growing-up
years, I maintained an unholy attitude for which Auntie whipped
my calves with a green willow switch, and I deserved every
whack.

Still, I wasn't a complete loss. I taught myself to read early on
and was a smart hand at filling a basket with blueberries.

By the time I was four, my hair had grown dark, unlike Mama's, and thick as a broom. When Auntie tried to drag a comb
through it, I screamed and stomped so that she braided it and
wound thick pigtails, like rope, around my head. It was sometimes two weeks before she took down the plaits, saddled up
with a comb, and rode into that rat's nest. The rest of the time,
my loose, fuzzy hair stuck out in all directions.

Later, my friend Finn told me that when the sun shone just
right, I looked to be wearing a golden halo. But it was like Finn to
say that. He was kinder than me, and he never killed anybody.

3

Next to Auntie, I loved Uncle Cunny best. He was no true relation but was a collector and seller of metal junk, and he tended to Auntie's house and drove over in his pickup truck two or three times a week. He plowed and built a back porch and nailed up shingles, and Auntie paid him in meals and by sewing buttons on his shirts.

But Uncle Cunny Gholar and Sister Shookie did not get along. Nobody got along well with Miss Shookie Lovemore.

After Sunday service, she and Auntie would tie on their aprons, and while they peeled potatoes and rolled out biscuit dough, they hissed and spat and fought royally. When she was riled, Miss Shookie quoted the Bible wrong, trifling with the Beatitudes until they suited her. Auntie laughed at her, but Miss Shookie kept her own commandments, calling my mother a sodomite and me the devil's babe.

Uncle and Miss Shookie went at it like cats, she creating scripture and Uncle calling her a sanctimonious sow.

Then Miss Shookie'd let loose with "You rusty old sinkhole" and "Pass the biscuits, you goddamned sinner."

Uncle Cunny Gholar was opposed to all things religious. He

declared himself a heathen to the core. So when Miss Shookie went to beating the table with her fork and laying down vague laws of the Old Testament, he'd arch his brows and look away like something more important had caught his eye. That sent Miss Shookie into a royal tear. One time she beaned him with her cast-iron skillet, clonking him good during a funeral dinner at the Oasis of Love Bingo Hall and Prison Camp Center.

The Center, in our closest town of False River, was a low square building with a sloped tin roof, and everything important happened there.

The racket, back in the kitchen, woke things up and spewed blood all around. For a while it looked like Uncle's funeral might be next. But Reverend Ollie helped Uncle into his Buick and drove him to Greenfield while Auntie and I sat in the back and pressed cloths to his head.

The doctor in Greenfield said Uncle would live, and Auntie, who'd been wringing her hands and praying to Jesus, slapped Uncle a good one.

"Fool!" she said. "You know better than to stand in the face of my sister!"

Even with twelve new stitches lacing his scalp, Uncle was not deterred. At one o'clock the next Sunday, he stepped in our back door, doffed his felt hat, and said, "Miss Shookie, you're looking particularly ravaged today."

"You hell-bent old fart," she shot back, peeling skins from a soft-baked yam.

"And you have the tongue of a spinster viper," he said.

"Well, I *never!*" Miss Shookie's chins bobbled mightily.

"Then it's plain you *ought* to," Uncle Cunny replied, ignoring the paring knife in her hand. "You'd feel considerably better if you did."

Aunt Jerusha sent Uncle the evil eye, and the conversation turned to the dreadful humidity we'd been having lately. Like the air wasn't a wet blanket every day of our lives.

In spring, the rain poured down and the False River rose up. The shallows crept into the yard and covered the chicken run and the vegetable garden with a thick layer of river trash and muddy ooze. In the following days, while we slogged around in rubber boots, hundreds of brilliant wildflowers bloomed on the river-bank and in our yard.

But the mud was a nuisance. Annually, I lost my shoes in the muck, causing Auntie to decree that I could just go without. Every time, though, Uncle Cunny drove me in to False River and treated me to a pair of ugly brown lace-ups from the Ninety-Nine Cent Store.

When the crops came up, I scrambled between wire-basketed tomatoes, chasing fat white worms back into the ground and tearing the patches off my overalls. Thereafter I was consigned to pillow-slip dresses and finally hopsacking, until Miss Shookie and Bitsy brought a cardboard box of washed-out hand-me-downs. I wore them with great pain—especially on Sundays.

The folks in False River were a holy lot, grounded in the Lord and the First and Last Holy Word Church. On Sunday mornings, Sunday nights, and for Wednesday prayer meetings, I wore Bit-sy's old dresses. I fidgeted beside Auntie in that hard church pew and learned that *We shall not be moved* ran together in one whole sentence. Still, I liked the way Auntie sang it, as if each word was truly the first and last holy sound.

Sometimes the Best Reverend Ollie Green came to dinner. He was a single man—round of face and shiny black, spiffed up in his striped suit with a flash of pocket-hankie color. He was loved by his congregation and could lift his voice to a pitch that shook our teeth. On an apple-pie Sunday, with Uncle Cunny at the head of our table and Ollie Green at the foot, I asked why he was called the *Best Reverend*.

While Miss Shookie and her pudding of a daughter helped themselves to the choicest parts of two fried hens, Miss Shookie gave the Reverend a beatific smile. "While some preachers are fair at divining and o-rating, others are better. We are fortunate as hell to have the best."

Dressed in his own natty suit, Uncle Cunny grinned.

I, too, depended on the Reverend.

More than anything, I longed to read. Words called my name. Because I wasn't old enough to go to school, the Reverend Ollie lent me volumes from the church library. After a while, Auntie asked Uncle to come twice a week in the afternoons and pursue other segments of my early education.

I excelled at three things—reading, backtalking, and making things up. With his pencil-thin mustache, and his pencil-thin self got up in a fine blue suit, Uncle sat across from me at the domino table. He taught me the basics of arithmetic.

My attitude toward numbers was simple: I could add as quick as I could scramble up the porch roof—but I would not subtract, and he could not make me. In my chair under the willow, I moaned and held my braid-wound head like an old lady with a migraine. "Uncle Cunny, why would we take perfectly good things away?"

"Girl, you are four years old, going on five," he said. "With a mind like a mousetrap, and the cheese just waitin'. If I tell you there are—" he held up his ringed fingers to count "—eleven trees on this property, and we take away three, you know there would be eight left."

"But, Uncle, these are beautimous trees, and—"

"The word is *beautiful*, Miss Clea."

"—they've been growing here longer than Auntie has, longer than her fat sister, and—"

"That's no way to speak of Sister Shookie," he said mildly.

I wiggled in my chair, then got up on my knees, put my elbows on the table, and leaned across. "But that's how *you* speak of her, and have you noticed, Uncle, that her name truly fits her? When she walks, she shakes like a bowl of Jell-O. I can't hardly eat the stuff without thinking of her bosoms."

I could see he was trying not to smile. If he'd let his mustache thicken, Uncle would be better at covering a mouth that gave away his feelings.

"The point I am makin'," he said, "is that there are eleven trees, and—"

"—An' we love these trees dearly. We ain't taking away any."

"*Aren't*," he said.

"Right. But I can tell you that if we planted four more we'd have fifteen, and if seven seedlings came up after, there'd be twenty-two."

Uncle sighed, as he seemed often to do.

I hated mathematics. In the evenings, I'd sit in the parlor with my head against Uncle's bony knee. Auntie clicked her knitting needles across the room and broke up our fights over five times four. The six times tables were ass-kickers to recite.

What I really wanted to do was kiss both their cheeks and scoot upstairs to bed. Then I'd sneak out my window, shinny down the back porch post, and make my way through the weeds to Mama's house, where I'd curl up on a cot, which I thought of as my own. Mama kept it on the back porch. I couldn't stay away from her house; as much as I loved Auntie, I just wanted to go home. On Mama's porch cot, I'd sit with my knees pulled up and hugging them tight. From there, I could hear my grandma's piano, and the burble of gin, and the sounds from inside, of what real loving was like.

4

On her side of the field, Mama's house was tight and hunched like a buzzard's beak; Auntie's was broad and gracious as a southern belle. I was never sure which one to call home.

I told myself I didn't care that I had no real place at Mama's, except on the long slatted space across the back of the house, where the screens were caved in. On my tiptoes, from there, I could see through the kitchen window. I loved to watch my mama move around the place—opening a drawer, smoothing a stocking, her long, fine fingers lifting a glass to the light. She was elegant to observe, cinch-waisted and graceful and delicate of bone. Her clothes hung prettily, like she'd stepped out of a magazine. Her pale hair was wavy, and even in the dry heat of summer, not one strand was out of place. I loved how her red lips parted when she spoke to gentlemen friends, her chin and neck sculpted from smooth white stone.

Sometimes she caught me and shooed me away. Other nights, I could have entered that house, poured a drink, and sat down, and she would never have seen me. I'd stand on the porch and study my arms and legs and wonder how she could possibly look right through me.

On rare occasions, we'd go upstairs and sit at her vanity. I wondered if I looked enough like her that folks would know I was her girl. One bad night, when she'd drunk herself to sleep and woke to find me staring, she leapt from the sofa and split my lip. Another time, she broke my thumb. Auntie called Uncle, and they drove me, grim and silent, to the doctor in Greenfield.

And still I went back. As time went by, more and more loving was performed on Mama's porch. One night I hid under the cot and waited till the grunting and smacking and pushing ended, Mama screaming so fiercely that I closed my eyes and stuck my fingers in my ears.

"Damn, honey," said the man who was with her. "'Pears to be somethin' under this bed."

Mama dragged me out while I banged my heels on the boards, and delivered a backhand that sent me tumbling. "Goddamn kid," she said.

Her scarlet nails had caught the side of my face. I could already feel swelling along my cheekbone, and a throbbing had set up just below my temple. I scrambled to my feet.

"Jesus Christ, look at you," Mama said. "Wearin' a goddamn pillow slip."

I said, "Jesus Christ, look at you, wearing nothin' at all!"

"That is my business." She pulled a sheet from the cot and covered her parts.

But the gent on the bed had his gray guard pants shoved to his knees, his own parts pale and slick, his hands grabbing for my mother. "Come here, Clarice," he said. "Let the girl watch if she wants."

"The girl doesn't want," Mama said, wiggling her feet into spiky-heeled shoes, and as I scooted down the steps, she aimed a kick at my backside with one pointy toe.

"Light me a damn cigarette," I heard her say to the guard.

On that particular night, Auntie stood in the yard with her hands on her hips. "How many times you got to hear it, girl? How many thrashings it gonna take? Don't go near that place! You ain't come back yet without bruises to show."

And she set off through the grass to stand tall against my mother.

※

Mississippi women could display gentility, but they were physical too, and purebred tough. Always, Auntie'd return with her hair disarranged and her eyes wide, and breathing hard. Then she'd sit in the parlor, wooden rockers screaming while she shot back and forth. I'd climb on her lap and curl into a ball, and she'd hold my sad self with her two strong arms.

When I felt truly lost—which was most of the time—I went out to the narrow lot and sat down in the weeds. From there I could observe both houses. After all, I had two eyes, didn't I? Two nostrils, two arms, two knobby knees.

The trouble was, I had only one heart.

※

One of Mama's customers carried a yellow valise.

Mama waggled her fingers at me. "Come on in here, girlie girl, and meet this young man."

I'd held back in the dark kitchen, but now I stepped forward.

"You work at the Farm?" I said conversationally, meaning the prison.

"Not anymore. I am not givin' this state another day of my labor."

"But—you're an ex-con? You've seen it inside?"

I had an inordinate curiosity about the Stuart P. Havellion State Penitentiary. It was one old plantation house and a tight bundle of outbuildings, all set on concrete blocks and surrounded by chain-link and razor wire. In the beginning it was a river-backed home, with four square miles of cotton fields that flooded every year. Piece by piece, they sold it off. Now the prison and its remaining land were called Hell's Farm.

Further, Webster defined ex-con as *freedom from conviction*.

"Guess I'll be gettin' on," the young man said. "They told me the bus comes through False River."

"On Saturdays and Sundays," I said. "You got three days to wait."

He shrugged into his thin coat. "Well, then, how far away's the next town?"

"Hour or two, if you got a car. We got a railroad station in False River, but my Uncle Cunny says trains haven't run here in twenty years."

"You know a lot," he said.

"It's a fact, I do."

The young man pulled a twenty-dollar bill from his pocket. "They give me two a' these this morning." He handed the bill to my mama. "The other one's got to do me till I get home."

"I'll walk with you a ways," I said when we went out. I pointed down the dusty road.

"Yes, ma'am," he said with a kind of bark. "I been the other way. Now I'm headin' for Memphis. You heard of that?"

"Tennessee. On the Mississippi River."

"Well, now," he said.

"You got a mama and a daddy up there?"

"I got a daddy."

"He know you been here?"

"You ask a lot of questions, missy. And no, ma'am," he said softly. "My daddy don't know I been here."

My heart ached for this former convict who could turn out to be a fountain of information. I wanted to know if what I'd heard was true—that the state swooped in and broke the whole house into cells. That a central basement had been dug underneath and fitted with instruments of torture.

It was commonly known that at Hell's Farm, the walls ran with moisture while the prisoners alternately baked with the heat and then came down sick with the damp.

"What did you do?" I asked him. "What was your crime?"

He looked down at me. "You don't want to know about that."

"Yes, I do."

"No, ma'am, you don't. Nobody goes to prison for anything good." He jerked a thumb to our right. "I guess that there's the actual False River?"

"You haven't *seen* it before?"

"No, ma'am. Not in the whole ten years. We didn't have windows where we stayed."

"Well," I said. "There's a creek on the other side of the farm. It's got real steep sides, and it's heaped with jagged boulders, and it floods in spring."

"Yes, ma'am, we sure know about flooding."

Personally, I thought it was a good place for a prison. The creek on one side and the river on the other would make it near impossible to escape. "Did you ever think about escaping?" I said.

"That's all we ever thought about," he said.

I kicked up more dust. "Did you ever try?"

"I did not. Nobody wants to be set upon by prison dogs—they got bad tempers and real sharp teeth."

"Did you have visitors?"

Everybody knew the assigned hours at Hell's Farm. On Saturday mornings and Sunday afternoons, junky cars puttered up and down the road, or families walked with brown-paper packages under their arms.

"No, ma'am."

"If I'd known you were there, I'd have come to see you."

"I reckon your mama wouldn't a' let you."

In that moment, I longed to deny the existence of my own mama. I recalled the Best Reverend Ollie telling us how Peter denied Jesus three times—and all before the cock crowed in the morning! Still, I was nothing like Peter, and my mama was not Jesus.

"It's what Aunt Jerusha says that counts," I told him. "She's real friendly. And smart. You ought to talk to her. You've got no place to stay and no money to speak of."

I was on fire with an idea. Nothing else could crowd into my head. He would stay with us and tell me everything, and I would write it all down so as not to forget.

"Missy," he said. "I ain't traveling back on this road for nothing."

"But you need a bed to sleep in, and a job of work so you can make some money and get home to your family in Tennessee—"

A car motor coughed. I looked around and saw Miss Shookie chugging down the road, heading toward us in her Chevrolet. Bitsy was beside her, and both were hunch-necked and squinty-eyed with curiosity. Miss Shookie leaned out a side window that hadn't rolled up since 1967.

"What y'all doin' here, girl? You take up with strangers, your aunt whup you alive."

"Miss Shookie, this man's starting a new life, and I was offering him a stay at our house till he gets on his feet —"

"He is on his feets, looks to me," she said. "Now, you git in this car, I'll take you home. Jerusha let you run so goddamn wild—"

But my own feet were planted solid in the dirt. "No, ma'am, Miss Shookie. This young man needs a firm chance, and anyway, I'm not getting in that smelly old thing."

"Don't make me get outa this car, girl," she said, looking pained. "All day, my knees been talkin' to me—"

She turned her attention to my companion. "So you fresh outa the joint, hey, boy? They give y'all's clothes back to you, do they?"

"Yes, ma'am."

"I told my gal Bitsy, here, they used them to stoke the fires of hell. You gone and made a liar outa me."

My jaw slacked. "Miss Shookie, the Christian thing to do—"

Miss Shookie's fat jiggled and rolled around. "Ain't no Christians at Hell's Farm, Clea June, and I know he's broke as a church mouse already. By the time these mens set out on this road, they money's spent.

"And everybody knows where."

5

I waited for the ax to fall. But, to my amazement, Uncle Cunny helped that young man up in his truck and drove him clear to Jackson. There, he told us later, he bought him a grilled cheese at a soda fountain and saw him off on a bus.

The weekend came around.

As always, I wore one of Bitsy's colorless castoffs to church. Those dresses hung on me but were ruffled and made of organdy, and that, Auntie said, counted for something.

After church on Sundays, I learned more than I did at any other time in my life.

That day, Miss Shookie was working alongside Auntie, cooking and sweating till their faces shone and their sweetly oiled hair was further kinked and matted to their shapely heads.

The night before, Auntie had simmered greens with butter, vinegar, ham hocks, and black pepper. Over those pots of steaming collards and thick custards, the bickering grew worse, and before long they were stomping around the hot kitchen, hip-shoving and wagging fingers and rubber spatulas. The subject turned to the chicken circus. I took a quiet seat at the table. This was a subject I ached to know more about.

It was said that Auntie had run away, when she was younger, and joined a traveling show. I could not imagine my steadfast Auntie doing such a thing, let alone what chicken circuses must entail. I visualized the dozen brainless guineas that belonged to the much-feared Miz Millicent Poole, down the road. I wondered if these were the same sort of fowl that had *also* joined the circus, and how in the world you made them *mind*, let alone do tricks. Auntie sometimes hinted there'd been trapeze artists, too, and midgets on stilts.

Although I often begged for more information, both misses would turn on me. *"You're not old enough to hear such things."*

At the table, today, they poured hot sauce on their chicken while their arguments and bellows rose to flat-out howls.

Even Uncle Cunny, who'd been mopping up his creamed corn, could not break up the ruckus. He lifted a slice of meringue pie from the dish, and hid behind it.

Bitsy said nothing. She was not my real cousin, of course, but was Miss Shookie's own, and Aunt Jerusha's true niece. Sweat always formed shiny on her face and neck. Even the backs of her hands were slick.

I hated Bitsy; she was pushy and rude and smirky, and whined constantly. She had ashy elbows and knees and coppery spots on her face, and looked to be made from inner tubes. A day never saw light when she and her mama agreed on anything, and they brought their fussing to our dinner table. Today Bitsy sat, shoving in biscuits and peppery soppings.

Ol' Bitsy was a whiz at eating with her fingers and thick lips and big teeth, and not bad with a fork. In two minutes flat she could work through three helpings of sausage and dirty rice. She fisted chicken and pork chops and ham hocks till the juice ran down her arms and dripped from her elbows. Her eyes, which seldom lifted from bowls of food on the table, were squinty in their surrounding flesh, and her hair was a Brillo pad.

If she hadn't been such a mix of irritations and disgusting things, I might have felt sorry for her. Instead, every Sunday, I endured her whining and tried not to watch her pull her dress from her crack. When it looked like Bitsy was about to make a comment, Miss Shookie backhanded her, smack in the face, no matter that she had a mouthful of mushrooms and cream sauce. Thus, it was normal for Bitsy to make one unholy mess, and she ate with a dish towel tied around her neck.

"Sister," Auntie said, "are you aware that your daughter stinks to high heaven?"

Miss Shookie lifted her chin and replied, "What you are smelling is those damn prison pig farms 'round here."

"Shit," said Auntie.

"Exactly," said Miss Shookie. "Have you know my baby girl uses my homemade deodorant."

"Lord, that's right," Auntie said. "Damn stuff simmers on your back burner till it rots."

Aunt Shookie's deodorant was made from sheep's fat, melted to a wax that was applied directly to the skin.

"Everybody knows," Miss Shookie said, "that deodorant is only meant to block the sweat glands."

"Bullshit, sister," Auntie said.

Miss Shookie wound up. She waved a large serving spoon and demanded to know—*now that they were comin' to speaking of it*—why Auntie had never wedded and bedded some upstanding church man.

Auntie said they *weren't* coming to speaking of it, but now that Shookie mentioned it, why hadn't she up and married Bitsy's father?

Then Auntie looked embarrassed, and to ease the tension, Uncle Cunny told a joke—a good one about three horses, a piece of string, and a beer. Bitsy laughed so hard she peed her pants, and Miz Shookie had to suds them at the sink. She carried on about what a small bladder her daughter had, but she laid into that washboard and was mad as hell.

While Uncle Cunny sat with his bottom lip between his teeth and his head in his hands, Miss Shookie stretched Bitsy's unders on the line, with six clothespins to hold them. I'd never seen such enormous drawers. I was embarrassed for Bitsy for more reasons than one.

I'd heard Uncle Cunny say Bitsy was aiming to be as stout as her mama. If she would slim down and adjust her attitude, he said, the girl might make something of her life. But I'd seen Bitsy kissing boys behind the church, one time letting a Farm guard lift her skirt. I held less hope for her than Uncle did.

6

On Potato Shed Road, my best friend was Claudie Maytubby, one of a family of thirteen, living mostly on food stamps, government cheese, and brown beans. Claudie was round of face and sturdy of body. She was black as a raven's wing, her hair short and four-pigtailed, and her two dresses were plaid and coming apart at the seams. I loved her dearly, but more—I coveted her.

Unfortunately she was double twin to her sister, Eulogenie, who had one arm. Those girls had come into this world with only three arms between them. They were joined together from one wrist to belly button like a French chorus line. Claudie was the bigger, tougher one while Eulogenie was smaller, with finer bones, shaved-back hair, and tiny teeth. Miss Shookie said that at some time in the womb, Eulogenie had drawn the short stick.

"After we was born," Claudie told me one day, "we got too big to be carried around, joined up as we was. Mama dreamed she heard Eulogenie saying, *'Go on, Mama, and give this here arm to my sister.'*"

I watched Claudie's big pink tongue move around in her mouth. "People came and wrote us up in their magazine. Then a doctor took us to Montgomery and cut us apart. We didn't share no internals, so that weren't no problem." She draped the coveted arm around her sister. It had a wrist and hand and five normal fingers, and underneath was the scar.

"After," Eulogenie said in her little voice, "they put us in two cribs."

Claudie said, "Eulogenie cried so bad, they laid us in one, and the nurses taped our good hands together, so we'd each know the other'n was still there."

Eulogenie's hearing was bad, her eyeglasses repaired at one corner with a gob of dirty masking tape. I was also embarrassed for her name. For several months she'd gone without, until her mama heard that word at a funeral service. I took to calling her Plain Genie, which fit her better. I knew that hurt her feelings, but I didn't care. I wanted Claudie to myself.

Sometimes, in our playing, we two would drift over to Auntie's place. But here'd come Plain Genie, hanging around, blinking her eyes and sucking her thumb. Auntie'd bring out jelly sandwiches for us all—Plain Genie too—and that irritated the living hell out of me.

The twins never came to our house on Sundays, or on Wednesday nights, so they never met up with Miss Shookie, and I was glad. Claudie was dramatic about everything. If God sent her a letter stamped with all the seals of heaven, she would have rolled her big eyes. She did that a lot, and I could picture her watching Bitsy at dinner. Those eyes would've wobbled out of Claudie's head.

Down the road from us, the Maytubbys lived in one-half of a duplex. Because the other half was empty, they had spilled into it too, and when the landlord found out, he boarded up the other side.

One afternoon, I sat with Claudie on their porch. Most of the Maytubbys were home that day, because Denver Lee was due to arrive anytime. Denver was the only Maytubby in the history of False River to go to college. I knew there was a boy younger than Denver, name of Roland, but they never so much as whispered his name.

The oldest girl, Alvadene, was fourteen and twice over a mama. She sat on the porch too, rocking and nursing her son at one breast. The boy was pig-suckling and naked but for a hank of diaper in the awful heat. His little sister dug in the dirt with a spoon.

After Alvadene, a girl had been born, but she died when she was one day old. A tiny hammered-wood cross was planted in the ground near the river. There was a gaggle of Maytubby boys too, and they all looked alike—shaved-headed and skinny and just now wrestling around in the yard, a tangle of knobby elbows and knees.

Today, like a leper touched by Jesus, Miz Maytubby had risen out of her bed. In the house, a brown-sugar cake was baked and sitting on the table. Newspaper was tacked over the windows to keep out the sun.

Auntie had told me the story about Denver Lee. Apparently, Mississippi Southwest sent a scout up one day to watch him play high school basketball. Here in False River, it wasn't his grades that had kept him in class but his strong good looks. The coach's daughter, Janelle, having checked out the contents of Denver's pants, made a deal with her daddy. She'd do Denver's homework, and for her keeping this fine, tall jump-man on the team, Coach would say nothing about their coupling behind the gym as long as she didn't get pregnant and nobody saw them. Over time, however, Coach paid for at least two trips to Greenfield—one to have his baby girl "scraped" and another to get Denver shot full of antibiotics.

On the basketball court, Denver Lee had pure-greased glide and lift. The college scout liked his looks and his moves, and said *Come on down.*

But Denver would have to leave Janelle behind.

"Go on and play ball for us," the grown-ups told him, and Denver Lee said *Okay.* He'd make money and bring home a truck full, and they'd all be rich. But he never did.

While Denver was away, his daddy passed of a weakened heart. Denver had a game that Saturday and couldn't get home for the burying. That winter, he wrote to his mama, saying he'd met this new girl, liked the look and feel and smell of her, and they'd got married by a justice of the peace.

Word got around.

"That's what them Maytubbys need," Miss Shookie said during a Sunday gab on our upstairs gallery. "Another mouth to feed. If that girl had any sense, she'd take Denver up to Jackson and forget this bunch down here."

Miss Shookie was always moving people to Jackson.

Today we were gathered for Denver Lee's homecoming.

"He bringin' his new wife," said Plain Genie in her slow voice, grinning with her pink gums and tiny teeth. "We got us a sister-in-law."

So we sat on the porch while the dogs slept underneath, and we waited in the heat, not wanting to start on the lemonade till they got there.

I leaned back on my hands. "Why's your mama stay in bed so much, Claudie?"

"She been laid up since we was born." Claudie waved a hand like the whole thing was of no account. "Our birthin' was that hard on her. She had no sense, squeezin' out two more after us."

I looked down to the riverbank, where the smallest boys ran

naked as jaybirds, their butts caked with clay dust and their bellies round. Claudie got up and called to them, "Y'all come on and cover your bidness now! Clean pants is on the ironing board."

"Poor Mama," Plain Genie said. "She lay in the bed and moan all day and all night. She say she goin' to die any minute."

"Any minute?" I said.

"For seven years now."

But their mama was up today, wearing a bathrobe and peeking out through the porch screen. I said to her, "How you doin' there, Miz Maytubby? You feelin' any better this day?"

"You're a dear child for askin'," she said. "Y'all, ain't that Denver Lee's car coming up the road?"

It was, in a cloud of dirt roiling thicker than bees.

"Hey, y'all!" Alvadene rose out of the rocker, the baby on her hip, a bead of milk on her nipple. The baby set up a terrible fuss.

"Girl, button your blouse," her mama said.

A red car pulled up, with more rust spots than paint. The top was down, and Denver Lee was waving like he was his own parade. He had a big grin on his handsome face, and the lady beside him wore a wide-brimmed hat and gloves and a yellow sundress. A slow buzz rose up. When Denver came round and opened his wife's door, she stretched out two long white legs, and the whole family drew back.

"Y'all," said Denver Lee, grinning, "this here's my wife, Lucille. Lu, this is Mama, and Alvadene, and Claudie and . . ."

The screen door had gone shut.

Denver rushed his wife up the steps and inside. I heard his voice in the dark kitchen. "Mama, I know Lucille is white, but she's a real lady, and she's got fine, wide hips. You got to get to know her, is all."

"Well, ain't we done in now," Alvadene said. She sat down in the rocker and flopped that one breast back out, offering it to the squalling boy. The little girl wobbled up the steps, climbed on her mama's leg, and peeled her shirt away from the other.

Claudie and Plain Genie shared a secret look. After a long, bare silence Denver came to the door. "Y'all come in now. Supper's on the table."

The boys scrambled in from their game of killing each other.

I knew this invitation included me too. The kitchen was tiny and filled with the heat of the stove and summer bodies. There were four chairs, a bench, and a piano stool squeezed around that small deal table. Miz Maytubby moved to the stove and back. The chairs were for grown-ups. Lucille was balanced on Denver Lee's lap. In this crowded house there was no prayer, no hymn, no *Thank you, Jesus.* Everybody reached and dipped and poured and dug in. Claudie and Plain Genie and I were passed cracked cereal bowls, and we ate with spoons and our fingers, standing up.

A great pot of black-eyed peas sat in the middle of the table, and Denver Lee rose to dish them out while a platter of corn bread went around, and another heaped with fried potatoes. Nobody said a word. Without Denver's help, Lucille wouldn't have got a thing on her plate, because soon conversation rose up about Alvadene's babies, and nobody spoke to, or about, Denver's new wife. Like she wasn't there, like she didn't count.

She was so pretty. Her eyes were big and round and green, and she kept touching Denver Lee, like she needed to feel something familiar under her hand.

When dinner was done, and I'd thanked Miz Maytubby for letting me join in, Denver Lee said he was going down the road to visit old friends, and he'd be back directly. Lucille's skin went so pale, she looked almost blue.

All the boys tore out the door.

The rest of us moved around the kitchen like I reckon women have for a million years. When Alvadene handed out dish towels, Lucille didn't get one. Nobody let her pour up the peas or wrap the last square of corn bread. Lucille sat down on the floor and tucked her legs under her, set to play with the babies, but Alvadene scooped them both up and took them off to bed. Claudie took over the washing, passed me a towel, and I dried the dishes and stacked them by the drainboard. Eulogenie put them away. Lucille rose from the floor, and with one hiccuping sob, ran out the back door.

They all stood, looking at the linoleum. I put down my towel and headed out too. I saw the door slam on the outhouse, and I sat down in the grass to wait. Time went on, but the door did not open.

"Miss Lucille?" I called. "You got to step out sometime."

"No, I don't," she said.

"That's one nasty outhouse. Denver Lee will come back, and you'll smell like shit."

She opened the door.

"I greatly admire your yellow dress," I said.

She looked me over, causing me to brush a crumb from my shirt and retie one sneaker.

"I don't understand," she said to me. "White girl, what are you doing here?"

"I'm friends with Claudie."

She sighed. "I'm wife to their oldest boy—"

"I know."

"—and I just wanted to play with the little ones." Tears filled her eyes and spilled over on her rouge. "I hoped they'd all like me, especially his mama. I tried to be polite."

"You were," I agreed. "Although you didn't eat much."

"How could I?" she said. "It's like I was carrying some almighty disease."

I smiled with one corner of my mouth while I searched for something to say. "They were excited when they got Denver's letter, saying he was married."

She looked at her sandals, at the hard packed ground. "I told Denver Lee to explain, that it wouldn't set right. This is Mississippi and—well, they weren't expectin' him to bring home a white woman."

"Just give them time." I got up to leave.

"Wait!" she said, the word sharp on her tongue. "You got any more advice?"

"Well—I can tell Genie already likes you."

"Oh. The skinny little thing with her mouth hanging open?"

I nodded. "That's her. And Claudie'll take to you. Look, Denver's mama will be back in the bed now. Go on in, ask how she's doing, can you get her anything."

"I don't know—"

"Then get you some cool water, sit out on the porch, and wait for Denver Lee. Go on, now."

"What's your name again?"

"Clea June Shine," I said. "I stay twelve houses down, at Miss Jerusha Lovemore's."

"She's white too? She your foster nanna?"

Auntie was neither. The air had grown cool. "No, ma'am."

"Then how come she keeps you?"

"My mama gave me to her. I reckon it's bad manners to give back a present."

"Girl," Lucille said with a small pink smile. "I bet you came tied up with a great big bow."

7

It seemed like the right thing to do that day, it being too hot to come out from under the willow.

Claudie came over, and we formed a plan. We would put on a show and do it up right, charging nickels and all. Three cents for the kids.

"I can't sing," I told Claudie. "And I sure can't dance."

"Hell you cain't," she said. "Anybody can dance, girl, just move with the music—like this." She commenced to hum something surprisingly deep-throated, her shoulders rotating like broken helicopter blades and the rest of her bopping up and down. Genie watched from among the oaks along the river.

"First thing we got to do is have microphones," Claudie said. And she took up a fat stick and broke it under her bare foot. She held one half to her chin. "What you wanna sing?"

"Well—"

"I can see you gonna be a joy kill," she said. "You don't got the beat."

"Which beat?" I said.

"You don't hear that music goin' on inside you, girl?"

"You mean—in my head?"

I heard plenty of things—story ideas and clever ways to say stuff, words I'd read in a book. "I guess I could tell a joke," I said. "I know this one about a horse and a piece of string. . . ."

Claudie handed me my half of the stick. "Hold it up to your mouth, like this, and say somethin'. Go on, now."

So I did, and we spent a while with her belting out songs and me yammering into a stick, saying memorized things like " 'Twas on the good ship *Hesperus* that sailed the stormy sea . . .' " and "For unto us a child is born" and "The war in Switzerland is ended, and now American troops are expected to . . ."

Claudie held up her hand. "They's a war?" she said.

"There's always a war. I'm like a radio announcer. Auntie said when she was a kid, they used to watch these newsreels before a movie, and—"

"I ain't ever been to a movie," Claudie said. "So stop your showin' off. Say something folks can understand. An' make it about me."

"Okay." I put on a haughty air. "Miss Maytubby from Atlanta, will you pass us the pork chops and the chutney, do you mind?"

Claudie's face was pure annoyance. "I ain't from Atlanta, and I ain't ever the hell had pork chops either."

My jaw fell slack. "You've never had pork chops? Ham? Sweet potatoes?"

"I had sweet-tater pie," she said. "Come to think on it, I never see y'all walkin' down to the highway for free cheese or beans. Y'all must be rich."

"We aren't rich," I said. But it stuck in my mind to ask Auntie later. "Aunt Jerusha made a bunch of money in the chicken circus," I said grandly. "Enough to live on for the rest of our lives."

"Anyway, you're s'posed to introduce me first thing."

"I'll be the master of ceremonies."

"Yeah," Claudie said. "That. And you can sing along some-times."

"How many songs are we gonna do?"

"Three or four," she said. "Enough to make it worth five cents."

"Right." I nodded. This whole thing was beginning to seem better now, and I was counting up the people we might invite— Aunt Jerusha, Uncle Cunny and his friends, the Hazzletons, the Oaty brothers. Miz Maytubby and Alvadene.

"We'll ask the Sherrards and their sister-in-law, Miss Minnie Roosevelt," I said.

I wondered about Miss Shookie and old Bitsy, and if Reverend Ollie would come—and what about Miz Millicent Poole? Nobody liked that crazy woman with her wild red hair and white scalp showing through. Her dresses hung uneven, and her eyes were red-rimmed. Oft times her nose was dripping, and she made no move to wipe it. Knowing Miz Millicent, she might take it on her-self to collect our money. It had come to me recently that she and my mother and I were the only white people on Potato Shed Road.

"Let's do this on Saturday night," I said. "At six o'clock. We can sing and dance on our back porch and put chairs in the yard for the audience."

Claudie grinned, her big white teeth shining. "Now you're get-tin' it, girl," she said. "Let's start with 'Rock Around the Clock,' I do that real good."

And she did. I was dumbfounded. For somebody who lived, as Miss Shookie said, in the lap of poverty, Claudie knew all the words, and the melodies too. She had the moves down perfect, the jiving and juking, and her feet pounded and ground the dirt while the top of her twisted separate from the bottom. It was better than what we did in church, even with our hand-waving and shouting *Amen*.

I stood there with a silly grin on my face, but then Claudie gave me a shove, and I took a shuffling step and then another and slung my skinny hips and tried swiveling them, and before long, I had it down. I wasn't as smooth as Claudie, though, because somehow the moving seemed part of her—like music was in her the way words were inside me.

It seemed, that afternoon, we were a kind of *temple*, and I wondered at that new strange word that had bloomed in my head.

On Friday, we tired of rehearsing and went off to wade in the green shallows of the river and make a plan to visit all our neighbors first thing in the morning, inviting them for that evening, lemonade served. It was suppertime just now, and I asked Claudie in, but she glanced over at Plain Genie, who was sitting on the bank, sucking her thumb, and Claudie said no, she and Genie would be gettin' on home.

I went in to eat and to tell Auntie the plan and that I needed drinks enough to serve all the people who might show up tomorrow night.

"And who's gonna pay for the lemons?" she asked.

"Don't we have some in the refrigerator?"

"We do not, and even if we did, child, you embarkin' on free enterprise, and you'd owe me for them lemons, you understand?"

"No, ma'am."

It was just Auntie and me tonight, Uncle Cunny off playing Friday-night poker.

"Cunny taught you to count out money," she said. "Tomorrow you go on over to the Tiger Market and buy six lemons. I'll front you the price. But you owe me what they cost, and you'll give it back."

I would split the nickels with Claudie, all right, but I was not about to take out the cost of lemons.

"And you do it before you girls share a penny. That way you'll both be paid equal."

"But, Auntie—"

"No, ma'am," she said, her feet planted in front of the stove. "That's how it will be, or it won't be at all."

To save my life, I couldn't make myself subtract the price of the lemons. Subtraction was unkind. Taking things away hurt something fierce, and I couldn't think why they'd teach such a thing in school.

I had an idea. I kept seventy-five cents upstairs in a sock, under my bed, and I would take that sock with me to the market tomorrow. Then, when we collected admission, Claudie would just have to give me half the price of the fruit. Everybody knew they lived off food stamps and ate beans every day. Not one of them owned shoes till they went to school, and their clothes came from the donation box behind the Oasis of Love Bingo Hall and Prison Camp Center.

Saturday evening was surprisingly cool. Uncle helped us line up chairs, and near six o'clock he drove down to the Maytubbys'. When he came back, he opened the door and helped Miz Maytubby and Alvadene down. A whole pile of Maytubby kids spilled out of the back. Then Uncle came to where I was standing with a cigar box, sometimes shaking it just to hear the coins rattle, and he counted his guests and dropped in two quarters. "Miz Maytubby," he said, "it'd please me mightily to help you to a seat on the front row."

I looked over at Plain Genie, and at Alvadene in her tight shorts and her blouse with the sleeves cut out and her bosoms straining against the buttons, and the baby asleep on her arm.

Miz Maytubby, I heard, took to her bed for weeks after Denver showed up with his white-lady wife, and even now, she looked as if she'd come straight from there, in a faded pink duster and barefoot, her hair slept on. In spite of that, she had a lifted and somewhat delicate chin and swipe of pink lipstick across her mouth. Claudie looked proud.

Mr. and Mrs. Sherrard and Miss Minnie Roosevelt came arm in arm, under a tattered parasol, and the brothers Oaty. At the very last minute, Miz Millicent Poole tottered down the road, her legs black and blue. She swayed into a seat. The Best Reverend Ollie paid her way. Auntie went to speak with Miz Millicent, then sat in the back row, Uncle standing, as all the chairs were taken. I was pleased with this turnout.

When everyone was seated, I flounced up on that porch and announced loudly, "Ladies and gentlemen, come one, come all—to the greatest show in False River! Starring me and Claudie Maytubby, who arranged *all* the dancing."

Then I looked over toward Mama's house, just to be sure, and was grateful to the core there was no sign of her. The last thing I needed was her stumbling over here in her boa and high heels, creating a scene.

"I'm pleased to present us both in our opening number, 'Ain't No Mountain High Enough.'" With that, we snatched up our make-believe microphones, which made some laugh, and launched into our number.

"'Ain't no mountain high enough, ain't no valley low enough . . . to keep me away from yooooou . . .'"

On that wood porch, we gyrated and jerked our hips and our thumbs like we were looking to hitchhike clear to Jackson. Everyone clapped, except Miz Millicent.

"Now," I said when we were catching our breath. "We're gonna dance while Miss Maytubby here sings 'Johnny Jump.'" And with that, we fell into swoops and dives and swan-arm gyrations, the great finale being Claudie bending over and me climbing on her ass. My bare feet wiggled up to her shoulders and she held on to my legs. We'd done this stunt a half-hundred times.

But it was then I lifted my eyes and saw my auntie. She'd grown pale of face, clutching air with her hands, and nearly turned over her chair. I lost my balance some, catching before I toppled, and shot a glance toward Mama's, but she wasn't outside. It wasn't that. Auntie was up now, her hand covering her mouth, backing away, Uncle picking up her chair, taking her by the shoulders.

"Jerusha," I heard him say. "Jerusha—"

Miss Shookie, who sat with Bitsy beside her, wagged her head and said, "Uh-uh-*uh*."

With the flat of her hand, Auntie slapped at Uncle, made for the side of the house, and was gone around the corner. Claudie, however, had taken her microphone and was announcing her own next number.

The lemonade, and some sugar cookies Auntie had made, were on the domino table under the willow. Everybody ate standing and went off home, and things would have been fine, except they weren't. Miss Shookie never said another word. She and Bitsy just got in their Chevy and drove away. In silence, Uncle took all the Maytubbys home. Claudie had a fine, flushed look to her face. I had taken those nickels and divided them evenly—five for her, five for me. The price of the lemons had come out of my sock.

I went straight to bed. I couldn't bear to question what had happened to Auntie. Whatever it was, I was sure it was my fault.

8

It was my birthday, and I wanted only to spend time with Claudie, but nothing could pry her loose from her sister, and anyway, her time was limited. Both girls went to first grade half a day. I, however, was turning six late and would not go to school for another year.

I envied the Maytubbys their big family and the way they all stuck up for one another, with the exception, of course, of Denver's new wife. But I was jealous of more than strength among the siblings—at one time Claudie *had known her daddy*.

It was with downright stubbornness that I persuaded Claudie to leave Plain Genie long enough to join us for my birthday dinner. No matter that it rained. I took Auntie's umbrella and went to fetch her, the two of us dancing back, jumping puddles and cowering beneath lightning, then screaming at the great claps of thunder.

In addition to it being a special day, I needed Claudie's help. I had a plan, and after dinner I would share it with her. It was a great secret and could not involve Plain Genie, who was weak and trembly and prone to tears. I was going to ask Claudie to go down the road with me to spy on the prison. I'd heard terrible tales of the folks who were kept there—crying out for their families, beaten to the bone, starved and wailing to be spared, and I thoroughly needed to see for myself.

Just now, though, dinner was on the table, and from my side, I lorded over the pork chops with boiled potatoes, candied carrots, and dumplings. I was beside myself—surely Claudie had never seen such a spread. I was anxious for my guest to try everything. Our good manners and a loaded table must be a rare delight for her, and I behaved as though I'd cooked every morsel. Auntie had baked a cake for the occasion. Uncle Cunny was there too, having dropped by in time to lick frosting from the bowl. Tonight he held Auntie's chair for her and touched her shoulder before he seated himself at the head of the table—things I never saw him do on a Sunday. And the rain came down. It beat on the window over the sink and the big parlor panes.

I was thrilled for Claudie. There were so many people in the Maytubbys' house, they took turns at the table. I was welcome there, but always seeing the short supply of things—a bowl of boiled peas with no snaps, and a long, thin corn bread—I politely helped myself to a spoonful. Waiting at home, I knew, would be thick slices of bread and butter, and Auntie's homemade apple butter.

Today, our table was set with Auntie's best blue dishes.

But when we sat, Claudie went on standing behind her chair. My big and solid Auntie spoke. "Would you like to sit down, Claudie, sugar?"

"She doesn't get to, at her house," I said, by way of explaining. "They don't have enough chairs to go around."

Claudie looked at the army of bowls on our table, pinched her lips together, pulled out her chair, and perched on its edge like a bird on a wire. Then Uncle asked a blessing, plain and simple.

"Yes, Lord," Auntie said softly, when he was done. I said, "Amen." Claudie's eyes were big, and she said nothing.

"You ever see so much food?" I asked her, heaving a great sigh.

"I never did," Claudie said. "You got more folks coming?"

"Nope."

Because she was our guest, Auntie asked first for Claudie's plate. "Would you like a little of everything?" Auntie asked.

"Well—" Claudie said.

While Auntie and Uncle heaped up spoonfuls for Claudie, I grinned like a fool. Claudie fingered her spoon and looked at it and set it back down, her mouth twisting, and when Uncle laid her plate in front of her, I thought she might bolt.

I wondered why she didn't take her fork and dig in.

Auntie's voice was soothing. She asked after Miz Maytubby—was she taking her medicine regular—and how was that handsome Denver Lee doing now that he was back at school?

"Right well," said Claudie.

"Child," said Auntie, screwing the lid off a jar. "Would you like to try my homemade chow-chow?"

Claudie said nothing.

"Goes real fine with the chops," Auntie said.

"Claudie don't know what chow-chow is," I said.

"That's all right," said Auntie, giving me a look. "Not everybody's got a taste for it."

"She don't know pork chops either. Or candied carrots."

Uncle murmured into his paper napkin, "The word is *doesn't*, Miss Clea. Not *don't*."

"But Claudie says *don't*." I was trying like all molly hell to make her feel welcome.

Silence fell on our table while Claudie stared at her carrots, then took one up in her fingers and closed her big teeth around it.

"Not like that," I said, laughing. "With your fork."

"Clea June," Auntie said. "The Lord made fingers before he made forks," and with that she plucked up a new potato and popped it into her mouth. She smiled at Claudie. This was certainly not the first time we'd sopped up cream gravy with biscuits, or cleaned bones with our teeth. But it was the only night that we ate a whole meal with our hands.

Claudie couldn't seem to get enough. Uncle passed her the chop plate and more potatoes. I marveled that she could put away so much food, and she bent to the work like she was shoveling dirt, digging deeper and deeper into the heap. I could not clean my own plate for watching.

By the time Claudie was gnawing on her third chop bone, her face was shiny with grease and the kitchen heat. She mopped up pickled chow-chow with a fourth buttered biscuit, and when Auntie offered, she slid the last three tomato slices into her mouth. At one point she rose from the table and walked around the kitchen. I couldn't think what she was doing, or looking for.

"Miss Claudie, I'm glad you came to sup with us," Uncle Cunny said. "I believe there's dessert, if you'd like a slice."

From the sideboard, Auntie brought the pink cake and, with her hair frizzing from the heat and all the labor of preparing a fine dinner, struck a match and lit six candles. Claudie's eyes bugged out.

I closed my own while I made a wish.

"What you doin'?" Claudie said.

"Haven't you seen a birthday cake before?"

Ever so slow, she shook her head.

"You make a wish and blow out the candles." And I did.

Auntie cut slices and set them on our plates.

Claudie lifted the whole triangle to her mouth. Auntie asked, would she like a second piece? *Yes, ma'am.* And the same to honey drizzled on the last biscuit, too.

While I licked icing from my fork, Auntie told Claudie that she had a few small things for Miz Maytubby, if she would be so kind as to carry them home, and Claudie said *Yes, ma'am* again. I knew what those things were because we'd often loaded baskets and grocery boxes with cartons of eggs and great bunches of greens from our garden, bread Auntie had baked herself. I helped tote them. But while she went to each door and knocked, I had to wait in the road. When I once asked why, Auntie told me I could visit when I learned to properly hold my tongue. I didn't know what that meant.

Just now I'd grown weary of the silence, so I took my own turn with Maytubby inquiries, like I didn't see Claudie every day of my life.

Having passed into my sixth year, I felt like a grown-up. I squared my shoulders and asked, "How's your daddy doin', Claudie? He still gone off?" And, "Lord, I ain't ever seen anybody *eat* so much!"

Claudie looked stunned. Her eyes slid to her near-empty glass of milk. "You know my daddy run off," she murmured. "He ain't been back since."

"He just up and walk away?" I said because this was a subject I was curious about. Especially since no one could even recount my own daddy's name. "After your little brothers were born?"

Claudie nodded.

"Clea June," Auntie warned. "Claudie, let me pour you more milk."

"Y'all got so many mouths to feed," I went on, repeating what I'd heard Miss Shookie say. "You think he'd go *before there was thirteen of you.*"

Auntie and Uncle sat frozen in their seats.

"We only twelve now," Claudie whispered, setting her biscuit down. "One died."

Thinking I could lift this gloom with a joke, I said, "Too bad it wasn't more."

But I knew it was wrong. The room fell away. I felt darkness run up past my neck to my cheeks, and was shattered at the cruelty of my own tongue. My mouth was my surest trip to hell. Here among the remains of dinner, around the crumbs and frosting and globs of honey on the table, God would surely strike me dead.

Uncle cleared his throat and said what a fine meal Auntie had prepared.

"I only meant," I said, "everyone saying times are hard, and with y'all livin' on welfare checks—"

"I believe dinner is over," Auntie said, and was on the edge of rising when a knock came on the screen and through its mesh I saw tall, skinny Alvadene, soaked in the rain. She had her little girl on her hip and a sweater over their heads. "I'm sorry to bother y'all, but Claudie got to come home."

I shot out of my chair. "No! It's my birthday, and she ain't done with her cake!"

"Eulogenie havin' a ringtail fit 'cause she gone."

My mouth turned so far down it hurt my chin. "Eulogenie doesn't get her every minute."

Alvadene said, "She got to come on. Eulogenie won't stop crying."

"I'll be goin' now," Claudie said in a whispery voice.

Auntie was on her feet. "I'll just wrap up some chops for your mama," she said, and she dumped the last two onto a square of waxed paper.

So softly I could barely hear, Claudie thanked Auntie for having her.

Only I could make a bad thing worse. When Claudie banged out the door and went off with her sister, I mumbled, "Y'all know her mama won't ever see those chops. Not with those nasty little boys on the place."

Auntie said in a tight voice, "Clea June, go outside and fetch me a green willow switch."

I wandered around beneath the dripping tree and stared at the bent and broken twigs. It was a pure wonder I didn't come out regularly, gather them all up, and chuck them in the river. But I knew, by now, that Auntie was just as likely to snatch up a fly-swatter, and that was worse.

I waited for her upstairs on my bed. From my attic window in the back of the house, I could see the top of the willow, the row of tall oaks, and the slow-running river with its green inlets. Something rustled in a mossy oak, and I imagined it was birds, flying off to huddle on their nests, in their own high attics. I bet they wouldn't spend their birthday night tossing with their legs on fire.

When Auntie came heaving and grunting up two flights of stairs, I sat in misery and already-pain where I knew welts would soon rise on my calves. The springs groaned when she sat down beside me. I hunched over, the switch drooping between my knees.

"Clea," Auntie said, "I can't think what you've gone and done to that girl, made her feel like she's got nothin'. Saying her family'd be better off dead. What possessed you?"

She didn't wait for an answer. "Every day, you are no more than her. When you act like that, it makes you less."

She was expecting me to agree, but I couldn't. For a while tonight I'd been happy. So—when we were most joyful, we ought not to speak? Why, then, had God given me a voice? When I grew up and had kids of my own, I would put corks in their mouths, or at least teach them to suck on their thumbs.

"Well," said Auntie. "I'm disappointed through and through. You go on over there and apologize, understand?"

"Yes, ma'am." This was far worse than switching—I had Auntie's hurt to mix in with my own.

She went off down the stairs, and I sat and thought on how this could not possibly be all my fault. Claudie eating with her fingers had started it. I went to the window, lifted the sash, and threw the stick out as far as I could.

The crickets came out and began to chirrup. I went down the wet drainpipe and on over to the Maytubbys'. I asked if I could talk to Claudie. "I want to say sorry and ask her if she's still my friend."

"Best you go on home," Alvadene said, turning away. "She don't want no part of you."

9

After what seemed like a hundred years, it was August.

I'd questioned the effectiveness of school from the start. When word came down that Miss Izzie Thorne from Birmingham, Alabama, would teach Years One and Two, Uncle Cunny and Auntie exchanged a look I couldn't read.

I worried that there would be something terrible about having Miss Thorne for a teacher, but at least I would have the twins nearby. Claudie was speaking to me, more or less.

"We goin' to first grade," she said proudly as the time got closer. They were older than me, though not any bigger.

"I thought you all did first grade last year."

"We did. An' the year before that. Me and Eulogenie, we gonna keep on till we get it right."

I'd worked with Uncle Cunny till I could add three columns and multiply like nobody's business, but Auntie predicted the sky would cloud over when Miss Thorne set to teaching me subtraction. Still, she said, it would do me good to see the world through someone else's eyes.

The first day of school came. I wore one of Bitsy's old dresses—thank the Lord, without frills or bows. My shoes were new and pinching, but I was pleased with the buckles and the click the heels made on our wood floor. I felt like I was tap dancing, just crossing the room.

I kissed Auntie 'bye.

On the way to school, Claudie and Plain Genie and I passed through False River, crossing the lawn of Red Roof Retirement, which was nothing but a smelly old folks' home. Half a dozen gnarled coots were on the porch in wheelchairs, drooling on their blankets and watching traffic go by.

Plain Genie loved it. "Someday I'm gonna live there," she said.

It was the only time I ever saw her sister slap her. Claudie drew back her hand and laid out a good one, Plain Genie falling over, then hunching on her heels to cry between her knees. Plain Genie had snot on her cheek and her taped-up glasses were coming apart. I bet it was her fault that Claudie was serving so much time in first grade.

Claudie helped her up, kissed her cheek, and, with Genie swiping boogers on the back of her hand, we followed the two-lane to the broken-down schoolhouse.

Like the rest of the county, it was a sorry place. The porch was falling off, and Claudie's foot went clean through when she set foot on the first step. The floors creaked and squawked with the weight of a hundred kids as we all filed in and dispersed into four rooms.

Maytubbys populated every grade. It was that way with a lot of families. Kids punched one another and clowned around while I found a seat near the window. I figured out quick that this room was divided, the left side Year One, the other Year Two.

Somebody had chalked straight lines and circles on our half of the green board. Beneath the window was a shelf of battered picture books, beads and string, and colored blocks. Right away the air went out of my lungs. There was not one dictionary, nor a single copy of *Jo's Boys*—which I was now reading—or Edgar Bertolli's *View of the Planets*. Instead, above our chalkboard, was a yellowed strip of alphabet. On the desks were sheets of paper with red and blue lines, and stubby pencils with the erasers gnawed off. There were first-year primers too, their covers gone and spines nothing but cotton stitch. The first page commanded: *See Jane run.*

"For the love of God," I said, and some of the boys snickered.

This room was a true learning injustice, and I could not wait to tell Uncle Cunny. No wonder none of the Maytubbys could read.

Miss Thorne stood in front of the room, tall and pointed, from her black patent shoes to her black chicken neck and long, narrow face. She rearranged our seating and moved Plain Genie, who was squinting through her taped-up glasses, to the front of the room, and a few long-legged smart-ass boys to the back. I was glad to keep my seat, because the window felt handy—an emergency exit if things got too bad.

Miss Thorne was new to our school and clearly did not know why Plain Genie had her head down and was sobbing mightily into her one arm, so I raised my hand. When she called on me, I rose and started in explaining conjoined twins and how, while each of these two Maytubbys had her own internals, they'd once shared an arm and didn't like to sit apart.

To my surprise, Claudie whirled in her seat. "Shut your mouth, Clea Shine."

"But—"

"You don't know nothin'."

"Claudie, I was just telling Miss Thorne the way of things. About the man who took your picture, and the doctor that—"

Feet stopped shuffling, voices died away.

"—chopped you all apart. How you cried, and they had to tape—"

"Shut up, shut up!" Claudie said, on her feet, in my face. "Don't you know us Maytubbys is private? We take care of our own."

I thought I knew the Maytubbys well. "I was only saying—"

Miss Thorne was rising from behind her desk.

Claudie was so angry, she was spraying spit. "You ain't ever liked Genie. But she's my twin, and we're plain folks, so don't you waste fancy words on us."

"—you owe me seventeen cents," I said, because it was all I could think of. "For three lemons."

Miss Thorne snatched her roll sheet. "Clea Shine," she said, "if you are quite through, I can speak to these girls without your help."

But I was wounded and definitely not done. "Miss Thorne, this room is a sad disgrace. You got no decent books. Why, look at that wall map—the Pacific Ocean is purely faded out."

There was not a sound in the room, from the hall or outside. Even the very air held still.

"Clea *Shine*! Take your *seat*!" Miss Thorne calmed herself. "I can see you are—knowledgeable." She spoke that fine word as if it hurt. "But you will keep your mouth closed, and you and I will talk after school."

I sat and sulked. Later, I might get a chance to ask if we were going to cover the wars in Europe and Korea and do science experiments in which we would make fog and arcs of electricity. But just now, around the room, all the girls smirked and made knowing faces at one another.

I slid into my seat and folded my hands. I dared not take a breath. Claudie had said I used *fancy words*? I was surprised to see so many big kids hunched over these little desks, and it came to me that most of them were repeating Year One—and many had probably repeated it before. Further, it was true that I did not like Plain Genie. She filled up my head with her whining. She was like the sticky Mississippi mud that sucked at your shoes. But did Claudie have to go and announce it?

For now there was nothing to do but suffer the indignity of printing ABCs on primary paper.

To my great relief, we went outside at recess, and although I looked for the twins, I didn't see them. On a square of blacktop, a couple of jump-rope teams had formed, but when I approached, they all stepped away or turned their backs or coiled up their ropes like they were done anyway, and that surprised me. I was a champion jumper.

At noon I dragged myself home for lunch. Auntie made me a grilled cheese, and while I poked it with my finger and tore at the crust, she asked me how the day was going. I said, "Fine."

She asked—*wasn't I hungry?* I lied and said we'd had graham crackers for a snack. I felt empty, all right, but grilled cheese would not fill me.

In the afternoon, Miss Thorne called on me to come to the chalkboard and copy down numbers. We would learn to add apples. While her back was turned, I added to each number a string of zeroes. Some in the class snickered, but when Miss Thorne looked, they went quiet as scared mice. She asked me why I had done that.

"Because, Miss Thorne, two apples aren't enough to feed a family. It would take bushels to fill the bellies of False River, so I thought it more useful to create two thousand—"

Nobody could shush a room like I could.

By three o'clock, Miss Thorne looked tired even though the

year had just started. Everybody else left; I stayed in my seat, my hands folded on the desk. With all my heart I hoped she'd ask me how this class should be run.

"Come here, Clea," Miss Thorne said softly. "I can see that you are an intelligent and outspoken young lady. And while intelligence is an asset, it sometimes causes problems for your fellow students. Beginning tomorrow, I want you to sit on the other side of the room. At the back. In the corner."

"But that's Year Two!"

Miss Thorne sighed. "Clea, you already know more than most of these first-graders ever will."

Why did that sound like a not-good thing?

"Tomorrow the principal will administer a test so we can officially pass you into Year Two."

I wasn't so sure. "I don't subtract."

Miss Thorne cocked her head. "Child, what is the capital of these United States?"

"Washington, D.C.," I replied, "though it wasn't always. It—"

"Don't worry," she said drily. "You'll do fine."

Outside, where the shadows were long and the day was closing down, Claudie and Plain Genie had not waited for me. What awful sin had I committed that everyone was treating me like the leper in the Bible—and where was Jesus when you needed him, with his outstretched hands and barefoot followers and his flock of sheep? But sheep didn't do well in Delta country, and Jesus would never come to False River.

Maybe Uncle Cunny had been wrong to instruct me in mathematics and history. I walked home, sad to the bone and not sure why.

The problem with second grade was that it dragged like a line of rained-on wash. Every Monday Miss Thorne spat out a new bit of history or geography, then hammered it in until I no longer cared. The pace was enough to make me yank out my hair.

I began to smuggle the Reverend's books to school in the back of my pants. I had finished *Jo's Boys* and proceeded to a biography of Louisa May Alcott. Oh, how I loved to think that that lady sat at her desk, penning pages of story just for me.

I had an idea. I would ask Auntie for a clean pad of paper, and I would write my own book. While I was miserable in one life, I would live in another.

In the classroom, I figured how to prop up my raggedy copy of *Dick and Jane for Year Two* and, in its shadow, cleverly conceal my copy of *Heidi*. I loved Heidi and Peter but was crazy about Clara, bound to her wheeled chair and waking up to the world.

I didn't care if I was caught. I had a greater problem—second grade meant subtraction. Miss Thorne had thoroughly explained the concept, but I balked. Day after day I left my mimeographed sheet blank.

Then one morning it came to me that, while I rested my chin in my hand, my other four fingers had nothing to do. I reasoned that each one might represent a number—pointer finger for single digits, the middle one fives, the ring finger tens, and my pinkie one-hundreds. In this way, I could stroke my face while removing oranges from a crate, or bread loaves from a basket, and not a single person in False River went begging. It allowed me to fill in the blanks on my paper.

More than once, I caught Miss Thorne watching me, eyes narrowed, head cocked, as I stroked my cheek. But I was ecstatic. This new method allowed me to add and subtract long strings of numbers without connecting them to my life in any manner.

I was already the most unpopular kid. I was never included in games at recess, and I'd developed what Miss Thorne began to call insolence. That word hurt me to the core, and I ran all the way home to tell Auntie that I was never going to school again.

I wouldn't come down from the attic for dinner. Auntie hollered and stomped, then spoke softly and cajoled. I sat on the top step while she reasoned away my mountain of problems— stupid books, baby classmates, that infernal slow-slowness with which they were teaching me. Auntie said my imagination was probably making it worse.

I didn't tell her that Claudie and Plain Genie ran away when they saw me. I stomped down the stairs, planted my feet, and said it square on. "Auntie, nobody likes me 'cause I'm too smart."

"Oh, Clea June—"

"I don't think Miss Thorne's ever heard of the Battle of Waterloo. Uncle should've left me soft-minded and ignorant. I didn't fit into Year One at all, and I sure as aces don't like Year Two. I don't belong anywhere!" I wailed.

"You belong here," Auntie said and hefted me, long-legged as I was, into the rocker and against her soft bosom. Through my fierce anger and my pain, I listened to the squeak beneath our weight, and felt Auntie's stoutness as a mighty fortress.

Miss Thorne, she assured me, had indeed heard of the Battle of Waterloo. Did I want Auntie to call and talk with her?

"No."

Did I need Auntie to walk me to school?

No. Through tears I asked, "But—could I have paper? And

pencils, sharp pencils?" The pages of my old notebook were written on, full of scribblings that seemed infantile. My two pencils were worried down to nubs.

"Well," Auntie said. "I suppose so. Meanwhile—would you like to walk over to the Maytubbys' with me? Look in on their missus, take them a jar of jam?"

Oh, misery, I thought. Plain undecorated hurt. I couldn't. I wouldn't. "No," I said. Then, "Yes, Auntie, please."

But friendship, it turned out, was dandelion fluff. I sat on the Maytubbys' porch and waited for Auntie while the children scattered, and I was left with my sorry and broken heart.

Claudie didn't talk to me for the rest of the year, and school plodded on, one day oozing into the next.

Then summer came.

It meant cool dips in the shallows, and the Fourth of July. Like everyone else along the False River, we lined up our chairs and drank lemonade and watched sparklers and bottle rockets zing over the water and listened late into the night while Black Cats banged and made all the dogs howl.

10

One night after dark, I slipped out the window and down the drainpipe and lattice, and over to Mama's house. I stood on the porch, looking in through the window. A single lamp was lit in the parlor and Mama was dancing to the radio—slow, bluesy music, her steps long and smooth. She had a bottle in her hand. The hem of her dress was caught over one wrist, lifted and whirling like a red wing.

I went in through the kitchen and leaned in the doorway.

"Well, hi, there, darlin'," she said. "Where you been?"

I didn't bother with an answer. I never did. She'd put me at Auntie's, so she damn well knew.

"Come on in here an' let me show you a few steps."

I eased out on that wood floor that was polished by my mama's feet, and a hundred men. I knew they paid for more than a dance.

She must have had a good day. "Come on upstairs, girlie girl, and let's see what trouble we can get into."

The steps were steep and narrow, and I wondered what it would have been like, growing up in this house. There was an old refrigerator in the kitchen, but I never saw food on her table and

I didn't know what was behind the cabinet doors. The bathroom was off the kitchen. I'd guessed it was for company. I'd used it a time or two, thinking of the men in gray uniforms who'd stood there peeing in the way that men do, hitting everything but the bowl. The floor was always sticky, and I dared not touch the seat.

Upstairs, there were beds in all three rooms, and each was made up with fine sheets and a pretty spread. In Mama's room, in her private space, every surface was filled with glass bottles of nail polish and rouge, eyeliner and hair color, foundation creams and stopper-topped perfume.

She sat down on a low bench in front of the little table she called her vanity. She picked out a few bottles. "Come over here, darlin'. Let's see what you look like all shined up."

That was a joke.

"Shine" was our name. I was Clea June, daughter of Clarice Shine who owned five hundred kinds of sweet-smelling things. "Go on and let that bottom lip hang down for me," she said.

And I did, while she swiped lipstick on me, and powdered and rouged my cheeks, and I closed my eyes tight while she brushed on color and thickened my lashes. She clipped earrings on my ears. I could feel them bump-bump against my neck.

"Now see?" she said. "Lookie there at your elegant self."

I opened my eyes. What I saw in that mirror stole away my breath. I *did* look like her, peach-shaded and rosy, scarlet cheeks and lips. She stuck a silver comb on top of my braids.

"Well," she drawled. "Don't you look fine."

And then it was gone, that soft curve of her mouth. It stretched out thin. "Go on now. Get out and leave me in peace."

She followed me down the narrow stairs, and sank to the floor like her knees were liquid. "'Fore you go, bring me them smokes, girl, and the matches too." She coaxed out a Marlboro with her long red nails. "Light it up," she said. "Go on. God, do I got to tell you six times? Put it 'tween your lips. Now do the damn match."

But I wasn't good at striking them, and pretty soon a lot of half-burnt matches lay on the floor. Finally, she showed me how to hold it, how to draw on the cigarette till I coughed, and the end sparkled and glowed.

She might be drunk, but here was something no other kid was privy to. She took the thing and puffed away while the taste roared terrible on my tongue and in my throat. My tummy clutched up. Mama sent streams of smoke into the air.

While I watched the rings, a noise rose up—not down the road, nor from the prison where sometimes a siren went off—but from across the bare field where weed stalks had long ago fallen and were stubby and wrecked.

This was hollering and common horn honking, and at first it sounded like plain joy riding. I went to the front window and looked out at two pickups bouncing around in the prison's far field. High school kids waved their arms and yelled, looking just like their daddies on a Saturday night.

But then here they came—bumping across the road, lobbing things at the house, and I heard an upstairs glass break, and over that, the boys chanting something I could not make out.

Then the words came clearer:

"In a golden wig, she smelled like pig, and"—what was that next?—*"wore her wedding gown!"*

Like a nursery rhyme, only ugly and cruel. They shattered bottles and thundered their good time, and here came more hits SPLOCK SPLOCK, and I opened the door. Color upon color ran down the wall. Something hit me in the chest and exploded into red paint and bits of balloon.

Then one fired past me. I looked back through the door and

saw Mama cross-legged, and around her the stuff puddled, purple and thickening, on her floor.

Then from the corner of my eye I also saw Auntie and wide Miss Shookie barreling across the empty lot, Auntie screaming and shouting and waving her fists. The boys took off in their fine pickups, bouncing back the way they had come, across the field and through the far trees.

"Beware the ho' with the painted do'!" Their voices spun out.

Auntie stepped up on the porch and grabbed me by a hand. Miss Shookie peered into the house, like a voyeur.

"Well, don't that just make it, that red paint on the girl," Miss Shookie said. "Puts me in mind of a scarlet letter. . . ."

Auntie let go of me long enough to draw back a hard fist and sock Miss Shookie a good one.

For a while after that, Miss Shookie and Bitsy didn't come on Sundays, but then they started again, and we all took up like nothing had happened.

Only it had.

11

Summers were too short, made worse by knowing September was ahead. Every August, I sat on the porch with my knees tucked up and, dry-eyed, cried my heart to death.

Auntie had little patience with people who whined and felt sorry for themselves. But if I said nothing at the Sunday table, Miss Shookie picked at me like a dry brown scab. Uncle Cunny was different. He watched over us all. Reverend Ollie told his flock that God's eye was on the sparrows. If that was true, maybe Uncle was God, come down to earth in a pin-striped suit. He smiled and he praised me, and he passed me the peas. I loved him with a heart so full that sometimes I worried that my aching might leak out.

I sat in the itchy grass and watched Mama's house. She hardly ever came out anymore, but probably laid up inside with her dress hitched high in front of a slow-moving fan.

When I was ten, they made Miss Thorne principal, and she taught Year Five. I was in her class.

Every morning, in charge, she stood outside to greet us, looking down at her broken porch steps over which someone had laid a length of plywood. But sometimes in January that old wood became slippery with frost so last winter Miss Thorne had dragged in a length of old carpet and had the older boys nail it to the slick plywood.

I was grateful to be sitting in the back of her room. She had her hair done up nice now, and she smelled of English lavender. I wanted to please her, and it came easy. I had long since left Claudie and Eulogenie behind. It was Eulogenie's fault. If Claudie wanted to stay back and read *Dick and Jane* till she was old and gnarled up, it was fine by me.

In this class, there were only four of us white kids. I watched the other three stumble over the simplest of spelling words and felt sorry to be counted as one of their color. After that, I couldn't concentrate on anything but my whiteness.

I wondered what that would be like, having shiny dark skin, pale palms, and pink crevasses on the heels of my feet. In the most secret places of my heart, I wondered too about their private parts, how far *dark* extended, and if their organs inside were the same color as mine.

I imagined I was one of them, my hair twisted up in a hundred tiny braids and threaded with beads. If I were black, I'd wear African clothes and sandals made from the tires of safari jeeps. I'd speak Swahili and lift my chin and be proud. My eyes would be big and brown, my lips full, my backside high and rolling when I walked.

I also wondered what it'd be like to come upon a colored boy and find he was the love of my life. I imagined kissing him, my hands touching his short, fuzzy hair. Like Lucille Maytubby, the world would abhor me.

It was then I knew there was a "them" and a "me."

It opened my eyes and tore me apart.

I suspect that Miss Izzie Thorne caught on to my thinking. I saw it in the way she looked at me—like I was part of some memory she thought was past.

That very afternoon, I went home, stripped off my clothes, and looked at myself—long white arms and pointy elbows. I pulled off my socks and studied my feet, whitened from winter. I thought of Auntie and dark Uncle Cunny, stared at the concaveness of my belly and the length of my legs. Deep in my bones I felt an ancient division and realized something I hadn't before. My lack of popularity wasn't because I was smart, not at all.

Nobody liked me because I was white.

❋

One fall afternoon, I was swinging upside down from a limb of the oak, when I looked over to see a face looking back. It had a long set of jaw and forehead bones, with skin so thin and pale I could see the blue veins. A lick of yellow hair hung like a question mark, and I'd never witnessed such green, green eyes.

"Hey!" I said. "What you doin' in our tree?"

"Ain't your tree." This boy had the longest of legs and was now sitting on a branch, just passing the day. "This tree's on the river, and can't nobody own a river."

"Our property's right down to the water, then."

"Show me," he said. "Where does it say?"

I let go of the branch and landed on the soft bank. "What you doin' up there, anyway?"

"I live here," he said.

I thought of the crows I could see from my window, and their high, raggedy nests. "People don't live in live-oak trees."

"Can if they want." He gave a great tumbling swing, sprang up on his feet, and hopped away among the branches.

"Don't you have a home somewhere?" I asked.

"You're lookin' at it."

"And how old are you?"

He sucked on his top lip. "Old enough, I guess."

Was this boy, I wondered, all right in the head? I should go in and tell Auntie to call the sheriff and maybe Uncle Cunny and his friends, besides.

"I got to go in now," I said. And I did, sidling away without turning my back.

In the kitchen Aunt Jerusha was putting a cold supper on the table—sliced cucumbers and tuna and bread and butter. It was just her and me. I sat in my chair and tore at a crust. "Auntie, how come there's a boy in our tree?"

She went on with her peeling and slicing. "I reckon he likes it up there," she said.

"Don't you think his folks want him to come home?"

"Doesn't seem the case, does it?" she said. "He's been with us since last night. I took him some ham and biscuits this morning."

"But, Auntie, people don't live in trees. Monkeys do. I read—"

She gave me a long look. "Child, there is one thing you got to remember in this life."

I sighed. Auntie's list of life rules was longer than my arm.

"First off," she said, buttering her bread, "are you seeing him with your mind or your heart?"

"That boy is trespassing."

She laid circles of cucumber on her bread, and salt-and-peppered them hard.

"Second, if it's not hurting anybody, jus' leave it alone."

"But—" Maybe, somewhere, this boy's ma was calling him.

Auntie took up a fresh peach. She pitted the fruit and sliced some on her plate.

I bit into my own and marveled at the warm juice. "But it's suppertime, and I'll bet he's hungry."

"Don't talk with your mouth full. Butter him some bread. And fill a glass with lemon water."

I also slid three peaches into my pocket.

When I went out, I was pleased to the bone that he was still up there, that he had not climbed down and wandered off to set up housekeeping in somebody else's tree. It was like having a wild and exotic bird. I bet there wasn't one other person along the False River that could say a yellow-haired boy had moved into their tree.

"Hey!" I hollered up. "I brought you some food. What's your name, anyway?"

"Finn," he said. "Hand it here, then."

"I won't," I said. "I'll lay it on the ground. You come on down, now, and get it 'fore the ants do."

I could see him through the branches. He wore cutoff jeans, a T-shirt of no color, and a ball cap fixed tight on his head. "I ain't coming down," he said.

"Then I brought it for no reason. I'll just throw it to the geese—"

"Wait," he said, and he stepped down, and again, till he was perched on the lowest and thinnest branch.

"How come you're wearing that hat?"

"This here was my daddy's cap." Finn gobbled up his dinner. Peach juice ran off his elbows. He tossed the pits away and drained the glass.

"You act like you're starving," I said. "Where's your daddy at now? Isn't he wondering what's become of you?"

He didn't answer but asked a question of his own. "What's your name, anyway?"

"Clea," I said.

"How old are you?"

"Ten and eleven-twelfths."

"Ha!" he said. "I'm lots older." Then he climbed to the top, and I saw no more of him that night.

※

The next day I sat with my back to the trunk. This was nothing like Claudie's friendship had been. Finn was older and therefore wiser, and he had secrets. I liked that. Up in his tree he could be quiet as a mouse. In fact, all the next day I heard nothing out of him and began to be concerned. Then came the rustling of leaves, and Finn suddenly asked about the multicolored house across the way.

When I said nothing, he came down a few branches and asked again.

I set down the book I'd been pretending to read. "I was born in that house."

"Then how come you're here?"

"My mama's Clarice Shine. After she birthed me, she brought me here."

"I heard about her. Seems a sad thing," Finn said.

"Don't you go feeling sorry for me, boy."

"Don't *you* call me boy," he said, "and anyway, my ma died when I was two days old. That makes us the same—your ma being dead to you and all."

That set me off like a bottle rocket. "She's not dead to me, and she sure isn't dead to all her friends that stop by."

"Friends?" Finn snorted. "You ain't noticed they're all horny gents, and most of 'em's wearing boss-man uniforms?"

By *boss-man* he meant guards. It was one reason I hated the prison worse than any criminal they might harbor there. "Mind your own beeswax," I said.

Finn sounded far away. "My daddy told me Clarice Shine has a red light and a real bad name."

"She doesn't have any red lights. And anyhow, I'll bet you don't have a daddy."

At that, he went silent.

"Finn?" I said. "Come on and tell me the truth, why don't you?"

He closed his eyes and was quiet for so long, I thought he'd gone to sleep on his perch. "He kilt a man. Where we was camping, about a mile downstream. In the night this fella was trying to rob us, and he held a knife to my throat—thing was *this long*." He held his hands apart to show. "My daddy kilt him. Somebody saw, so they come to get him. Cops drove up where we was camping. They had these dogs—we heard 'em snapping big teeth."

"Oh, Finn."

"My daddy gave me his ball cap, and he said, 'Son, you run over yonder and climb up in that big oak. You'll be safe as long as you don't come down.' So I did. And they took him away. I been here ever since."

I could think of no words that might aid him or comfort either of us. But that night I carried Finn a sliver of pie, hoping Auntie wouldn't miss it from the dish. He didn't seem to mind that I woke him, and I'd brought along my blanket and pillow. Auntie found me under the tree in the morning.

In the two days that followed, the rains came down and soaked everything till we lived in a world that was spongy underfoot and inside our lungs. Just before noon of the second day, two deputies pulled up in their black-and-white car, and got out and stood in our dooryard, looking up at Finn.

"Don't you bother him," I said from some distance. I carried an umbrella. "He's got our permission to live there, and he isn't hurtin' anyone."

The cops talked in hushed-down voices, saying the boy was fourteen and white, and who in the world would take him in, and the county sure as hell had no place to put him. And then I heard the rest of the story.

Finn was kin to the Sarasons, who lived one county over, and they'd come looking for him, to tell him the court had given his daddy a free lawyer. That man spoke up for his daddy in front of the judge, but he couldn't get him off, him being guilty as hell. The Sarasons sure as the devil didn't want Finn.

In the end, Uncle Cunny and some of his domino pals fetched a ladder and climbed up there to rig a canvas tarp over Finn's head. I climbed up too. They hammered together a platform so Finn could lie down, and for the first time I got a look at the world from his angle. It felt cool and fresh. Up here, there was nothing but the shifting of leaves like silky green clouds, and the way my heart beat, and then skipped, and then beat again.

Aunt Jerusha brought Finn a bar of Palmolive and a towel—plus a bucket of wash water and another to do his business in. I privately wondered what would happen when the shit bucket was full, and I resolved to be Finn's friend and companion even when this part of the yard began to stink something awful.

12

In the side yard, Auntie kept geese, and they were mean as hell—three long-necked, splay-footed honkers bent on flying at me with their necks stretched and throats hissing, and beating me to death with their hard, vicious beaks. Trouble was, they ran loose on the place, and it was my job, twice a day, to round them up from the river or from the field across the road, and herd them home. Auntie'd had their wings clipped so they couldn't fly away, but they tried, running across that yard like they were about to lift off, making noises like whole pits full of snakes, and they made my life miserable.

On the other hand, they gave Jerusha no more grief than a trio of slugs. They adored her, and she them. In addition to feeding them a fistful of grain each day, she parched corn in the oven, and I guess those geese smelled it, because they stood at the back step like that meal was the Second Coming.

The two small females were called Sophie and Robert. When I pointed out that Robert was a boy's name, Auntie said nothing. When Auntie said naught, it was a done-and-set thing. The two girl geese spent their days pecking happily at Auntie's dropped

clothespins or the hem of her dress, and she'd stroke their long
necks and smile at their husky trumpeting.

But that almighty big gander she called St. Augustine, and he
was pure delinquent, scarfing up the choicest potato peelings,
chopped cabbage leaves, and cracked eggshells.

"Here you go, sweet Augie," Auntie cooed, stumping out,
throwing him a fistful of popped corn. "A treatie for my boy."
And so it went. Every time he nipped at my ankles or carried off
a shoe, I took up a stick and threatened that bird good. But when
I wandered out one morning and caught him ripping, one by
one, the pages of *David Copperfield* that I'd left out on the domino
table, I took up my switch and ripped him a new one.

Auntie was away, carrying a basket of bread to Miz Millicent
Poole—she being caught in the fist of the grippe—when a couple of Uncle Cunny's pals passed by in their truck, and they
jumped out to pry me off that bird. Auntie must have heard, because she didn't speak the rest of that day, and that very evening,
Uncle Cunny came and nailed up a chicken-wire pen and a
lean-to to shelter the geese and hold their water pans. Sophie and
Robert settled down inside, but the big gray gander had a mind
of his own, and he broke loose more often than not.

Even from my room in the attic, I heard Aunt Jerusha cater-
wauling one early morn and flew down the stairs to find her rav-
ing in the yard. Clipped wings aside, Augie had apparently flown
the coop.

"Oh, my sweet Jesus," Auntie wailed and flapped her hands.

"What?"

"He's been *stole!*"

I groaned.

"You get on down the road, Clea Shine, and find that gander."

"But, Auntie, I haven't had breakfast—"

"Nor will you, lest you come back with my goose!"

"It's not my fault—"

"Was no love lost between you," she said. "Now, start by the Farm. Check the creek behind and zigzag through the fields. Go to town if you have to, and ask at the fellowship hall." She filled my pockets with corn to lead him back.

From the oak tree, I could hear Finn laughing at me. *Damn him.*

It didn't seem likely to me that a goose would have any truck with the Oasis of Love Bingo Hall and Prison Camp Center, but I would stop there and inquire.

I couldn't think why they brought prisoners to the hall on Tuesday and Saturday nights just to call the bingo numbers, unless that was Mississippi's way of rehabilitating. Sometimes convicts were paroled, I knew. And the Farm kept a pig business and a truck garden beyond the trees. They sold vegetables along the highway too, but I knew little else. When a man was given a life sentence and rode in on the shuttered blue bus, I guessed he stayed till he died, at which time the guards took his body out and pitched it into the cemetery across the creek.

"Damnation," I said, making a crappy face at Finn. Up in his tree, he made one back.

I set off, scraping the dirt with my stick and watching dust clouds rise and keeping half an eye out for that goose.

I inquired at every door. Nobody had spotted a runaway bird.

Unless he'd slipped under the fence and found himself incarcerated, he was not down at Hell's Farm, or trapped in the coils of wire, or, as far as I could see, stuffing his gullet in the prison's garden. A lot of men were out in their orange uniforms today, chained and clanking when they moved in their hoeing. I watched until a fat woman guard looked up and hollered and waved a big black club.

On the far side of the farm, Devil's Creek had cut through the land, and it emptied into a particularly deep section of False River. I worried that Auntie's goose had been wrung by the neck and thrown in that creek, fretting not so much at the loss of the goose as that I would have to find and retrieve him. I went on around the Farm and approached the steep bank. I did not see him in the water below, nor splayed anywhere on the sharp rocks. Still, I was afraid of the place, and the narrow bridge that spanned the creek. I made my way along the edge, peering through my fingers, lest I encounter, on the other side, human skeletons still clad in orange and rotting in the slime.

I did not find that bird lying dead on the road or any cow track, or paddling in somebody's water trough. In town, I briefly checked the empty buildings and lots and asked around. He wasn't poking through the canned goods at the Ninety-Nine Cent Store, and he sure wasn't playing canasta with the ladies at the Oasis of Love.

At about noon I found him—grinning, if a goose could grin— munching lettuce leaves and collards in Miz Millicent Poole's garden. He had trampled her tomatoes and plucked early grapes from her vine and was honking in a victorious but sickly way, and I hoped he had a bellyache that beat all.

Miz Millicent would not take kindly to the trodden mess. I'd not had much to do with her in these years because she was tall and pinched, the color of a parsnip, and she smelled bad. A strange odor came out through her pores and rose on her breath. Auntie told me once it was malaria. I asked if a doctor couldn't do something for her, but Auntie said things had invaded Miz Millicent's bloodstream, and they weren't likely going anywhere.

Miz Millicent's red hair was thin and stringy so that her pink scalp showed through. Weekly, she put on a hat and sashayed down to First and Last Holy Word, where she supervised Sunday school teachers, picked hymns for the service, and bossed everybody. She told the Best Reverend what lesson us backsliding folks needed and, in all matters, which way was up.

But on many days she was sickly, and Aunt Jerusha walked down the road with a slab of pound cake or half a sweet-potato pie. Auntie'd step up on the porch and tap lightly on the door. From the other side, Miz Poole spoke softly, weeping. But if I was there, and if she saw, she'd begin to screech, "Jerusha, don't you bring that child in here! She got germs and vermin crawling. You don't come in, little girl, you hear me, now?"

Auntie'd give me a look that said I'd better back off and pretend to admire Miz Millicent's hydrangeas, and nod my head at her bobbing zinnias like they were the finest I had ever seen.

Secretly I thought Miz Millicent was a loon, and she scared the living daylights out of me.

But today I was alone, and I had a clear purpose, and I spotted a broom on Miz Poole's porch. It seemed like a fair thing with which to chase a goose from a garden, and I grabbed it up and rushed into the grapevines and, although we were near the same size, I beat that bird up one side and down the other. He flashed his wings and hissed and flew at me and I swung again, catching him upside the head. He turned to run, but I whacked and whaled until he flat fell over. Then I let go the broom and took hold of his neck. I jerked him across the road and into the field, and I laid down on that thing's head, his one eye like a bright bead, taking my measure.

I went back to Miz Poole's and onto her porch and knocked on her door, intending to apologize for Augie's behavior and her ruined fruit and torn vegetables, and to tell her I was sure Aunt Jerusha would make up for it all. I'd have laid my nose to the screen to see was I bothering her, but a vagueness of smoke had boiled up inside and was escaping through the screen. Then the door jerked open, catching my cheekbone hard, and her hand shot out and yanked me inside. Her eyes were a back-and-forth marvel of wild and jerky, and colorless in their gone-awayness. Smoke pricked my nose and made me cough. I looked around for a flame, but it was something else, a glass contraption. Something inside her had gone terribly wrong.

She opened her awful mouth and screamed in my face, and I screamed too. I backed up. And up again, against the door, but her crook'd fingers reached out, curling for my shirt, the tip of my nose. If she caught me, I would surely roast in her oven.

Her mouth came close. I could smell her bad teeth and her smoky breath, feel her thin lips on my ear. "Don't you ever tell what you seen here, girlie. Don't you ever speak my name—else you're mine, you understand?"

I nodded. True fact. I would never tell, I would never set foot in her yard or on her porch again. And never, ever would I look her in the eye.

I didn't run until I was well clear of her place, and then I picked my feet up and put them down in clouds of dust, and I didn't stop until Auntie caught me in her arms, and I backed her into the rocking chair, where, big as I was, she held me and waited for an explanation.

Auntie had the grace not to ask if I'd found Augie. In my heart, I felt Miz Millicent had probably wandered into the field, found Augie, and done him up for her supper. I couldn't stop shaking, and my mind was a mess. Over and over I saw that smoke, and smelled that pipe. I knew there were things like what I'd just seen. But—this was the righteous Miz Poole with her hymns and her holiness, a woman who everybody minded and feared!

"Look at me, Clea," Auntie said. "Something happen down at the prison?"

"No, ma'am."

"You go into town, then? Something there?"

I shook my head.

She held me closer. Tighter. "The church?"

"No, ma'am." *Don't you ever speak my name. . . .*

She held me out to look me over. "Somebody hurt you?"

I shook my head.

Whatever it was, we would rock it to death. "You go over to your mama's, child?"

"I didn't, I swear."

"Hazzletons'? The Bishop place? Miz Maytubby all right?" By now Auntie was shaking too. "Talk to me, Clea! I can't he'p you till I know! Something happen by the river?"

"No'm."

She quit rocking. "You stop at Miz Millie's, did you?"

I held my breath while her mind switched gears, and her knowing rose up and filled the cracks in the walls.

"She—told me never to speak it." I clung to her strong shoulder and buried my face in Auntie's neck while the rockers creaked.

"Oh, baby girl. You saw somethin' you shouldn't have."

My stomach rolled like thunder does. "Yes, ma'am."

"It's a sickness, doncha know. After all these years, Millie Poole can't help it. I'm sorry you had to witness that."

"But she's so—"

Auntie sighed. "I know. The addiction is where she finds her courage."

"It's *not* courage, Auntie—she's plain mean. And scary."

"Those things aren't real, child."

Not real! I'd feared Miz Poole; now I feared her twice over. Uncle Cunny had helped me read Sherlock Holmes. I knew what opium was. Miz Millicent Poole was not an English detective; she was an addict and a junkie. I wondered if she'd made a pact with the devil.

13

Auntie never set eyes on that goose again.

Although my world was growing bigger, it was also getting smaller. I was banned from going to Mama's house. It seemed wrong that Auntie would lay down this rule, and for a while I stomped around upstairs with the distance of two long staircases between us.

To Auntie's credit, she filled my mind with plans for the upcoming Fourth of July picnic. Auntie pronounced it *JOO-lie*, and when I commented on this, Uncle tapped me on the shoulder and gave me the eye.

I did know how to fry blueberry pies, and the day before the picnic, I washed and sugared a pan of fat berries, set the oil to heat, and stirred up flour in a bowl, cutting in bits of lard. Uncle Cunny, who loved my fried pies, peeked over my shoulder and rubbed his hands together. He was the only one who could make me smile.

By suppertime, the house was filled with smoke from my frying, and hand-sized crescents with crimped edges rested on squares of waxed paper on every surface in the kitchen and the parlor, and on plates on the first twelve steps that led to the second floor. Uncle, who had eaten five pies, refused supper and sat groaning in his chair, fingering a cup of weak tea and rubbing his belly. Auntie finally brought him the Pepto-Bismol while I started a new batch.

"Clea?" she said, looking things over. "Don't you think we have enough?"

I studied my handiwork, the steaming, lightly sugared half-moons, and replied, "One more batch."

"Then you'll eat something," she said. "I'll slice us that ham in the refrigerator and a tomato from the garden. Take a fork and score those cucumbers, will you? I've got the beets pickled with onion for tomorrow, and we'll make potato salad in the morning. We'll use mustard and vinegar—I don't trust mayonnaise in the summer heat. Tonight, Cunny can have thin soup after he's digested all those pastries."

With this last pronouncement, Uncle gave a big sigh.

I'd been skeptical about holding a picnic in False River, the town's main feature being cracked foundations, which were all that was left. There was part of a brick train station, and a weedy lot that was once the city park. It had a sand pit and two huge dead trees.

But Uncle and his buddies had taken scythes and lawn mowers and turned the whole thing into a respectable rectangle of green. They erected several dining canopies for shade, while Mr. Hazzleton hammered a couple of booths, where cold drinks would be passed out. I knew what that meant. There'd be one with lemonade for us, and at the other, gents—and some ladies—could neaten their soda pop with gin.

There was to be a great wooden tub of ice for striped watermelons, and long tables made of planks and old doors on saw-horses. The ladies would cover these with oilcloth while ladders went up for the hanging of red, white, and blue bunting.

Most important, three gents from Greenfield were coming down with their instruments. In return for a fine dinner and a free outpouring of Mr. Hazzleton's booze, they would play for the folks, and we might dance on the grass. I asked Uncle what instruments they would bring.

"Well, the bass fiddle," he said. I knew what that was, with its great, deep plunking. "A regular fiddle and a slide trombone."

I was picturing a golden horn winking in the sun, when Uncle gave Auntie a secret grin.

"What?" I said.

But Auntie just smiled.

At one o'clock, she came downstairs in a pink flowered dress, with a bit of ribbon tying up her hair. She looked like a big, shiny doll.

Uncle said to her, "My, you look pretty." And he went and kissed her on the cheek. "Jerusha, you smell like a summer day."

"Go on with your smooth self," Auntie said, but she took a paper fan and cooled herself. "It *is* a summer day. Now, quit actin' the fool and get this stuff loaded up."

So we began to carry out the baskets and hampers and covered bowls. I got into the bed of Uncle Cunny's truck and spread things around, then I sat down in the middle of the picnic food with my hands holding it all, while Auntie and Uncle climbed into the truck, and Uncle drove the road as slow as he could.

There were already folks in the park when we arrived, and we had plenty of help laying out our stuff, Auntie preening and saying "Get on now" to every last compliment. But she was smiling something fierce. I hung back, with one eye on the Maytubby boys, who were kicking up sand, and a gaggle of kids playing chase in a nearby lot. Claudie and Plain Genie were there too. But mostly I watched Auntie. She wasn't born here like the Reverend, but she'd adapted to False River like she'd been no-where else. To look at her, and to listen and to know her, you'd never think she'd been with a circus. While I could imagine her feeding and watering chickens, and putting them to bed, I could not imagine her teaching them how to do tricks. I re-solved to inquire further about that entire affair. Someday, I might even write about it. Meanwhile, I'd fry pies for every-one and be less like Mama and more like Auntie in both word and deed.

By two o'clock, the picnic tables were loaded with platters of ham and spicy fried chicken. There was pot roast too, with tiny potatoes and onions, bowls of salad and cauliflower and corn casseroles, and at the far end were the desserts.

The Reverend offered up a prayer that rose into the dead trees and caught on the pointy branches. The blessing wailed and boomed and spilled out over the people and the roads of town, and I'm sure the patients in the old folks' home could hear and join in, and maybe the ones passing on the highway too. It set-tled like sweet rain over the food. Then all our *amens* floated up to join it. Renewed and hungry, we took our forks and our paper plates and walked the line.

A time or two, Uncle and other men chased off a stray dog that came sniffing around, and while we sat on quilts, eating, a truck pulled up and three men got out with big black cases, and Uncle Cunny said, "Well, looks like the band is finally here." They declined to eat until they'd played some, and they tuned up their strings.

And play they did, firing us up with "Oh, Susanna" and other tunes I knew, and some that I didn't. Auntie and the other women sat in metal folding chairs and tapped their feet and swayed with the rhythm. The band broke for dinner and paper cups of cool drink.

When they were rested and ready to start up again, Uncle took from the seat of his truck a similar case, and pulled out an old brown guitar. If that wood had ever been shiny, it wasn't now. He perched himself on the edge of a chair while I watched in wonder, and messed with the strings. Then the band lit up with a fast-and-classy "Down by the Riverside." I especially liked this song, with its single line "Ain't gonna study war no more."

Uncle played marvelously, with a plastic pick. He leaned into the music and over the guitar, and he set it afire with strumming born of his heart and soul. Like he had just then found a way to let himself loose.

And then, of course, the dancing started, and Auntie was swept out of her chair. Uncle gave up playing to catch her up, and then danced with Claudie and Plain Genie, and finally me too.

He smiled. "I got to get back to playin', so I saved the best for last."

"Uncle Cunny," I said. "You ever been married?"

"No, ma'am, I have not. You lookin' for a husband?"

I blushed. "No, sir. Not a man in this world would want me for a wife."

"Child, why would you say a thing like that?"

"'Cause it's true. I hardly know who I am, Uncle Cunny."

The music had subsided into nothing, and I turned to look.

There was my mama, stumbling through the sand on her spiky heels. "Don't let me interrupt," she sang out. "Hey, can anyone join—without an invite? I'm sure that was just an oversight, y'all bein' such good neighbors."

I could see that she carried her own plastic glass and was drunk as a lord. I ran and grabbed her wrist. "Please, Mama, go back home," I said.

But she didn't see me, didn't hear. Times like this, I wondered if I was even there.

"Len Hazzleton!" Mama called out. "You servin' liquor over there? Come on, now, fill a lady's cup."

Reverend Ollie was on his feet. "Miz Shine, why don't you come here and sit awhile. Enjoy this fine music, let me fix you a plate."

"Don't give me any of your horseshit, Ollie Green. I ain't hungry, I come for a drink."

Miz Bertha Hazzleton was incensed. She stomped over to the counter and on around and took her mister by the ear, leading him out of our hearing. I knew what she was doing—she was laying into her man for even knowing my mama. So—Mr. Hazzleton had been over to visit her too.

Unsure what to do, I ran to Auntie and sat in her lap, too big, too long, sticking out like a blinking sign.

Mama waggled her fingers at the musicians and plucked her skirt up to her pretty thigh. The music started, and she pranced to the beat like a damn circus pony. This was not the waltz I'd seen her glide into when she was alone, this was high-stepping and stupid, and I wanted to lie down in that mowed grass and die. Then she spied me.

"Baby girl!" she called. "Come on over here and light your mama a new cigarette."

A hundred eyes shifted from my mother to me.

"Clarice Shine," Aunt Jerusha said, rising from her chair, though she had first to unload me. Auntie was wide in the beam, and it was a sticky day, and it took her a minute too long to get loose from the chair. Mama put her hands on her tricky hips and let out a snort.

I think the ground passed under my feet. Gone was the beating of my heart, the squeeze box of my lungs. I was suspended in this time and place, but not quite.

"That's it, darlin'," Mama said, her voice pealing like bells, and she pulled her blouse from her considerable breasts as though her skin was all sticky in the heat. She moved easy, like a cat, taking in the heavy food tables, and she pulled a box of matches from her skirt pocket. Her eyes were sharp and fixed on Auntie. "Fire me one up, Clea. Then go on and light one for yourself."

Auntie's eyes, however, were wild and shifting, and she moved faster than I've ever seen. In one blink of an eye, her big hands scooped up a pie, and in another blink, that coconut cream landed SPLAT on Mama's frilly blouse, the goo thick and yellow, oozing down her front. Mama let out a yell, the way soldiers might yodel when they charge into battle, and she took up a plastic pitcher bought from the Ninety-Nine Cent Store. She rushed at Auntie and dumped a gallon of sweet tea on her head.

Black curls plastered to her face and neck, Auntie went down hard on her rump. She sat there, sputtering and bleating like a drowning man.

All around me, horrid gasps rose up while Mama's laugh was long and wheezy. The music faded.

While other ladies struggled out of their chairs, Aunt Jerusha reached out and grabbed those white ankles, and in front of God and everybody, she took my mother down.

But Mama cabbaged onto the corner of a tablecloth, and food crashed around them as they rolled and kicked. Auntie wallowed in Miz Hazzleton's macaroni salad, but pretty soon had Mama thrashing on the bottom, those white legs winding around like snakes. They slammed into a second table. Slices of watermelon toppled off, and milky coleslaw. The ground was muck.

Mama bit Auntie's shoulder and drew blood. Then they went at it harder, their shoes coming off and buttons popping while they grunted and tussled on the ground. Mama's toenails had been polished a shiny red, but now her feet were muddy, in the slop and the goo. The soles of Auntie's pale, wide feet were slippery with pink frosting and molasses-baked beans.

Uncle Cunny came running, hollering, "Stop!"

The other men, cowards that they were, held back, their cigars stubby and wet and going to gray ash, grins wicked on their faces.

Miz Poole sat in a canvas-backed chair, and her red hair stood up in all directions. Aunt Jerusha lathered Mama's face with a whole custard pie.

I guess the basic shock had worn off, because they all crowded in then, ladies screaming and pulling Auntie off Mama, the gents getting hold of Mama's arms and bare legs and blushing furiously, not knowing what to do next.

"Get on out of here, Clarice Shine!" Auntie shouted. She was sucking in breaths and dark red in the face while the ladies all nodded, huffing, stiff-lipped and fiery-eyed.

Miss Shookie waddled up. "Clarice, your kind lays a bad name on everything. We all know who you are, and what you do."

Millicent Poole surfaced. "—Your black soul's seein' *hell*," she shrilled at my mama.

"—Jezebel! You leave our men alone."

"—And our *sons!*"

"We ought to rail you out of town!"

And on it ran, till Mama spoke up. "Y'all afraid of me? Well, you got reason. Where you think your men goin' when they run out for smokes?" Mama laughed. "'Fore long, one whore won't be enough around here. So go on, then, take my girl! Raise up another'n in your goddamn midst!"

All the ladies looked aghast. I knew that word. Webster said *aghast* denoted horror, a sharp halting of thought. For a while that awfulness hung in the air. And then everyone turned, and their eyes fell on me.

This was the second time Mama had given me away. I stood there, hugging my elbows, my eyes on the ground. My jitteriness had smoothed. I had gone inside my head, to a place that was usually safer than this, but today even that was filled with sorrow.

In the end, Mr. Hazzleton brought his Ford around and three or four men, looking sheepish, piled in with Mama.

"Just seein' her home, sugar!" They waved to their wives.

By the end of the day, the park had emptied out, and banners hung in tatters. It was the worst Fourth of July in history. Half of False River was not speaking to the other half, and nobody at all was talking to me.

14

That night I heard folks. Teenagers, I thought, in their daddies' trucks, driving back and forth over Mama's lawn and in the field across the road. From the attic, I watched them lean out their truck windows and swill whiskey from glass bottles. Then they clambered out, took buckets from the back, and pried the lids. This time whole gallons. I could tell the color, easy, because when it hit Mama's house, it ran like blood in the moonlight. And they sang, a kind of drunken chant. I climbed out on the porch roof and tried to separate the words.

Clarice the ho' tore down the do'
The guards had come to town—

Another roaring pass and more buckets tossed, the cans banging against the clapboard, rattling on the little porch. I closed my eyes tight. I could not imagine what daylight would bring.

In a golden wig, she smelled like pig
And wore her wedding gown . . .

I curled up on the roof like a baby waiting to be born, and pressed my hands tight over my ears. I turned my back to a new night breeze that had risen and even closed my eyes to a curve of white moon. But I could not block out the revving of motors or the hard clump-bumping of those heavy trucks in the field. And I could not help hearing the wild, wild shrieking:

The ho' she screamed, and the dead all dreamed
of a scabby roll in the hay . . .

Laughing and wild screeching among those boys—until the retching. Then they bumped away, back to False River and whatever rocks they had crawled out from under.

Beware the ho' with the painted do'
If you ever pass this way . . .

Until the picnic, I'd thought my mama was an end-of-the-road secret. But it wasn't so. Long ago, word had spread like a plague on the river, where it was carried down to every last person along the Pearl and probably the gulf. Everyone knew. In fact, for a long time—maybe since before I was born—they'd been privy to much more truth than me.

There was no place to run, no air, no release. I crept back through my window, into my room. I lay on my bed and pulled the sheet over me, but the smell of wet paint was in my nose and my head.

I made myself a deep and dark promise: I was never going back to school. I wasn't welcome there—or anywhere. And it wasn't because I was smart, or white.

I was a Shine, and everybody knew it.

15

Summer was over, and autumn came. In the end, I lost the battle and went back to school. Still, I spoke to no one there, and I did not answer questions when asked but sat like a bump on the wooden seat. Finally, the teacher came around and talked to Auntie, and they both looked worried. Auntie asked me to try harder to take part in my learning. After that I did my homework and penciled answers on tests, but away from home, I hardly talked at all.

In the evenings, I sat on Auntie's upstairs gallery and took to watching the neighbors—the two Mr. Oatys in particular. They lived in a shotgun place, a distance along the road. They took care of their father, who drooled and talked in a way that never made any sense.

Those brothers were funny old geezers. Every day they walked the mile or so into town and carried odd clanking jars in all their pockets—coats, vests, and pants. Nobody knew if the bottles were empty or full.

One early morning, a haze lay around. The Oaty brothers drove by with two pigs in crates that slid around in the back of a borrowed truck. There was one black pig and one pink that they'd probably bought from the prison and were taking to the slaughterhouse in Greenfield.

I had nothing to do yet as Auntie was laundering in the electric washer on the back porch. I could hear its hum, clunking as it changed cycles, and I wandered down to the river, and followed the loamy bank north and east, dragging a stick in the dirt. Wash was the one thing from which I was exempt, having been instructed to commence stripping beds one morning, and having worked into the tub the afghan that lay on Auntie's bed. Her mother had knitted it from purest wool. The whole thing came out knotted and less than half its size, so that Auntie roared and stomped and beat me about the legs with a wooden spoon. I hid in the attic until better times, which meant dinner, when she'd settled down to a moan. Thereafter, the actual wash was not my job, although I was frequently called from a book to pin it on the line or to gather it in.

I set out, with my book, for a particular place where I liked to read. Not far from home, Little Duck Creek meandered into the False River, and there I came upon the back of the Oaty place, no more or less down-at-the-heels than the rest. I liked the looks of a shed they had, with the door propped open. The dirt floor of that spot was wallowed out and lined with a blanket, and it made for comfy reading. I was settling in and idly keeping an eye turned to the back door of the house when something moved and caught my eye.

There were times when it had proved to be in my best interest to mind my business, but I crept out of that shed among the willows and approached, stealthily. There was an opening beneath the house, the space set with bars, and, from between them, eyes in a pale, pale face stared out at me.

I could not think of a word to say nor a thing to do but squat there in the yard and stare down at this small person—a boy, I thought, and not very old.

"You workin' at something under there?" I said. "Fetching a snake or a cat?"

He just looked at me.

"I say, what you doin' down there?" And I put my face close to the bars, looking in upon a strip of soft light from the sun that was now lying low, and saw a filthy quilt and some other things scattered about.

"You sleep under there?" I asked, incredulous.

He said nothing but tilted his head like a curious dog.

And sure enough, there was a pan, a kind of dog dish, and another that had run dry of water, and it came to me with breathlessness and heartache that he did, indeed, live under this house. It was more than I could fathom, or stand, and I rose up on legs that were stiff as those bars and backed off like he had pox and it was spreading.

And I ran as fast as I could, carrying home with me that terrible secret, that sudden burning knowledge of a dark underground prison, so hung up with stomach cramps that I pulled down my britches and squatted among the weeds, my bowels emptying in the high Thompson grass.

I'd missed our meal, but Miss Shookie hadn't missed me, and she was fussing with the supper dishes when I made a showing, and I figure she mistook my silence for remorse, because no one said anything to me that night. I kept silent for most of three days, taking Finn's biscuits and honey, buttered sweet corn, and grits, just laying them under the tree, muttering, "You better get these before the ants carry them off," and him scrambling down long enough to nab them.

"What's the matter with you?" he finally said. "You stopped talking altogether? Ain't like you."

I went down on my knees under the tree and wrapped my arms around myself.

"What?" he said. "What is it?"

"Finn," I said, "it's almost my birthday. And if you'll come outa that goddamn tree, I got something to show you."

"You watch your swampy mouth," Finn said. "I know Miss Jerusha, an' she'll wash it out with soap."

"You'll be saying worse," I said, "when you see."

He eyed me sideways from where he swung like a monkey. Finn sure had this tree thing down. "This some trick?" he said. "You thinking to lure me down and—"

"No trick," I said. "You coming with me or not?"

"Not," he said.

"You're the sorriest thing ever, Finn. I got something I have to do, and I sure could use your help with this mission."

"You're shinin' me on," he said.

"I'm not," I said, and walked away.

Finn came down that tree like it was slicked with butter and landed on his feet, scooped up the cold potatoes, and crammed them in his mouth. "Mmrrrmph?" he said.

"Don't talk with your mouth full."

"I asked—" He took his time chewing and swallowing. "Where we goin' and what's so almighty important?"

"You got to see this to believe it."

And I took off, this time in a straight line down to the Oatys' house, thankful that nobody along the way questioned where I was going in such an all-fired hurry, and when we reached his short fence, I stood and looked over the pickets.

"There," I said. "Around there."

"I don't see nothing."

"Under the house, can you believe. Lord, Lord, Finn, there's a kid, smaller than me and starved half to death. If he's not dead by now."

"This one of your stories, Clea?"

"This is no made-up thing, you sorry piece of garbage. You got to get closer."

"What if the Oatys come out?"

"They've gone to slaughter some hogs."

"Well, what if their daddy comes out with a strap? That ol' man don't talk plain, but he's meaner'n twelve snakes in a barbecue pit."

"He won't touch me or Auntie'll be all over him when she sees. Come on, Finn. Don't be a sissy."

The day had darkened, storm clouds clotting the sky like an angry face.

"Okay, then," I said. "I'll rescue him alone."

"Wait," Finn said. It was the first time I'd noticed his high-top tennis shoes, no socks, his tanned and dirty legs. Finn on the ground now, a real boy, a person. "Okay, I'm comin'."

"Then keep down and be quiet."

And there he was, that white, white kid, with his face close up and scared—scared of us, I saw. Had it been me under there, I'd have had a stranglehold on the bars, screaming and shaking them like tomorrow depended on it. Or maybe this kid had already given up on ever being rescued. Maybe he didn't care anymore.

"Holy—"

"Hush," I said. "You're scaring the bejesus out of him. He's real shy."

"He's in a dang cage under there!" Finn said.

"Well, not a real cage. You reckon he just plays under here?"

"Behind bars?" Finn said. "He's got a damn dog dish."

I held my tongue, squatted down, and reached a hand toward the bars, but the pale white boy shrank back, his tongue sticking out between his lips like a thing too big for his mouth. His eyes were huge and round, his spiky hair without color, and he had no eyebrows nor lashes.

"Something's bad wrong, Finn," I said. "Listen to his breathing."

"He ain't right, that's for sure."

"What's the matter with him?"

"Born wrong, I guess," Finn said. "Come out upside down, or strangle-held."

"What's that mean?"

"Never mind. You're too young to know stuff like that."

"I'm not, either, and I wish you'd quit saying that. I'm old enough, and if you'd just tell me things, then I'd know."

"I 'spect he had his mama's cord wrapped around his neck."

"Neck's scrawny as a chicken's," I said. "Wouldn't take much to cut off his wind."

"Hell, he prob'ly don't even know what we're saying."

I reached my hand inside the bars. "Come here, boy. There's a shed over there, Finn. See if there's a saw."

Finn came back with a funny look on his face. "There's not one, and anyway, you can't saw through those bars."

"What's the matter with you? Walk around and see if you can find another way."

"Clea, you been reading in that shed yonder, haven't you? That's how you found him."

I made a face. I never lied to Finn. "I have. It was already a good spot, a hole dug out with blankets and all."

"Clea, you see that chain fastened to the wall?"

I had not.

"I think they kept the kid in there, too," he said. "Probably at first. There's a hammer in there, but listen. Things ain't right here. If we don't get him out fast, I'm goin'."

"Not me," I said. "I'm not going without him."

"Well, other side of the house, there's a crawl-through. It's nailed over with plywood," Finn said. "Maybe we can break in there." He went to the shed that had once been my reading place but which now turned my stomach.

He came back with a claw hammer and we both looked at the eighteen-inch piece of board. "I don't know," he said.

"We can free this boy. Did I tell you my birthday's coming, Finn? I'm going to be twelve. And I can do anything I want."

What I wanted was to beat the wood with that hammer till I got that kid out. So that's what I did, Finn holding his breath, lest the old man come running. At first the boy didn't want to be loose, so I had to flatten myself out on the ground and go in after him, which was bad because the place stunk so.

He could hardly stand up, and he was wheezing something awful. I took his hand and led him home. Finn carried the hammer *in case*, he said, *he had to fight off the Oatys.*

If Auntie was surprised to see the boy we called Wheezer, she never let on. This one took the cake. He was filthy. He froze up, clutching himself, when Auntie tried to take off his clothes, so she filled a dishpan with water and wiped him down the best she could.

In his filthy rags, he sat at our table while Auntie, as an early birthday present for me, stirred up a pan of fudge clotted with walnuts.

Turned out Wheezer loved fudge, but Auntie, who wanted to

spoon-feed him oatmeal with milk, said *Not too much, it could make him sick.*

He stayed the afternoon and through dinner. When Auntie had him full of mashed potatoes and gravy and chopped-up roast beef, she had no choice but to call Social Services and report the Oatys.

Before dark, the children's superintendent, Miss Pilcher, came in her county station wagon. She parked in front of Auntie's house. Miss Pilcher was tall and high yellow and flabby of jaw. She had fatty eyes that trusted nobody and nothing, and no one liked her in return. She asked who had found "the boy."

I said I did, as Finn had eaten his dinner on the back porch step, where we all had joined him, and he'd long since gone up to his tree.

Miss Pilcher gave me a look and said she could not let a minor sign the papers and stuck them under my auntie's nose. But Auntie said she'd had nothing to do with the freeing of the young man who'd lived under that house.

Miss Pilcher said *Then what did Auntie expect her to do with "the boy,"* and we all looked at each other while she flapped her chins and talked on about the foster care system being grossly over-loaded. In the end she packed Wheezer, like freight, in the back end of her station wagon and took him away. He knelt with his face to the window and lifted one hand to me.

I worried that with no one to take him in, Wheezer might soon be living under a bridge in Mobile or in a rough park in Birmingham. On the other hand, what if one day the foster care system unloaded itself, and had all kinds of room. Then what would happen to Finn—and to me?

Later, we all went down to the Oatys' place, including Finn and the sheriff, who had so far said nothing, and we looked around. The Oaty brothers acted sorely put out, claiming they had seen "no kid, no pale wheezing boy," and they knew nothing about it. They got downright huffy and, while the older Mr. Oaty sat on the porch, drinking from a straw and dribbling on his baby bib, we all took turns crouching down for a look under the house. There wasn't a sign that anybody'd been under there.

My stomach turned over, and I cried out, insisting that was where we'd found him. My voice rose to a caterwaul, until Finn came up and took hold of my hand. "She's right. That kid was livin' in there."

After the sheriff grunted and sucked in his belly fat and crawled under there, he came out saying the earth was packed hard and warm, and there were chicken bones and other garbage scattered around. The Oatys lied and said they'd gotten real bad about throwing trash beneath the house.

The sheriff said he could also tell by the smell that somebody had regularly urinated and defecated under the place.

The Oatys looked at each other and then at their pa. It was possible, they said, he had done that too.

✳

That night, I went out to sit under the tree and talk to Finn. The night was full of cricket sounds. I could not think what they'd witnessed that was good enough to sing about. This world was unfair, and people were sick and stupid and unkind to one another.

"Sometimes they are," Finn agreed from above.

"It's a waste of being alive!"

"Ain't always so," he said. "Sometimes people are downright funny."

"Wasn't nothing amusing about that kid." I was indignant to

the soul. "And that damned Miss Pilcher—I hate her, Finn. She ever comes back here, I swear I'll ..."

Over my head, Finn's branch was bouncing something awful, and when I looked up, his eyes were alight, and he was laughing.

"There wasn't one thing funny today, Finn," I said.

But he laughed some more and pointed toward the house.

The light was on in my attic room. The window was raised and there, between the pulled-back curtains, stood my wide Cousin Bitsy. She lifted her shirt and presented her great bosoms for Finn and all the world to see. They were big as watermelons. Her broad, flat nipples were the color of creamed coffee.

Finn rattled and roared and couldn't tear his eyes away.

I went into the house and said no more.

16

It was a strangely warm fall, with nothing happening that was near as exciting as the finding of that kid at the Oatys'. Nights, we lay awake on top of the covers, while below us the False River was a green sludgy wallow. It stank mightily.

Our side of the big Pearl was Mississippi; the western bank was Louisiana. Occasionally, but not often, a sigh of wind might drift upriver from the Gulf of Mexico and cool off both sides. The Pearl itself was a wide and rolling body of water that did a mysterious thing. In no hurry to join the Intracoastal Waterway, it appeared to spread out into a lazy swamp. All along the Pearl River, dead trees stuck up like pointy fingers, and thick green scum settled on its surface. It smelled like vinegar and dirty socks but was still good for pulling a catfish or two. But the miles and miles of marsh were deceiving. The currents underneath both False River and the Pearl were amazingly strong.

Autumn was our regular season for bad weather, most of which came up from the Gulf. With landfall, every storm seemed to sprout arms and legs that groped their way up first the Pearl, then its elbow, the False River, with whirling black clouds and rain that blew east to west. Wind ripped off shingles and shutters, and carried away lawn chairs and plastic swimming pools. It brought down thick branches of trees that had been growing in their places for aeons.

Afterward, convicts came in their orange-striped suits that looked like pajamas, to repair the roof of the Oasis of Love Bingo Hall and Prison Camp Center. They straddled its peak, though they were chained at the ankle and issued hammers and nails while two guards stood by with batons and walkie-talkies in hand. Below, on the ground, stood two more guards with rifles. From time to time, the prisoners were allowed a cup of water from a jug.

Everybody knew what kind of search would go on before these men were allowed back onto Hell's Farm. Any tiny thing they had found and were smuggling back was called contraband and worth a miserable month spent in the basement of the Farm's big house.

One windy early September day, when the gale was fierce and flattening the weeds, Auntie and I were closing windows on the third floor in preparation for rain. We looked out and saw Mama bobbling across the field.

Overhead, the black sky began to boil.

Uncle Cunny stood down in the yard, where he'd gone to drag the domino table up on the porch. Mama held something flapping in her hand and was walking herky-jerkied, but not just with the wind, and Uncle left the table and went over to meet her.

I ran down the stairs and out the back door and caught up.

"Afternoon, Miz Shine. Can I help you with something?" Uncle Cunny said.

"You, Cunny Gholar," Mama said in her thick-tongued voice, more difficult to hear with the shrieking wind. "You get in your truck an' go on home now. This got nothin' to do with you."

"No? What's that you got there?"

Mama was holding on to a paper that was snapping and already ripped by the gale, and she made an attempt to flatten it, but it only tore more.

"I want for that child, Cunny! I did a wrong, just givin' her away. Now I've wrote me up a bill of sale."

Uncle Cunny and I stood still in that grass with our mouths dropped open. I looked up at him with eyes so wide they hurt.

"You—what, ma'am?" he said.

"I want for that child. She ain't worth much. Two hun'ed dollars be fine."

I must not have been hearing right. Could things like this happen?

"You tell Jerusha Lovemore she owes me for her." She raised her voice more. "You come on out here now, J'rusha Lovemore! Two hun'ed dollars set it right!"

"Miz Shine, you best go on home and get some rest," Uncle Cunny said between his teeth. "I'm sure yo' just under the weather now, and don't know what you are saying."

"Oh, I know," she said.

Uncle looked at me and patted my hand. "Get back inside, Clea. It's fixin' to rain. I'll be there directly."

And he let go of me, got Mama turned around, and they set off together, she leaning hard against him, her voice still carrying on the wind. Leaves were whirling around my feet.

"Where you going, Uncle Cunny?" I called.

"I'm seein' a lady home," he said.

The rain came upon us, and I watched it soak them and slash all around as Mama stumbled and Uncle picked her up, and when I got wet from watching, I went in and slumped down in a corner of the parlor. The rain ran from me onto Auntie's floor. I hunkered there with my hands over my head. Auntie tried to raise me up, tried to jerk me alive, but I would not stand or sit, nor look up, down, or sideways.

Uncle Cunny came back then, and they talked in fierce voices and moved into the kitchen so they could holler and yell, and I heard Auntie cry out, *"She guv her to me, fair and square!"* And I thought I felt the floor move under my feet.

Auntie and Uncle went out into the rain and were gone a long time, so long, in fact, that I got up with stiff knees, and, still wet, I climbed to the third floor, where I crawled under my bed and lay flat on my belly.

A while passed, and I heard Auntie's shoes on the stairs. She came in where I was and got down on her knees. "You can slide on out now," she said.

I did not reply.

"She was drunk," Auntie said, "and meant nothing by those ignorant words."

I closed my eyes tight.

"Uncle Cunny took that paper from her and tore it in a million pieces, and it flew away across the river. Ain't that good?"

"It's good," I said. But I would not come out.

Auntie let herself down, and she just lay there, on her side on the floor, with her head on an elbow and her wet stockings steaming, saying no more, just keeping me company.

✳

In the days that followed, even my breath shut down. I held it close to my chest, like my lungs and my heart were afraid to let go. I ate little and slept less. Conversations were few, and mostly with Finn. I was cold all the time.

Sometimes I sat on the side porch and looked across the field at the house where I was born. One evening, when fall was tightening down into winter, I took up a towel to give a hand with the dish drying, and I asked Auntie, "Whatever happened to my daddy?"

She paused with her hands deep in the suds. "He went off."

"But where? He went off *where*?"

Auntie looked up and out through the window. "Just down the road. One day, he set out with a suit of clothes on his back, and wearing his best black shoes. She never saw him again."

"What was his name, at least?"

For a moment she was silent. "Nobody knows."

"Did he live with us, with Mama?"

"Not really, baby. He was just passing through."

"He never married my mama?"

Auntie missed only half a beat. "He did not."

"Auntie, Mama's a ho', ain't that right?"

"*Isn't*," Uncle said real soft. He still sat at the table, sipping his coffee. I guess he thought, with this one more time of correcting me, he could put off me hearing the answer—or Auntie's giving it.

"Isn't she?" I said.

"Child, do you even know what a whore is?"

"I guess I do." I ran the dish towel around the rim of a glass that was white and pebbled and saved just for my milk. "I've been over there and seen what all they're up to, those guards from the prison, and others too."

Auntie looked sad. "You've gone and growed up before your time."

She meant I knew too much. But I didn't know as much as Finn. He was the expert at everything. Almost.

17

The following Sunday, Miss Shookie came to get us in her car. At First and Last Holy Word, the Best Reverend Ollie was in fine form. He didn't wait for the sermon to move souls, he took the pulpit, reared back with his eyes shut, and laid into the day: "Oh, mighty GOD!" His voice was a trumpet. "Let us SEE the enemy, Lord. Let us KNOW him by his wicked heart. Lift us HIGH, Lord, above the temptation to give in to him, oh, yes!"

A bit stunned, the congregation murmured, "Amen."

"Make us STRONG, Lord, to serve you better in these *daaaaaaaaays* of tribulation. Make us more as we labor in your service, in your vineyards, in your temple, oh, YES!"

Now we were in tune, and the church went in motion with raised arms and fluttery, floating hands, and the hallelujahs that swept on and on.

"Yes, Jesus, oh, yes, Lord . . ."

The Reverend bellowed, "Keep us NOT JUST AFLOAT! We'll step OUT, Lord, as Peter did—"

And here came the choir, all six of them humming and backing the prayer. I wondered how they'd known to do that: "Fishers of men, oh, fishers of men—"

I didn't think the Reverend was talking about regular fishing.

"—Lift us to WALK on the stormiest seas!"

Miss Shookie cried, "Oh, Jesus . . ."

"Amen and —"

"Lord, Lord," said Auntie.

Webster's definition of *amen* was *So it is.*

On this morning the Reverend was full of something, and I wasn't just thinking the Holy Spirit. Everybody loved him. He was a good man with a fine and lucky life. But what did he know of stormy seas? Had he ever been afloat and alone, and not seen the shore? Had he ever found a hole in his goddamned boat?

"Amen," said the Reverend. And with that, we were primed, ready to be preached to, saved and re-saved. Dedicated once more.

The choir sang. The congregation sang. I wondered what would happen if Millicent Poole suddenly led us in *"Clarice the ho' . . ."*

I drew a stubby pencil and tithing envelope from the rack in front of me and began to scribble. When Auntie saw me and swatted my hands, I went on writing, trying to remember the words.

—*And wore her wedding gown.*

※

That night I told Finn, "I'm gonna do something bad."

"I'll help you," he said.

"How, when you won't hardly get down from that tree?"

"I would," he said. "I did for Wheezer."

"Finn, why don't you come down from there and live with Auntie? She's told you you can."

Among the leaves, he shook his head.

"Your daddy surely didn't mean for you to stay there forever."

"Anyway, I see enough of you," he said. "I couldn't take any more."

That hurt my feelings. "What—you watch me through my window, do you? The way you watched Bitsy?"

"I seen you once." He looked away. "You ain't got nothing, girl; you only twelve."

"So—you planning to sit there till I get me some shape and then take a picture?"

"No," he said. "I don't have to wait. Bitsy'll take me down to the river anytime I want."

"Bitsy?"

"Yeah, and she's got more goods than you."

"Finn!"

"What?"

"Listen," I said, "I'm gonna do something bad."

"How bad?"

"Enough that they might take me away."

"Who?" he said, his green eyes widening. "What you gonna do?"

"Well," I told him, "you hang on to your tree."

18

I kept the sash of my window greased with Vaseline.

I found the drainpipe with my toes, and shinnied down till my foot touched the trellis. Auntie's roses were climbers, gone wild up here and still thorny, although it was near winter now and all the flowers were gone. Silently I stepped down and down, and set my feet upon the cold December ground. There was a cowardly moon this night, with piled-up clouds like the sky was full of shuffling hunchbacks. The wind was up. I heard it rustling the grass and rushing the river along.

I had worn narrow paths in the tall grass between Auntie's place and Mama's, and even in the pitch black I found one easy and made my way by whatever magnet leads us home.

The lights were on in Mama's house, ramping yellow slats from the windows to the weeds. If there were frogs croaking or night birds singing, I could not hear them. The whole world was lost to the racket and thump of tinny music from an old stereo player.

I pulled open the creaking screen door and stepped onto the porch. The narrow cot was stripped bare to the mattress. I turned the knob and went into the kitchen.

The music wobbled, uncertain then plunking made to sound like falling tears or rain, and I thought about Uncle Cunny's lightning fingers on the strings of his guitar at the picnic, the groaning tables on that Fourth of July, Mama's bill of sale flying up in the wind when Uncle tore it to shreds. I thought of how Auntie lay down on the floor.

Over the years, the presence of me had given them all hell. The only thing worse was the presence of my mother.

Mama to child, blood into blood.

In the living room, cross-legged, Mama had an audience. Two guards in Farm gray were sprawled on the sofas. They all looked bleary with their drinking, their glasses in hand, sleepy-eyed, with smug smiles on their stubbly faces. Mama sat alone on the floor. The paint stains were still there.

Her filmy pink dress lay at the foot of the stairs, one nylon stocking on the arm of a chair. I felt the same—a piece of me here, a shred of me there.

My mother sat in her panties and bra, showing crotch and cleavage, the feather boa around her neck, the end hanging down on her bare silken back.

"Mama?" I said.

But her chin wagged and sagged to her collarbone.

"Mama?"

I hunkered down and looked at her face. Her eyes were half open, showing a vague light in the window, but the rest of her had gone away. A lit cigarette hung on her bottom lip. A fire waiting to drop down. I wondered how many hundred times in my life I'd be required to see that she was safe when she was drunk. My years—and hers—stretched out long in front of me.

I took the cigarette from her mouth and puffed on it, carried it through to the porch. I lay down on the bare mattress with one arm under my head, the way Mama's gents often did, and looked at the ceiling. I held the lipsticked butt in front of my face, flicked the ash away, and watched a thin trail of smoke rise up. There was nothing to think, because I'd thought it all, fretted and angered and grown pain in my belly till there wasn't room for anything else. I put it away only when I was so tired that I couldn't carry it. And then, minutes later, here it would come again—the who-am-I, the where-am-I, the work of keeping Mama away from everyone else, the never-ending fear that Auntie would grow tired of me, that Uncle would feel I was more trouble than I was worth.

But if they came to their senses and put Clea Shine down, where would she stand? On what actual ground did my feet belong?

I turned over on my belly and rubbed the glowing end of the cigarette on the floor.

I thought I heard a thousand hands clapping. Around me, the skinny house shuddered and whined. Was I dreaming? No. The dry kitchen wall was a plane of fire, flames rocketing from the knotholes.

Someone was screaming. I tumbled off the cot, trying to clear the fog and recall where I was. I scrambled across the floor toward the kitchen, but a man crashed through the door, his legs burning. I rolled away and twisted. His hair was gone, and his back was raw red and black char.

I felt for the door and believed I was in the kitchen. Black smoke rolled over my head. Sparks were everywhere. In seconds, the fire had eaten the table and was licking at the cabinet doors. Someone was lying spread-eagle on the floor, face gone and fire lapping at his clothes. I tried to squeeze past. Flames raced along the kitchen ceiling and into the living room. Through the throat-burning smoke, I recognized Mama. She had passed out in her spot on the floor and toppled over. The boa was on fire.

I lunged ahead, feeling for her. But now the front wall and the roof had caught fire, and I rubbed at my eyes while the ceiling groaned. Plaster and brittle beams of wood came down. And then the front door crashed open, and a rush of air ignited all that was left, and I was skidding across the floor, into smoldering weeds. I rose to my feet and was running. *Running.*

I cowered down and hid in the grass by the river and cried and breathed, and didn't breathe, and retched and hiccuped while wood and tall grass and everything that had been there before crackled and burned and was no more. Firemen roared up in pumper trucks, and I both watched and hid my eyes while fire-men, and the man I knew to be the county medical examiner, carried out bodies in bags.

I heard my name called, over and over, in pleadings and screams, *Clea* becoming six syllables, then ten.

Toward morning someone picked me up, coated with ash and snot and filth.

The air was gray, the field burnt; the house was rubble. Through the dark haze of a bad fairy tale, the only light shining was an occasional glimpse of the Farm's razor wire. There was no *Mama's house* now, to block the view.

I tried to make out the guard turrets, the big brick house with its torturous dungeons—the place where, in short order, I would be going.

Through the long hours of that day, Auntie rocked me. I was too long in the leg but scared beyond caring. Uncle brought tea and made me sip, though I wouldn't raise my head from Auntie's shoulder, where her dress had grown soggy from my tears. The tea only caused me to choke and cry more. Auntie told him to come with wet washcloths, and they tried to clean my arms and legs, but I clung to her with my fists and my knees. My hair stuck to me, and I wet myself and Auntie too. By the time they got me into a clean nightgown, my tears had made ashy stains on everything.

Instead of her usual lumbering around with a face full of muffin, Bitsy sat in a chair, and Miss Shookie moved about with a strange quietness. Neighbors came, even the younger Mr. Oatys, who acted like they'd never in their lives kept a boy under their house.

The ladies of the church stopped in, the ones who had hated my mama so hard on the Fourth and called her names and wouldn't speak to their husbands. Before long, the sheriff came too—he'd been over at the fire—looking sad and sorry that he had to ask questions. I could answer none of them. The horrid and flabby Miss Pilcher arrived in her green county station wagon, and with her was the hated Millicent Poole. She'd been on the telephone and among the neighbors, making calls and fanning flames. Like everybody else, she had first been next door to stand and cluck over the smoking embers, and now they all tracked in the sticky ash.

I was very afraid and had no one to whom I could confess my fears. I recalled how Miss Pilcher had taken Wheezer away. She had a high nasal whine, like an animal call. Miss Shookie called her a harpy and turned her back on her. Miss Pilcher shook a sheaf of papers and then her pencil and finally her fist, but Auntie kept her arms tight around me. In the end, Miss Pilcher said, "I'll be back, and *then,* by God, I'll have a court order."

Auntie shot back, "And I'll have a lawyer by suppertime. I'm responsible for the girl—you go tend to more important things."

But I wondered if there was anything more important.

The mood in our house stayed dismal and gray.

The most unfathomable thing was—Miss Izzie Thorne took time from school and came to be with us. We held a wake for my end, for the death of me. They sat on the sofa with me wedged between the skinny Miss Thorne and my rotund aunt. They sipped their coffee, and although I could not drink, I was given coffee that was mostly milk. Auntie said I had the tremors bad enough. Even in my misery, I could not take my eyes from Miss Thorne, her broomstick legs with their cotton stockings, her flat-heeled shoes, and what Auntie called a Marcel wave. This woman, who had corrected and chastised me in the classroom, sat daily now, looking like she wanted to say something but wasn't sure what.

Uncle stayed over in one of the two rooms on the second floor. Miss Shookie did too. I think she was afraid some big thing would happen, and she might miss it. Or maybe she was just there in case Auntie needed her.

But Uncle's presence was for me. He sat in the chair by the window and oversaw the road, announced any comings, and helped Auntie and Miss Shookie in the kitchen. He peeled carrots and onions that made him cry. At the table, Uncle's small antics had once sent me into peals of laughter. Now, when Miss Shookie called us to dinner, I begged off. But I was not excused. To please them, I took up my knife and fork and cut my roast beef or a wedge of melon into tiny pieces. I could not eat. When the conversation turned frightening, which was most of the time, Uncle laid his hand, palm up, on the table, and I slid my smaller one into his. Right-handed Uncle—who, because of

Claudie Maytubby, had once eaten his supper with his fingers—now ate with his left. For my benefit.

He did not sleep well; none of us did. Nightly, Auntie checked the locks on the doors—a thing I had never seen her do before. Uncle walked the hall below me, then down the stairs to the kitchen, where I heard the toilet flush and water run.

One week later, a volunteer fireman ducked in apologetically and said they were still over there, patrolling and checking, beating down hot spots. Twice, a pumper truck came out and those men hooked up their hoses and sprayed things down, kept the earth damp and sparks from starting up grass fires.

If there didn't come a rain, they said, and this wind kept up, they expected bad things to happen not only here and in the weeds next door but also for the neighbors, and in the prison gardens and as far as the hog farm. Auntie took them into the kitchen, talking softly but long and hard, and crying some, and therein my heart ached. Not for me, or for the old house across the way, but for what Auntie was feeling, and my great fear that it might separate us. But Auntie had said that both she and Miss Izzie Thorne had once made a brave stand, and maybe now they would keep me safe from harm.

I didn't know what she meant.

The greater question, one that plagued me like a worsening case of flu, was whether I deserved to be safe from harm. In her entire life, my mama never stood up for a single thing, and I'd hated her in ways no words can describe.

For the county workers and other visitors, Auntie made thick pork-roast sandwiches that they ate at our table. Their faces, full of pity and concern, sucked the breath right out of me. Auntie directed me to cut slices of cake and refill the tea glasses. She brooked no backtalk, and I did as I was told. But, oh, my soul—

those days were almost intolerable. The kitchen was full of a heavy purple sadness, though nobody but me seemed to have trouble breathing.

At night something cold wrapped around my heart. My eyes refused to close. During the days, my mouth was dry and glued shut. My soul was black as tar.

Reverend Ollie Green, whose books I'd once borrowed, came to visit. He lifted me up and set me on the sofa, and told me God loved me, but I knew he was lying. God loved the Reverend because he was good. God loved Auntie because she fed sandwiches to His flock. And He loved Uncle Cunny Gholar because, with Uncle's fine humor and his pencil-thin mustache, everybody did.

Neighbors and folks who knew Auntie, and had heard of our troubles, drove from as far away as Jackson and Hattiesburg and Slidell, Louisiana. They whispered gossip with Miss Shookie and ignored Miss Pilcher's green station wagon in the yard and her presence in our house. They unloaded angel food cakes and green-onion salads and crisp-browned casseroles. Some sat in our parlor with their Bibles and prayed.

Auntie kept the lights turned low. My hands and feet were freezing, and my backbone shook. While Auntie made endless pots of coffee and sliced loaves of the neighbors' pumpkin bread, Miss Pilcher sprang a half-dozen more visitations on us. Every time, she came armed with a clipboard, a sour face, a camera, and a fresh white glove.

Finally, folks were thinning out. In ones and twos, they drifted away, closing the screen door gently. Millicent Poole, though, stayed on. Every day she was the first to arrive and the last to leave. She had long crooked fingers that kept reaching and plucking at dust motes and lint, and she looked like she wanted to get me alone. She told Auntie, in her rusty voice, that I was overrun with Satan's demons, and less than a candidate for foster care. I'd be placed in a home for miscreants, for schizophrenics and delinquents—*and then prison would be the best thing for me.*

Otherwise, she said, I'd turn out just like—that knobby finger turned to the kitchen window, through which we could see the heap of charred scrap—my mother.

Auntie said that was not possible, that I was Jerusha Love-more's daughter.

But a dozen things in the room said otherwise.

"Oh, for Christ's sake, Jerusha," Millicent Poole said one evening while she drank up our tea and scratched at her arms with her long brittle nails. "You're as blind as you are ugly negroid."

Auntie dumped me on the floor and turned on the enemy. "And you, Millie Poole, are a hateful white woman in a colored church. You got no business in False River, no kindness to extend. You got no love, no joy, no thanks, no sex. Get on, now, outa my house and away from my girl."

Auntie's words should have flowed like syrup and settled around my aching heart. They did not. I watched the two of them, nose to nose, and wondered why Auntie did not remind Miz Poole that she was also an opium user and a candidate for jail.

From the door, Millicent Poole pointed one curled and yellow nail at me. "I curse you, girl! The church and all of False River curse you. In the name of the archangels, I brand you a minion from hell. You will crawl this earth on all fours because you are not worthy to stand. When you come of age, you will pay for what you have done.

"That is," she said, as Auntie's hands went for her throat, "if you're not dragged to hell before that."

Uncle got there first, and he rushed Miz Poole clean off her feet, bundled her out the door, and, with the sole of his Sunday shoe, booted her on down the road.

�֍

My fear of going to prison was greater than all nations. As soon as the sheriff decided how guilty I was, he would come for me. He'd put me in chains and walk me along Potato Shed Road, while everyone crowded up at this end, nodding and saying, "I told you."

Inside, I would be strung by my thumbs, or hidden in a dark and moldy chamber in the earth. All the things I'd heard or conjured about Hell's Farm rolled over me now—I'd eat bread with blue mold, and have nothing to drink. I'd be allowed no pencil, no paper. They'd work me mercilessly, slitting the throats of hogs in the boiling sun. I'd run out of tears, dry-sobbing and gagging, then scrub toilets with toothbrushes while they lashed my back, as they lashed everyone's. I'd spend a hundred years cleaning up the blood.

It finally came to me that I was an orphan, that Mama was no more. I had done something amazing. I had subtracted by one.

Some nights, Auntie shuffled up to the attic with quilts and a pillow and made a place on the rag rug by my bed. When she rolled over, she grunted.

"Auntie?" I said.

"Close your eyes, baby girl. Get some sleep."

"You won't let them take me away, will you?"

"I won't," she said.

But it was a false promise, and I was sorry I'd made her give it. She would not be able to stop them when they came.

✖

I lived in a fog, but I knew when officers of the law drove up and walked the burnt land. Uncle Cunny and his friend Ernie Shiloh told me, should I be questioned, to keep my mouth *shut!*

My eyes were so dry and sore, I could hardly blink.

One afternoon, when two firemen had dropped by, and while talk went on in low voices in the kitchen, Bitsy climbed to where I was hiding. I worried about her great bulk crashing through the attic floor. But she sat on the top step like the Great Wall of China, an immovable thing.

Everybody visited the scene of the fire—and me—like we were tourist attractions. I wondered, when they locked me away, would Auntie walk down to the prison to see me on Sundays with a brown-paper package under her arm. I also wondered, now that Mama's house was gone, *where would the guards go for a fine, fine time?*

Auntie'd say, "Don't mind, baby girl. It'll all get better."

Sometimes, though, she'd looked me in the eye and read my thoughts.

"Whatever you do," she said, "don't run away. I tried that, and I'll tell you, it's bad, *real* bad."

But I overheard Auntie say, "Cunny, I should have seen this coming. I think about takin' that baby and getting out of here."

Uncle Cunny said, "Don't—"

"Only thing that stops me—"

The silence was empty, like maybe Uncle had reached out and grabbed all the sound. Or maybe the words rushed back into Auntie's mouth as fast as she said them.

Maybe she'd never answered him at all.

19

Six months passed. Miss Pilcher came in spring, but Auntie took up a stick and ran her off. I went to school and back, and handed in papers, but I understood nothing. There were no thoughts left to attach myself to. I drifted inside a kind of cotton wool.

Then, one night, Auntie came up two flights of stairs. The springs squeaked and groaned as she lay down and arranged herself beside me on the narrow bed. We pressed together and looked at the steepled beams of the roof.

"Clea June," she said, "you are twelve years old. You're old enough to know about the chicken circus."

I smelled the starch in her cotton nightie.

"It was truly a circus, and it looked so fine, posters up all over town. The outfit was owned by this big white man," she said. "They pulled into the fairgrounds over in Greenfield. Our daddy took Shookie and me, and we bought tickets and candy floss. Oh, girl, how I loved it. My head was turned five ways from Sunday. There was a big striped tent on poles, and ringside seats that folded up, and they put on matinees in the afternoons. At night, they performed under colored lights."

I waited.

"They had an elephant trainer, and a man on stilts. The fella who owned it was the ringmaster, too. Most of all, I loved the way those people lived, travelin' in vans, pulling popcorn machines and midway games. They set up housekeeping behind the big top."

I found voice to ask, "Were there really trained chickens?"

For a time she said nothing. Then, "There were. They were tiny little things billed as *pygmy chickens*. They wore pink ruffles and swung from a trapeze and walked tightropes, and twenty or thirty would pile up on the backs of fancy ponies. They had this little playground too, with a seesaw and a merry-go-round. After the show, people could come outside and watch."

I wiggled over on my side and put one arm across Auntie. She laid her big hand on my elbow. I could not think why she'd kept this such a secret. Or why she was choosing to tell me now.

"They had these trailers they kept dark inside. They'd outfitted the walls with shelves for nesting hens. We called the shelves *pans,* a dozen setting hens bunched on a pan. Two, three hundred chickens in one trailer. Then we went in and took the eggs, kept them under hot lights, and hatched them out."

I pictured fuzzy yellow chicks. If they'd grown up to be pygmies, I couldn't imagine how small the babies must have been. "And you taught them to do tricks?"

She shook her head. "There was no such thing as a pygmy chicken, Clea. After a chick hatched, we bundled it tight in gauze strips to keep it from growing. We gave 'em just enough feed and water to stay alive."

I felt my eyes scrunch up at such cruelty to something so *cute*.

"Sometimes, they grew knobby and deformed, and we kilt

those right off. The rest lived and slept and shat in their bindings. We—we drugged 'em heavy to keep them from screaming."

"Chickens scream?" I said, my voice cracking.

"They surely do.

"When enough time passed, and we knew they wouldn't grow no more, we unwrapped each one and cleaned it up. We were poor teachers, and the chickens were bad at learning. But we got paid for every one that performed and, in the end, if they wanted to eat, they had to do tricks—hens and roosters, ducks sometimes. If one died, we threw it out for the dogs."

I pressed my face to Auntie's arm.

"—And, my goodness, people loved those shows. Rich men came in big limousines, smoking fat cigars. Some gave us their whole paychecks to stay late, squattin' by the pens, feeling for bones and plumpness under the feathers. That ringmaster did terrible things to those birds, squeezin' the life out of them. Sometimes he fired 'em out of cannons. Lord, feathers and bones and bits went everywhere.

"Folks wagered to see which ones would survive. The old man hired kids to clean up the mess. Later, lots of folks came down with tuberculosis from handling those birds."

I snuggled closer, laid my temple on Auntie's collarbone. I felt as though I'd fired that cannon myself.

"But the birds were the least of it," she said, sighing. "It was the 1960s and '70s, and folks were really coming to see us Negroes."

I lifted my head to look, but her eyes were closed, her lashes bristly.

"You see, times were changing in the South. Us colored was s'pose to be able to ride in the front of the bus. Eat at cafeterias and soda fountains. But there was so many white folks that held on to the old ways; they paid good money to see us pretend civil rights had never happened. And there we was, our eyelids painted glittery white, down in the circus ring, actin' like field hands with a make-believe outhouse and buckets of slop, barefoot and wearing mammy bandanas. Like a hundred years had not gone by."

A white man had paid my auntie to do that. She was big and fierce, defiant and defensive. So protective had Auntie been of me in times of tribulation, it hardly seemed possible.

"So we obliged. That's what we was, Clea June, without an ounce of self-respect. Clown slaves to them customers, and to them damned chickens. It pains me to recall how some of us walked on our hands with those birds balanced up there on the soles of our feet."

"Did you do that? I mean, did you walk on your hands?"

She snorted. "I could not. Sometimes I carried a microphone, though, flippin' those birds like they was flapjacks in a skillet, bowin' to 'em, sayin' *Yassuh, boss* and *No, ma'am, Miss Sally.* I was ashamed, you see that?"

"Yes."

"When a single black man carried on that way, it was like all of us disrespectin' ourselves. This one fella, he had a shoe-shine box, and he went around polishing those chickens' feet. That nearly kilt me, 'cause that's what my daddy did. But those people in them seats kept on clappin' and throwin' quarters on the ground."

Listening to Auntie, my heart was heavy, pressed down with a sorrow I knew something about.

"The rest of the time, we was half killin' those birds in the chicken trailers, spinning down and down. Some folks stood all they could and tried to run away. Every time, though, he caught them and beat them bad."

I could not imagine how this story might end.

But Auntie was done, and she got up off the bed. "Enough for tonight. You turn over now and go to sleep."

"But—you can't just stop there."

"It's my life," she said. "And I can. Hush, now."

20

The next day, the rain came. I walked home from school, watching cracks in the road fill up with water, and realized it was the first time in a long while that my eyes had seen anything.

I could not wait for bedtime, and feared Auntie would have a change of heart and not tell more of the story. But she had begun and seemed determined to plow through.

We lay, that night, listening to rain on the roof.

"Where was I?" she said.

"Chickens. And performing, and some folks running off. Oh, Auntie," I said, bundled against her dark bulk. "Weren't you scared?"

"Mighty scared."

"Did you try to run away too?"

"Not at first, baby girl. I told you—I'd already left home, and look where it got me. Truth was, I'd run away to join the circus 'cause I didn't want to be somebody's maid. My sister Shookie worked in a laundry, steam in her face and bleach in her lungs. Always folding other people's clothes. Me, I couldn't stand to watch my daddy shine shoes, not one more day.

"My fam'ly cried on the day I left, but I thought performing would be rich-making and fine. And if I saved my money, before long I'd be wearing diamonds and rubies. Instead, my daddy and my sister were sore ashamed. I took in money, all right, but I made myself small with what I did. Then one early mornin', I'd had enough. I went into the trailer and apologized to those chickens."

I felt my eyebrows fly up.

"Yes, ma'am. For all I'd done. For what I *hadn't* done. Then I said my prayers and crept into the ringmaster's tent and stole his whip. I beat that man within an inch of life."

I reached up and laid my palm against her round cheek. "He deserved it," I said, but Auntie only looked sad.

"He rolled on the floor and put his arms over his head and cried like a baby. I guess the rest of 'em heard, or maybe they looked in and saw, 'cause all of a sudden there was a hundred black folks pilin' out of those tents—the cookshack, the privy, the elephant pens. I had turned 'em loose.

"The po-lice came. They had a bullhorn and billy clubs. Said we were makin' a public racket 'cause we was camped in a parking lot. They started swingin' those clubs, breakin' bones and splittin' heads, and they hooked up fire hoses and sprayed water on us. A lot of folks slipped and fell on the paving."

"Were you hurt, Auntie? Was anyone?"

I could hear wheels of remembering turning in her head.

"Firemen tried to wash off the streets before news reporters came, and the TV people, 'cause the red blood was all mixed up with that water. Folks were wet and bleeding, and trying to figure which way to run. Another thing—somebody had turned those chickens loose. They got trampled and smashed under people's feet."

I moaned and sorrowed in my heart for those birds.

"Some black folks came rushing out of their houses and ran right into the middle of things. They tried to help—Izzie Thorne was there. Then others too—white folks—and there was a lot of screaming and crying, and fistfights broke out everywhere. That big striped tent was in rags, and —"

"Miss Izzie *Thorne*?"

Auntie nodded. "By startin' that fiasco, I'd done everybody wrong. Them that could walk got up and ran in all directions."

"Wait," I said. "Did Miss Thorne work for the *circus*?"

"No. She lived down the street, and she came running out, took some in and kept us hid."

"What happened to the man you whipped?"

"He was lookin' to have me arrested. His arm was broke and some of his ribs. The po-lice drove up and down the streets. They figured anyone who didn't live in that town was suspect, 'cause no matter what that ringmaster told 'em, the po-lice said, 'No one woman could inflict this much hurt.'"

At the corner of her mouth, Auntie grinned a little, and I grinned too.

"That night they come pounding on Izzie Thorne's door. She opened it like nothing had happened. She acted like she didn't know a thing. And all the while, there I was, living in her back bedroom. I hid in the closet—so I know how you feel, Clea girl, when you slide under your bed, and you can't come out.

"I'd peek between the window blinds, though, and see them officers in the street. They wore helmets and had guns, and they weren't afraid to shoot. We cowered down in those houses. My heart was broken. I saw I'd made trouble, that what I'd caused was just another riot. Accordin' to civil rights laws, all that street fighting in the South was supposed to be over. But it wasn't."

"Auntie!" I breathed. "I'm so proud of you." And I was proud of Miss Izzie Thorne too, and understood things better now. In the years she had taught me, seeing me every day at school, it was no wonder it hurt her to look at me. "What happened after?"

"I was real sorry I'd made Izzie unsafe. I remembered back when coloreds were ridin' the bus to Jackson, and I wished with all my heart that I'd not joined with the circus but had gone with them, learning to fight fists with peacefulness. But now I was terrified, afraid the fighting and bloodiness had got in my bones. So I come back here. We thought our generation would see the last of the problem." She gave an odd snort that came up from her belly.

"Aunt Jerusha! You were like a—a freedom fighter!"

"Everybody fights for freedom, some way."

"You were a part of the *sit-ins*?"

"Time for that should have been long past. The point I am makin'," she said, turning to look me in the eye, "is that it was my fault blood run in the street that day. Pride, baby girl, surely goes before a fall. Leavin' that circus, I felt I had to do what I thought was right even though it caused wrong. And I'm guessing that's what you did too. Oh, Clea, I'm not saying you can strike a match and make your troubles go 'way. Because, after, you got to live with it.

"Sometimes, though—when you've put up with a thing until you can't stand it no more—I know what it's like to have to do *something*."

I'd begun to cry, fat, rubbery tears, my mouth twisted up.

"Promise me," she said, "you won't strike a match again unless you've got to find your way in the dark."

"Yes, ma'am."

"Say, '*I promise*,' Clea June. And keep your word to this old woman."

"I promise," I said.

"And you won't tell nobody about the circus?"

"But—I'm proud of you. So why can't I talk about it?"

" 'Cause it's nobody's business but mine," she said.

I understood, now, why Auntie had been so horrified that night, to see Claudie and me performing on the porch.

"All right," I said. "But, Auntie, one thing—when you got here to False River, did you stand up at First and Last Holy Word and confess? Did you say what you'd done?"

"No," she said softly. "I never did."

21

If Auntie or Uncle knew I'd so thoroughly lost my way and couldn't get back, they'd worry themselves sick. If Millicent Poole knew, she'd call Social Services.

I finished the school year, kept my head down and myself to myself. Because I slept by day and lay awake at night, sometimes I dozed off in class. When the teacher prodded me, everyone laughed. I also labored to keep my eyes open during Sunday church, and on particularly bad mornings, it was only Reverend Ollie's bellowing and the choir's foot stomping that kept me from sliding out of my seat and onto the floor.

Nobody wanted to miss evening services. Not only was pot-luck at six o'clock, Sunday-night church was for confessing sins.

Our church building was small. It had a double row of scarred wooden pews, a piano, a pulpit, and folding chairs for the choir. Weekly, Millicent Poole posted the numbers of the hymns we would sing, and, with the tithing envelopes, we marked those places in the hymnals while the Reverend welcomed us and prayed on and on.

After one church supper of spoon bread and baked ham, we sat in those hard pews, fanning ourselves and waiting for the weekly confessions to begin. Before the night was over, the Reverend would spread his great arms and invite us all to the altar to confess any sins and be renewed in the faith.

On these occasions, Millicent Poole, who was Sunday-school superintendent and sat in the front row, would rise to her feet, the better to witness our angst. In the background, the come-on-down piano music would be lower than low, the twangy notes rolling, like sin-seeking fog, among the pews. That last chorus might go on forever, calling and calling, *Sinner, come home.*

When I was very young, I'd considered concocting a sin just so I could rise from my place on a Sunday night and bump knee after knee as I made my way up the aisle and into the Reverend's embrace.

On this night, however, Miss Shookie was the first to stand, one hand on her hat and the other on her daughter. As they stumbled by, Bitsy's swollen eyes slid to mine, and a terrible heat rose in my neck. God help me, this had nothing to do with the fire set at Mama's. This was new. I was guilty of tattling.

Miss Shookie led her daughter to the altar.

Millicent Poole popped out of her seat. The Reverend spoke softly to Bitsy—Miss Shookie not missing a word—and he flagged Miz Bishop to let up on the chorus the twelfth time around.

"Dear hearts," the Best Reverend said to us all, "our own Bitsy Lovemore has come forward this evening to confess her sins. Lift your voices, and make a joyful noise."

The congregation shook off their surprise, and a few hallelujahs wavered off the walls. Miss Shookie yanked at her girdle and straightened her dress.

Poor Bitsy. She was bland of face with a walrus body, and nobody liked her.

The night before, the heat had been sweltering. Under our willow, where Auntie was pouring cold pop for the grown-ups, Cousin Bitsy mumbled that she was going for a walk. A *stroll*, she called it. She did this often, and I thought it odd that a girl of her size, whose only exercise was to bend both elbows at the table, would choose to walk anywhere.

I followed her, for the purpose of spying. Maybe a hundred yards along the road, she stepped into the field and waited while a flashlight beam bobbled through the grass. In a clearing of old cornstalks, a prison-guard uniform was already being shed. Bitsy rucked up her dress, and shadow fell into shadow as she and the fellow went to rolling and grunting on the ground. When it was over, and they were both breathing hard, Bitsy got to her feet, caught me watching, and snarled, "Brush the goddamn grass offa me."

I said, "I'm going to tell."

"Christ! Just get the straw out of my hair." She pulled down her dress and stepped into her drawers.

But I didn't tell—not right away. All through last night, I savored the secret.

I wondered if any boy would ever want me the way the Farm guards apparently wanted Bitsy. Would any boy be interested at all? Would they call me on the phone or take me to the movies or hold my hand? Probably not.

Folks would remember my mama, and word would go around that I was free—or maybe they could pay me. They would chant their songs about me—the next Clarice—and write my name on bathroom walls.

Today, at our Sunday noon meal, I opened my mouth and

announced that this morning in church, all of First and Last Holy Word had been able to see through Bitsy's dress. These astonishing words fell on the dishes, on the tablecloth, and in my lap. Thereafter, it was hard for us all to concentrate on our barbecued ribs with Uncle Cunny's family-recipe sauce. All but Uncle eyed Bitsy's chest.

"Law," Miss Shookie said, rolling her eyes to heaven and looking shamed. "I do right by this girl eight days a week."

Across the table, Auntie got over the shock and took to studying Bitsy with narrowed eyes. "Sister, your daughter is no more *girl* than I am."

Indeed she was not. Guided by the devil, and making things worse, I proceeded to recount last night's tale of the naked prison guard, how the grass had broken and lay flat beneath them. How Bitsy had come up with straw in her hair and her underpants in her hand.

Uncle Cunny pushed back his chair, saying he'd just finish his cake outside.

At first nobody said anything about Bitsy's nakedness in the field. Then Auntie loudly announced that *Lord, Lord, it was time her niece wore foundation garments,* and she'd just loan her some till her mama could get her to the Big Woman's Store over in Slidell.

Now Miss Shookie was double-offended. "I have you to know, my baby girl is wearin' a slip!"

"A *half*-slip!" said Auntie.

Miss Shookie squeezed her eyes tight and moaned and wailed, "Oh, no, *Jesus!*" and keened and clutched her midsection. "*Lordy,* I can't afford no brassieres for this big girl."

Dinner was over. I followed them all into Auntie's bedroom, which was right off the kitchen and boasting a polished bureau, a treadle sewing machine, shelves crammed with antiques, and a high bed with a knobby chenille bedspread. Auntie rummaged in her drawer and came up with an undergarment the size of industrial machinery.

"Off with that dress, girl. Shookie, you should be ashamed, lettin' your child's titties hang loose. It's no wonder the men's been looking through and worse. Now, you put your arms in here, girl, that's right, go on." Auntie lifted and pushed and worked the straps, and pretty soon she had both Bitsy's arms going in the right directions.

"Now," she said, "bend over so's we can get you tucked in. That's how they do in fine department stores."

"Sister!" said Miss Shookie. "What obscenities you doin' to my baby girl?"

"What you already should have!" My aunt fumed and grunted. "I ain't the first what's had my hands on these things."

And with more heaving and molding on Auntie's part, and several snaps and protesting *womps* of elastic—along with whistling from between Bitsy's big teeth—I witnessed the holstering of Bitsy into Auntie's brassiere with the heavy-duty stitching. Auntie, inserting her knee in Bitsy's back, proceeded to fasten the six hooks and eyes.

"Oh, Lord *Jesus*," wailed Miss Shookie, hunched on the bed with her hands to her face. "My baby girl is gone and growed up!"

And here came the misery, and down fell the tears, Miss Shookie alternately flapping her hands and weeping into the hem of her own hiked-up skirt.

Auntie said, "*Baby*, my ass. Bitsy needs to confess her sins, that's what."

So now here we were—some fifty people at Sunday-night service, each holier than the next and waiting to hear what Bitsy Lovemore had done.

She put her hands together, one over the other, like she was fixing to sing. Then she got right to it. "I been loose," she said.

Her mama gave her one of those *uh-huh* looks.

Bitsy took in air and let it out of her cheeks. "I been wrestlin' the gents and gettin' down on the ground. Ain't had no bed." Her voice carried, wistful. "We do it however we finds a way."

Miss Shookie backed off by one sanctified step, pulled a fan from her purse, and cooled herself mightily. The congregation went into fits of shuffling while I wandered in a land between horror and wonder.

I, after all, was guilty of far more sin than Bitsy was.

And I wondered what it was like to be her, just now, if she cared what we thought, if wearing a bra hurt. Bitsy pinched her see-through skirt. Her face was bland and fat and shiny. "If y'all are wonderin' who fornicated me—"

She turned to the choir. "That one and that."

Two pimply-faced boys ducked into their collars.

"And him in the back—"

I swear she sent death rays over the congregation. "The Oaty brothers had their way with me, and the manager at the Ninety-Nine Cent Store. Miz Sherrard's old pappy—oh, and two of those Maytubby boys."

And still more—the high school gym teacher, three guards from the prison, the mailman in False River, on and on.

When Miss Shookie's knees looked weak and bendy, and she was close to buckling under her daughter's load of sin, Reverend Ollie guided them both to a seat, raced through the benediction, and sent the rest of us home. Auntie made me wait outside while she and Miss Shookie conversed with the Reverend.

On the way to her car, Miz Millicent Poole clasped my wrist in her bird-bone fingers. "Just you wait, girlie," she said. "Your turn is comin'."

On the way home, there was a great sighing and a muffling of words. Miss Shookie drove. Then she paced the length of our parlor and kitchen, and wept and had to be comforted. Again I had made everything wrong, and nothing could be righted.

When they were taking their leave, and Miss Shookie was rummaging for her car keys, Bitsy came by me.

"You don't know, girl," she said. "You ain't ever gonna know."

"Know what?" I asked.

"What it's like to be somethin' nobody wants."

22

Years have passed.

Last night in the rearview mirror, Luz looked like a refugee—sharp cheekbones, round glasses with black frames, green eyes, and no fat to speak of on her bones. She wears her hair in pigtails.

She and I laid Harry on the backseat of my Honda in a nest of shirts and jeans, and tucked his blue woolly around him.

"You okay, honey?" I said.

My daughter nodded and said disjointedly, "Harry has trauma, Mom. Mental suffering. Pain." At eleven, Luz is our dictionary.

I wheeled out of the hospital parking lot.

"Well, talk to him. Let him know we're here."

Luz asked, "Are we going to live in our car now, Mom? 'Cause I knew this kid, he and his dad slept in their Bronco."

"We are not," I said.

Because of yesterday's tropical storm, most businesses were shuttered or vacated, a few doors standing open for coolness in its wake. Just west of the city, in a less wind-damaged neighborhood, we found the Starlight Motel. There were no lights on anywhere. A man lounged against the portico, a flashlight in his hand.

I paid thirty-seven dollars and fifty-seven cents for two candles and a lighter and two beds in a room, where I tucked Harry in with me. Luz and I ate stale Cheese Nips with peanut butter and drank Diet Pepsi from a vending machine that someone had pried open with jack handles and crowbars. Harry ate nothing. I left the bathroom light on.

When the kids were asleep, I dumped our possessions on the floor, emptied out the black plastic bag, and carried Thomas's things down to the Dumpster. My heart was twisted sideways.

Screw this damn storm.

Today, while I laid out lesson plans, my house was collapsing, my babies were in danger, and my husband was in his office at the college, humping a cute young thing. *Well, fuck Thomas Ryder.* He can deal with the mess that was our house on Lilac Lane and our homeowner's insurance while he's finding the next target for his heat-seeking dick.

But that mess, that beautiful ruin, was our home.

And last night, in the face of trauma, mental suffering, and pain, I passed up Call. Meditation. My center quaked.

All night my daughter wheezed lightly in her sleep. I walked the cheap carpet and lay stiff as a board on the motel room's bed, my mind cluttered with junk.

Where will we go? We can't go back to Lilac Lane—the storm blew out the windows and brought the staircase down. The only other thing is to travel upriver. Terrible things wait for me there—the chicken circus and the curling black smoke. If we go there, I'll be arrested. I'm old enough, now, to be convicted and sentenced, to serve my time. The big question is—while I'm locked in prison, will Aunt Jerusha care for Luz and Harry?

Now, at first light, I feel trapped in my fear. The three of us put on yesterday's clothes and drive to McDonald's, Harry silent and eating nothing. I slip a straw into his milk. "Drink for Mama," I beg him. But he does not.

Luz and I pick at a foam tray of pancakes and scrambled egg and thin sausage.

"Mom. This food will keep us strong," Luz says. "Durable, un-yielding."

In the orange plastic booth, I hold Harry close. He hugs his blue woolly, that has dried overnight. He looks so sad.

23

All that we own is in the car, what I grabbed from the laundry room as the ceiling came down.

Luz says, "Mom. Where are we going?"

"False River," I say. My voice is not helpful. The words come out stiff. "See if you can find it on the map."

She pulls a map of Mississippi from the pocket behind my seat—finding anything is a no-brainer for Luz. Her interest is up.

"Is that a town?" she asks.

"Yes."

"What's there?"

How much should I tell her? "I lived there with my aunt."

In the rearview mirror I see her mouth fall open. "You have an *aunt*? I have a great-aunt?"

"Yes and no."

"Mom!"

"You'll see."

I'm a wreck. And to make driving harder, it appears yesterday's storm cut a wide path along the coast. The season has come early, and that does not bode well. Through downed trees and debris, we make our way east to the lazy Pearl. In spite of attaching itself to the gulf, the mouth of the river is pure trickery—wide and dark, with forests of dead cypress and green slime that pricks the nose. On the eastern bank of the Pearl is a two-lane, and it's there that I suck a long breath. And turn north.

Power lines are down, blocking the roads, creating detour after detour. Twenty miles on, in Carterville, shingles have blown off. Most houses squat under blue-plastic tarps while people live on their lawns and beside the road, under lean-tos and canvas canopies. A sign on one downtown storefront reads GENERATORS—SOLD OUT.

After that, the road is narrow and hilly, cut through miles of pine forest. Here, insects swarm in tandem, flying in our faces and up our noses. I wonder if the storm has brought them out. They cover our windshield in a thick, dead mass. Even the wipers don't clear them away. Carefully, we drive into a community, and at one intersection Luz rolls down the window and asks what these bugs are and why they fly in pairs.

An orange-vested worker bats at the things. "Love bugs," he says, grinning with his mouth closed. He waves us through.

"Very scientific," Luz says, forlorn. "If I had the right book—"

"I know." As we'd backed the Honda out, through the downpour, Luz's *History of Greece* had flapped wetly on the lawn.

In these little towns, it has not taken long for help to arrive. Trucks are parked with their back doors opened up, people working food lines, offering sandwiches and juice and tampons and diapers. Bonfires burn windfall in almost every yard. Patients at a nursing home are lined up on the porch, watching electrical crews, watching smoke rising, watching us. In front of a ruined beauty shop, a woman in pink clam-diggers sits, talking on her cell phone and smoking a cigar. A man with a hammer builds on to his outhouse.

While we drive, Luz and I eat slapped-together sandwiches of peanut butter, but we must find something tempting for Harry. We pull up to a grocery store, where the doors are propped open and the inside is dark. Customers go in and out. No one here seems flustered or panicked without electricity, not the clerk or the shoppers, though the shelves were near bare. Feeling guilty, I buy only four apple-granola bars and a couple of jars of baby-food custard. Our needs are less than other folks', and I hate to take anything.

In the parking lot, a woman says, "Y'all doin' okay?" She thrusts a plastic gallon of water at me.

Another hands me a slip of paper. "Here, hon, this'll get you a quart of milk for the kids."

I take them both, and collect our quart, which we drink on the spot—all but Harry.

Gasoline, in this town, is limited to five gallons per customer. I top up with the five. North of here, there is almost no traffic. We drive on until a siren whoops behind me, and I think my heart will stop and I'll die. A cop gets off his motorcycle and comes to my window. My knuckles are white, my throat gone to dust.

"Ma'am?" he says. "After this next town, there's no gas for fifty miles. Just wanted to warn y'all."

I nod faintly and keep my breathing steady and tell him we're fine. Plenty in the tank. I sit there until he gets back on his motor-cycle and rides away. Then I blink away tears and creep along. Behind me, Luz gives Harry water from a jiggling plastic spoon.

By that night, we've driven out of the damn bugs and have ar-rived at Cain's Crossing. This place has dried up. A double row of store windows are painted over. Railroad tracks run along a grassy strip in the middle of town. I wonder if trains even come here anymore. In one day, we've gone only a hundred and twelve miles.

The heat has been terrible, but it's cooler in the evening. We've agreed to sleep in the car tonight—not that we have a choice. There's not a motel room to be had. We're fortunate to find a city park, where people are camping, and we get in line for the toilets. A woman tells me, "Night before last, tornado come through, touched down, took my kitchen plum off, that's what."

I tell her, *So sorry,* usher my kids into the john, latch the door, and we three take turns over the hole. Harry pees too, and I take that as a good sign.

Under the trees, there's a raft of kids piled on two swings and a slide. They're laughing and shrieking and playing chase while Harry holds my hand, eyes shuttered down, and he sucks his thumb. I sit in back with the kids and spoon vanilla custard inside Harry's lip, but it oozes down his chin and onto his shirt.

On concrete tables, folks' groceries are laid out in inventory— boxes of dry cereal and crackers, some cans—and a few grills are lit, sleeping bags and blankets waiting to be unrolled. It would be a refugee camp except, for these kids, this seems to be a lark.

"Luz," I say. "You guys want to walk around for a bit?"

"No," she says, speaking also for Harry. "Get in the car, Mom." She's scared too.

"Let me stand here a minute. I need to stretch my legs."

We roll the windows down and lock the doors in senseless contradiction. I lay the passenger seat down as far as it will go and tuck Harry in there, giving Luz the back. It still isn't enough to accommodate her long legs. She sleeps fitfully. I can hear her hard breathing. Finally, I wake her and hand back her inhaler. I lean over the seat and stroke her dark hair.

They want to be at home, of course they do. But the roof fell in—in more ways than one—and we cannot go back.

When Luz is asleep, I listen to the trill and call of night things in the trees.

Over the years, the Sisters of Mercy have created a kind of stillness in my mind. We address that quietude as "coming to Call." It's preceded by prayer.

Thank you for the lives that were spared in this town, for my children— their strong bodies and their beautiful minds, for the Sisters of Mercy who'll wonder where I am.

I'm not sure that my little guy is all that healthy, but in the last couple of decades I have learned that we humans chant things into being. We summon them to us. It's the law of attraction. Heartfelt thanks, given in advance, sets gears in motion and allows things to come. I learned this the hard way: to plead with God only affirms the need.

Where Thomas is concerned, though, I'm hurt and angry, and while I know that dwelling on this will only bring more suffering, right now I want to wallow in my pain.

Thomas is a teacher. I see his lying eyes and his cheating heart and all the other things people have ever written or sung about. I've gone from numbness to dreaming up fifteen methods for killing the co-ed. I've got to get some sleep. Long into the night, I search for ways to bend myself around the steering wheel without also banging my knee on the gearshift.

Thank you, God, for Harry's voice. His four-year-old voice. I know it's in there.

I mourn the collapse of my marriage, hope for rescue trucks to drive up with ladders and hoses, men with hammers to patch things up. I wipe my face with the heels of my hands. And I listen to Harry suck his thumb.

24

A round three o'clock, we arrive in False River.

The liquor store is now a drive-through. The electricity's on here, which allows the shack to live up to its bargain: BANANA DACKAREES TWO/FIVE. Six or eight cars and a pickup are in line. I do not see a single highway patrol or sheriff's department car. It will take two minutes for word to get around.

The barbershop has burned to the ground—recently, judging by the blackened mess, the stinging stench, and puddles of water that haven't yet dried in the heat. The Ninety-Nine Cent Store is now Family Dollar.

The schoolhouse still stands, but the front door and the windows have been boarded up and spray-painted with profane things. Miss Izzie Thorne's plywood steps are gone. Everything else has been sucked down and covered over with the green kudzu.

Harry's asleep in the back. Luz is beside me, not saying a thing. I hold my breath and turn onto Potato Shed Road.

I never realized how narrow this asphalt lane was—but, then, I have never driven it. The field on the right is an expanse of browning stubs where corn has been harvested. On the right, a couple of homes have been torn down, or have fallen down, and are just a chimney or two. I try to think who lived here long ago, but my heart is banging, and my memory is mush.

Some porches are collapsing under rusted washers, and yards are littered with rubber tires and lidless camping coolers, plastic toys, and, in one case, a trampoline. Gardens have gone to seedlings and weed. Was our lane always like this? Were our neighbors poor white trash? Were we?

Jerusha's, of course, is the last in the line before the quarter-mile to the prison, and flowers are planted all around, in old coffee cans, plastic bowls, and ceramic pots. I pull into a short driveway, next to a blue Kia. My lungs ache; my chest hurts. I try not to look at the guard towers up at Hell's Farm, the big central brick building, or the rolls of wire that wink in the down-turning sun. I look, instead, at the red salvia planted around a front door we never used. And I think, *Let home be where they take you in.*

I get out of the car and lift Harry and walk Luz around to the back of the house, see the willow and the big mossy oaks along the slow river, a new domino table that nearly makes me weep. I'm carrying a sleeping Harry, his long legs dangling and his face sweaty at my neck.

The screen door opens.

Auntie comes down the steps, wiping her hands on a dish towel. Behind her is an older Miss Shookie, her flat face set in a permanent frown.

Auntie's hair is mostly gray. She's a little thinner but still tall and straight and looking me square in the eyes.

She puts her arms out and says, "You give me that baby."

25

I leave the parlor where Auntie's rocking Harry, because it's more than I can bear to see. We've drunk glass after glass of sweet tea, said stilted *howdy*s and almost nothing more. In the kitchen, Luz is watching Bitsy. If it is possible, Cousin has only grown larger over the years. She wears a purple muumuu, and I can no longer see where one part of her leaves off and the other begins. On the drainboard she butters slices of bread and sprinkles powdered sugar on top—something to hold her till meal time, I guess. Bitsy hands a slice to Luz—an offering that nearly bends me in half.

Auntie's got something roasting in the oven. She gets up, leaving Harry curled on the cushions of her chair, and I wonder if, in all my years, I ever had the privilege of sitting there alone. I excuse myself and go out to perch on the back steps. I have not yet had to offer explanations.

My stomach's wrenched tight.

In the last few years I lived here, every day seemed a week long. I recall how I found some solace in baking. The rest of the time I moved as though blind. I did my homework, and at night

I read until my eyes were so tired, I thought they'd jump out of my head.

I was invited to a party once, and because Auntie'd bought me a new dress, I went. The house was crowded and blaring with music. Kids passed secret things in the kitchen and danced in ways that bumped breasts and ground hips—I would have danced, too, if anyone had asked me. Instead, I sat in a corner and drank 7Up, a little pile of crackers in my hand. At ten o'clock we all moved toward a bedroom, where they were playing a game, going into the closet in pairs.

We'll close the door; it'll be fun. Come on, Clea. They grinned like cats and wanted me to go first. But the music banged in my ears and hurt my head. *Beware the ho' with the painted do'* . . .

I walked home in the dark, sat by the river until after midnight, then went up to my bed.

Finally, on a Saturday, Auntie came to the attic and said, *Clea June, get on your feet and find you a job.*

I did just that. I started working after school at the Ninety-Nine Cent Store. It required almost no thinking. The new manager was a short, fat, and fussy man with a screwy haircut. He said I seemed smart enough to run his cash register and give customers their change. I pushed buttons on that machine from four in the afternoon until closing at nine. Sometimes I wished there were words on those keys, so I could ring up receipts that said who I was.

Thank you, I told them, as I'd been instructed. *You come back, hear?*

When there was nobody to check out, I pulled a bottle of cleaner and a roll of paper towels from under my counter, and I made clean circles on those big front windows. I moved a rack of houseplants there, and the philodendron and tiny violets grew like crazy. I brought over the garden trowels and boxes of plant food too, and arranged them in a semicircle and stacked flower-pots and bags of potting soil. And I asked each customer, *Find everything okay?*

Every night I'd come home to find my dinner kept warm on the back of the stove. Those last years, I hardly ever saw Claudie or her twiggy sister, and I never saw Finn. He'd left the oak tree, and we heard that he lived in a shack in the woods, and he sel-dom came out. I guess he mourned his daddy that much.

Here in the yard now, I see that a few tree limbs have cracked and split from the oaks. I recall that the big one was Finn's tree, how he leapt among those high branches. The first time I saw him, he was hanging upside down. The rope ladder is gone too, but a couple of planks from the old platform remain.

Auntie pokes her head out the door. "Come help me with sup-per," she says.

"Where's Luz?"

"Upstairs in the attic."

I wonder if my bed is still there—my dresser, my things. "I'll get her."

"Leave her be," Auntie says. "We'll call her when it's ready."

Miss Shookie is spooning up string beans with lengths of pur-ple onion.

I ask, "How you been doing, Miss Shookie?" I cringe at the limpness of my question.

I'm old enough now to call her by her given name, but some things never change. Others do.

Shookie's hair is now cropped and dyed burgundy. She wears a slash of lipstick the color of blood. "You ought to be embar-rassed comin' here, girl."

I take the bowl of mashed potatoes and set it on the table.

Auntie brings a platter of sliced roast, a great bowl of gravy, and I cannot help but look at Bitsy, who's already in her chair, pulling a roll to bits.

"I'd like to bed Harry down on the sofa with his blue blanket while we eat."

"No, ma'am," Aunt Jerusha says. "You bring that boy to this table."

And so I do. Luz takes the place where I once sat.

It's when Uncle Cunny Gholar comes through the door, swinging his hat in his hand, that I lose my togetherness. Right at the table, my face caves in. Uncle stands there, startled, while I catch tears with the tip of my tongue. I don't care that his hair is white and his face is old. I lost my way. And now I am found.

I only half rise before I am in his arms. He stumbles but catches us both, and we rock back and forth, and I gulp deep breaths, and my heart beats again.

I wipe at my face, but I'm dripping and a mess.

"Take your seat, Cunny," Auntie says softly, for I see that he's weeping too. "We all need a good meal."

Shookie heaves an impatient sigh.

"Luz," I say, with what dignity I can gather, "Mr. Cunny Gholar. My daughter, Maria-Luz Ryder. My son, Harry."

Uncle comes around and takes Luz's hand, holds it tight to his heart. He lays his other on Harry's head. Harry leans forward, puts his chin on the table.

Uncle hangs up his hat—a fine black bowler with rounded-up sides. He pulls out his chair and says, "Shookie, I see you were first to the table. You leave anything for me?"

"You fractious old goat," Shookie says.

For now, I am home.

Then still another man stomps up the porch steps and on in, and my heart rushes to my throat for fear someone has called the law. He nods apologetically when the screen door bangs, and dashes up the stairs. Then he's down again, pulling out a chair, smiling at me. Auntie looks at me too, quick-like and full of meaning, and passes the roast beef to this tall blond man.

"You remember Mr. Francis Stengle," she says. She loads potato on her fork. "From down at Oatys'?"

I do not recall.

Auntie eases the fork to her mouth. When she's chewed and swallowed, she says, "You called him Wheezer."

The man grins and wrests the gravy boat from Bitsy.

Then I *do* know, I remember. This handsome man—that fair hair, the pale skin. "Oh, *God!*" I say.

The Oaty brothers kept him under their house! Finn and I went down to set him free—but some rescue that turned out to be. Social Services hauled him away—that awful Miss Pilcher and her green station wagon.

"Francis lives here now," Aunt Jerusha says. "He's the chaplain down at the Farm."

Hell's Farm! The penitentiary?

"*Wheezer?*" I say, and in spite of my fears, that's funny somehow—for us both, I guess, because we share crooked smiles and wide-eyed looks. It's hardly a name for a grown-up man with rolled shirtsleeves, a strong jaw, and curly hair on his arms.

"Hey, Clea," he says.

"These are my children," I tell him, breathless.

While I pick at my roast beef, I cannot take my eyes off him. I'm overrun with memories. Wheezer's a pure miracle. And he's sitting at the same place where my friend Claudie once sat. I remember that night too, all of us eating with our hands, that Alvadene came in from the pouring rain and how, with my running mouth, I ended a friendship.

Harry, between Auntie and me, leans back in his chair. Auntie has put bits of meat and potato on his plate, a couple of green beans. She watches him for a time, then goes to the refrigerator and brings out Jell-O, which she spoons into a pretty yellow plastic bowl. Harry watches the stuff wiggle. She puts the spoon in his hand, curls his fingers around it.

"Lord, save us," Shookie says. "Clea June Shine, you've spoiled that one rotten. And the other hasn't got an ounce of meat on her bones. They both need a good tonic, and some discipline, you ask me."

"No one asked you, Shookie," Uncle says softly.

"It's Clea *Ryder* now." I wonder if Auntie's sister always irritated me this much.

How Luz could use discipline is more than I can see, and she and I exchange faint smiles. But Shookie's words pinch because I truly have no idea what my little guy needs.

"Harry," I whisper, "will you drink some milk?"

Harry hooks an arm around the yellow bowl.

Aunt Jerusha says coolly, "He can have milk when he's tried my lime Jell-O. Go on, now."

Amazingly, Harry's thumb slides from his mouth.

"That's right," Auntie says, as though she and he are the only two in the room. "And there's more if you want."

"Stuff's nothing but sugar water," Shookie says.

Harry touches the wiggly green with his fingers and licks them for taste, and although the thumb pops back in his mouth, he eyes the dish with interest.

The conversation is surface-thin. I thought I was hungry, but my belly hurts, and I've twisted my paper napkin to shreds.

When supper is done, and we're clearing up, Harry takes the yellow bowl, slides from his chair, and wanders into the parlor, where he sits on the floor by Auntie's chair—*criss-cross-applesauce*—spoon in hand and the bowl in his lap.

No one says a word.

❋

Apparently, Wheezer occupies one of two rooms on the second floor. Shookie and Bitsy have taken the other. I wonder how long they've been living here, and if they contribute to the cost of things. There might be Social Security from Shookie's years of laboring in laundries, but I doubt Bitsy's worked a day in her life. And I know nothing at all about Bitsy's daddy.

Until now, one scrap of logic has escaped me—when I am arrested, who will pay for my children's room and board? If Auntie takes them, who will buy their groceries, their clothes, pay for tennis shoes and Luz's inhalers?

If I'd thought of this before, would I have brought them up-river?

Just now I need to make up the beds. There's a double in the attic that Luz and I will share. Harry, still gripping his spoon in his fist, will sleep on a camp cot pushed up so tight, Luz and I will have to climb over the foot of the bed.

I snap out pristine sheets, find old pillows in an upstairs closet. I dump the black plastic bag and sort the kids' dirty clothes and wonder how much time I have. I wonder if, downstairs, Shookie's the one who is making the call.

❋

The sun stays up late in this part of Mississippi, but it's dusky in the attic, with its four small windows. I put the kids down early.

Luz has a flashlight and a borrowed book. I pull the quilts to their chins even though, in the heat, they'll soon kick them off. Auntie climbs the stairs with cold glasses of Ovaltine for them both.

Luz says, "Maybe I can get Harry to drink."

I kiss them again and go down to find Wheezer sitting out under the willow.

Wheezer's looking up at the lighted attic window. "Great kids," he says, when I sit down.

"Thanks. Harry was two when we got him. His father was a police officer. Decorated—so I have that to tell him someday."

Wheezer waits.

"Harry watched him gunned down on a street in Chicago. He had no other family. The sisters—I work with a sisterhood—"

I smile, remembering. "They told me he had a thatch of brown hair, was a thumb-sucker, and kept asking for his daddy. Thomas—my husband—well, we already had Luz."

"Smart girl there."

"Yes. She was eight by then, and we thought, *What's one more?* So we took him and started the paperwork. Watched him, you know, for trauma. But in six months he was calling me Mama. And he—he called Thomas dad."

I look at Wheezer to see if I'm saying too much. "He seemed okay until—"

Harry is nowhere happier than in my lap, or snugged up next to me, with his elbow on my thigh and his chin in his hand, as though he is the greatest thinker in the world. My favorite photo on our refrigerator was a close-up of the kids' faces, a pencil clamped between Luz's teeth, Harry sporting a peanut-butter smile.

"—until this storm."

I am wrapped inside myself. Uncle comes out then, and takes a chair. He must be telling a joke, because he and Wheezer roar with laughter and slap each other's knees. Auntie and Shookie come too. They still gather under the willow after supper.

Auntie says, "There's lemonade—"

Not for me. I want to sit here, hugging my elbows, not recalling. I don't want to remember anything.

26

"I suppose I need to explain," I say.

Wheezer and Uncle move to get up, but Shookie and Bitsy seem settled in.

"Y'all stay," I say. "You might as well hear."

"Clea," Wheezer says, "you don't have to tell us anything. We're just so damned glad to see you—"

"Yes, she does," Uncle says. "She owes Jerusha that."

I nod. I'm wearing a short-sleeved blouse, and I wonder if they're looking at the scars on my arms. "Well," I begin haltingly, leaving things out. "I went to Mexico. And then Belize City."

Auntie seems surprised. Shookie looks like I've already lost her.

I recall the tramp steamer and how I had dragged my belongings ashore and stood on the street bridge and watched the fish markets below. I wandered past shaded government buildings and bare city parks, and watched children play in filthy ditch water. I strolled along Barakat Street, where funeral parlors had dark, open doorways. In the daytime, the grille fronts of tiny *farmacias* were pulled back to admit customers, and, upstairs, black women sat alone at open windows.

"The city was—wonderful. The people had amazing faces. I was wishing I had a sketch pad and pencils so I could sit on the curb and draw them. But I was never really an artist. So I bought an old Polaroid at a flea market, and I took pictures of tourists at bus stops and on the dock."

I don't look at my listeners.

"I wrote these clever captions across the bottoms and sold them for fifty cents American. Four photographs paid for my room for a week. The house where I lived was on Mortuary Lane."

I cannot help but smile at that memory. For my two dollars I'd gotten a narrow bed and a bowl of clean water every morning, an outdoor toilet, and my turn at the backyard shower twice a week. At its highest point, Belize City was thirty-nine inches above sea level. From my upstairs window I watched the ocean sweep the flat beach and lick greedily at the end of the road.

I knew one thing in Belize: I was alive.

"Um, some days I caught the bus inland, or up to Progresso." I don't tell them about the armed soldiers who stood outside the bank, or the razor wire coiled around an elementary school that was pinkly stuccoed and blinding in the sun. Or that on one corner, hundreds of cartons of eggs were stacked under the overhang of a stall. Quarters of beef hung from hooks in meat markets, where packs of wild dogs leapt and snarled and helped themselves to the lowest parts.

"The afternoons in Belize City are wicked hot," I say. "Over a hundred degrees. And by night the mosquitoes are thicker than soup. Worse than here—"

I knew this would be hard. But I'm coming to my favorite part.

"One day I stopped at a street infirmary to buy a bottle of

water, and I saw these women with blue scarves tied around their heads. They—did everything."

"What everything?" Shookie asks. She *is* listening.

"They took temperatures and bandaged hurts; they handed out tortillas; they dished up soup on the beach. They rocked babies and played hopscotch with little girls. They sat with the sick. They were the Sisters of Mercy."

"Catholics," Shookie says, and snorts.

I'd thought so too, and I was turning away that day when a nun caught my sleeve.

Take their picture, she'd said, pointing to a mother and a little boy, waiting their turn in a plastic chair. *She is dying.*

So I did, and gave it to them with a light kiss to both their foreheads—the boy's sweaty, his mother's hot and dry—and then I sat on a bench with Sister Anne Benefactor, sharing her cheese sandwich.

"No. They were all denominations and were starting a new group."

"What kind of group?" Auntie asks.

"A new branch of the sisterhood. To learn to do good works. I—I was surprised that I've had to *learn* to do charitable things. I was thinking, *My Aunt Jerusha was the queen of charity.*"

Auntie frowns.

"I was never like you," I say, intending a compliment. "If I were to become a Sister of Mercy, I knew they'd have to—teach me the ropes. I stayed to help. And went back the next day. Pretty soon I was Sister Clea Gloria. *Gloria,* meaning the bliss of heaven, a circle of light."

And at last—*at last*—I was no longer a *Shine.*

"Never heard of them," Shookie says.

I look away, to the place where Mama's home once stood. A couple of people stand in the grass there. "Other things too. We do driving and housekeeping for shut-ins, take groceries and bedding to people who sleep on the floor, in the park, under bridges. I've sat at the prison hospital with fourteen-year-old inmates while they tore at their shackles and gave birth. I rocked crack babies who skidded into the world screaming and shivering."

I've done it again—said more than I meant to. I'm still pretty bad about that.

I get up then, and go in to pour a glass of lemonade while I pull myself together.

More than three thousand Sisters of Mercy, most of them laywomen, are stationed at various camps in the United States, Mexico, and Latin America. So many things I love about them. They work for humanity, and they work on themselves. They know there is a God, and they accept one another. I have become more patient with my Pentecostal sisters, the brimstone-fearing Baptists, and the Catholics, who always seemed the most inexplicable of all.

I like thinking: *Nobody's wrong.*

One day Sister Anne Benefactor said to me, "Life is a great mystery, Clea. Under the surface all things are connected with everything else. With you. With the Source. And it all understands you. Remember that one well-chosen word can replace fifty others."

Lord, Lord, what a revelation. I'd spent an entire childhood prattling.

Try as I did, I never mastered stillness. The sisters assured me that almost nobody does. But we do keep on trying. Eventually, those few minutes of silence, twice a day, calmed me to the point that I was moved to write a book. Thanks to Sister Anne, I chose my words carefully.

Every night in my room, I picked up my pen, and words fell onto the paper.

I wrote about Mama.

I wrote about Claudie.

I wrote about the First and Last Holy Word Church and Millicent Poole, with her thin hair and her army of demons. As I wrote, I learned. Words were tricky things: Nothing else had the power to put a man down. Nothing could pick him up so quickly.

Because I had a degree in English—I barely remembered earning it. Those were the bad days with knives and scissors—the sisters assigned me the job of teaching people to read. I especially loved the older folks, who'd spent a lifetime never knowing the power of words.

And I loved Belize City. Three times a week, Sister Margaret Redemptor, who was also the real thing in the way of nuns—one of three externs assigned to lead us—gathered us all at the foot of the great cathedral's stone stairs. She ordered us to climb the steps on our knees, pausing on each to reflect on our work and the state of our souls. But my mind grew restless on those steps, and I repeatedly turned my attention from my soul, to the holes in my jeans and the blood and the calluses that had thickened and yellowed on my hands.

We sat at the top, hugging our torn shins. No one had brought alcohol wipes or Band-Aids. But Sister Anne kissed our knees and wept over them. I already had raised silver scars on my body to remind me of my past. Here in Belize, I wasn't cutting myself anymore.

Before we left for the States, we crept up the steps one last time. At the top I sat, while the others prayed, and I looked out

over the city and the deep, dark forests that lay beyond. Sister
Anne came and laid a hand on the braids I still wound around
my head.

"In your heart, Sister Clea, which do you think God loves
more—you on skinned knees, or the way you open old eyes to
written words?"

I rose and went down and sat on the grass and knew that my
heart was gloriously filled, like the rich insides of a Boston cream
bun. Then we all walked back to town and into the tropic-wet
furnace of another day.

I'd decided I would stay with a collective that intended to meet
weekly in lower Mississippi. One of our group, whose home had
been in Biloxi, was eager to get back. She was divorced and had
an infant son who, all this time, she'd carried on her hip and
breast-fed under the banana trees. But her mother missed her
and wanted to see the child. Instead of thirteen, we would be
twelve.

Sister Margaret Redemptor led us back to the United States,
crammed in a small boat, and swamped with seawater. We came
ashore in Dandridge. Most of us needed housing. *I did.*

And we searched for a place to meet once a week.

We found the back room at Fong's Chinese Wok.

I carry my lemonade outside.

27

When I take my seat under the willow, there is a silence that no one else fills.

Wheezer reaches out, laying a hand over mine. He's being kind. But it wasn't *him* I ran away from in the night. He didn't wonder where I'd gone or if I was alive. It wasn't his butcher knife I took.

What was it Auntie had said about Wheezer?

... *The chaplain down at the Farm.*

With the back of my hand I wipe sweat from my face and tell them about the collapse of our house in Dandridge. I skip quickly over Thomas, try to make the story funny—"It was a two-story monstrosity. One repair led to another. We needed contractors and an electrician and inspectors and roofers. We'd each decided to cut back on one activity per month so we could pay for all that.

"Luz was spending too much time over her books, so we'd told her she had to sign up for basketball. Naturally, when we each made one sacrifice, she gave up the team. And Harry—he gave this big sigh and said he'd been thinking about getting a rabbit. But now he would not."

"So he talked, before," Wheezer says. "Harry talked."

"Oh, yes. My goodness, yes. When—when the storm came, we were under the dining room table. I could hear the windows breaking upstairs. The big tree on the lawn came down, and the neighbors' too. Then these cracks opened up, and the ceiling came apart under Harry's room, and his things just—fell through. His braided rug, his rabbit, his slippers. The legs of his bed. There was so much dust. After that, he wouldn't eat or talk. I took him to the hospital, but it was crowded there, and they said trauma. Lots of people with trauma. So we—came here."

Mercifully, nobody asks me more about my husband.

"Dammit to hell," Wheezer says. He's looking at the people next door.

Auntie sits up straighter in her webbed chair. "News does travel."

On the other side of a half-acre of tall grass, two figures stand where my mother's house used to be. One is stick-thin, curved of shoulder, and flapping her arms. Knees bent, her arms are raised like she might fly away. She's squawking and wailing, making the noise of a hundred sick chickens. Her hair is wispy and white, and beneath a cotton gown, her veined legs are a road map. I know who she is, and I know the man with her, dark and dignified and leaning on a cane. Millicent Poole and Reverend Ollie Green.

My throat has gone dry. "What are they doing?"

"Millie Poole," Shookie says. Her voice is smug. "She's shakin' up Satan."

Wheezer, still leaning forward on his chair, gives me a devilish grin. "Miss Millie comes down every so often so she can—dust the place."

"What?"

"She's riddin' the property of demons, Clea. She thinks after your mama and those others died, it left bad juju. She's afraid it'll spread down to her place."

"Y'oughta go over," Cousin Bitsy says, "say hey." It's the first time since I arrived that she's spoken to me.

That hundred feet would be the farthest I ever walked.

Auntie shrugs. "Place belongs to you now. Do what you want with it."

No, thanks.

Auntie says stiffly, "Now and then Cunny has Ernie Shiloh come and mow down the weeds. He hauled off what lumber he could use."

"Uncle," I say, "I owe you for that."

"No," he says. "You settle with Ernie."

I remember how that charred flooring and timber stood across the narrow field for so many years. What an awful thing to have next door. No wonder I went away and lived on the curb and took razor blades to my arms. The truth was, I hurt so badly inside, I needed someone to see. It took me God's long time to learn that.

I realize suddenly that the night has grown cool. The Reverend lifts a hand and stumps into Auntie's yard. His smile is huge. He hugs me and calls me Sister Clea, an appellation accorded grown women in the church. I imagine he's retired and been replaced by now.

Millicent Poole scuttles over too, her feet in dirty bedroom slippers. She's sighted me, and she shakes a crooked finger. "That fancy car—I shoulda knowed it was you!"

Her voice is raw—probably from years of drugs. "That's all

right," she rasps. "Don't you bother to get up, little girl, or say *howdy-do*. All these years, I've done your work for you. See that concrete, them broken pieces?"

The old flooring. Part of the kitchen. A piece of staircase, lying on its side. A broken pipe.

"Bad spirits live under there," she says. "You should be prostrate in that field, begging forgiveness. Doing good works."

I do good works.

"Now, Millie—" the Reverend says.

Millicent lifts her chin, her frail self wobbling. "Girl, you're just the devil in one of his clever disguises. You get yourself over to church on Sunday and confess your sins. You're a grown woman now—" She paws the air, catching rays of light and dust that only she can see. Her knuckles look swollen and sore. "It's time you paid for your sins."

I recall the gray goose that ate up her garden that one day, and how I tried to do right. I think of the opium pipe, and how afraid I was. Although I could now make three of Miss Millicent and could knock her over with my hand, no time has passed. I need somewhere to run.

The screen door creaks open. "Mom," Luz says. "Harry's having nightmares again."

I go to my children.

My heart feels like some rickety place. Like there's nowhere safe to put my feet. It has something to do, I think, with the way my houses keep falling down.

28

In the morning, there's bacon and a spoonful of scrambled egg on Harry's plate. He has his spoon in his hand; he slept that way. I was fearful that he'd poke his eye out or run it down his throat, but he's using it now to chop at the yellow egg.

Auntie's at the stove, turning hotcakes. She says to Harry, "Honey, you go on and pick up that bacon in your fingers. That's the way it's done around here."

And Harry does. He takes an almost-bite. I want to fall on the floor in relief. Now, if we can get him to talk . . .

Luz has already eaten. I pour a cup of coffee, hug Harry, and kiss the top of his head, and Luz's too.

I try to figure how many years I've been gone. In this big kitchen, not much has changed. No dishwasher has been added, no microwave. I wonder if I'm welcome enough—or at home enough—to run dishwater in the sink for the washing up. I do it anyway, and squirt in liquid soap, begin to dunk the sticky plates. On the porch, a dryer has been installed alongside the washer. I guess the clothesline, where I used to play among the sweet-smelling sheets, isn't used anymore.

Auntie brings the plate of hotcakes and the warm syrup jar.

She stirs sugar in her mug and gets right to it. "Clea, all of us, we read your book."

The book. I began it the day Dr. Ahmed gave me the steno pad in the hospital. When it was finished, I called it *Halo*. I'd changed the characters' names, at the urging of my editor, and I'd fudged with the places, making up towns, renaming the river. I hadn't fooled anyone here, nor did I expect to.

"You said bad things about us."

"No." I sip my coffee. Too hot. "I said bad things about Mama. I needed to say them."

"You ran off," Auntie says, as if she has a whole list. "In the dead of night."

To save myself.

Those were the bad years. After False River, before Belize.

I went to live where nobody cared, just sat on the sidewalk and watched shoes go by. I had street people to learn from. When it rained I held cardboard over my head. I could walk two blocks to a food line, and when I needed to pee I went around to the alley, although most didn't bother.

That was just the beginning.

"I went to college," I said. "Got a degree."

Luz has been watching me, her eyes big and round. She knows about the book and has asked to read it, but I won't let her. Here in this house, though, things are going to come out.

I set my coffee down, give her a smile, and watch Harry toy with his breakfast. In just the last couple of days, his face has grown pale, veins blue at his temples, his eye sockets too big. I've heard of children who had to be fed intravenously, and that also makes me afraid. Fear breeds fear—had I not learned that myself, bound to a bed in a psychiatric ward?

What we put into the world, we get back a thousandfold.

When I've finished my coffee, I'll go upstairs to Call, and I'll give thanks, in advance, for the return of Harry's appetite.

Meanwhile, I say, "One bite, little guy?"

He rubs an eye with the flat of his hand.

I'm no more rested than when I went to bed. Last night I lay awake, thinking that Millicent couldn't be more wrong. Whatever sins my mother committed, and wherever she is now, she made her hell right here, where I could see it. I sometimes stepped inside it with her.

Being *away* from here was what saved me. I'm grateful to those people who reached out to me in the streets and clinics and basements. And among the Belize Sisters, I learned that life is the hard part. As will be the next life, and the next. Only between is there real, true rest.

There was always comfort in this house. Aunt Jerusha and Uncle Cunny gave me what was never required of them, and as soon as I calm my nerves and screw up my courage, I'll walk next door, find whatever concrete or timber may be left, and I will spit on it and curse it.

Then Miss Millie will have something real to work on.

After that, I'll have to deal with the law. There's probably no statute of limitations on murder.

I sit at the table and swallow a mouthful of coffee. My eyes are on my boy. I say, "I think babies remember God."

Auntie looks over at me. Bitsy has come down, and she fills a plate.

I say, "I wish Harry could tell me what God looks like. Or that he could show me heaven on a map."

No one says a word.

"I think that's why they can't speak," I say.

Bitsy pours syrup.

I smile, making conversation. "Babies have these funny little toes and dimpled bottoms. They're—you know—fresh from the earth and the sky and wind, but not allowed to speak of it. I wonder where that memory goes."

Over the rim of her cup Auntie says primly, "They say we got brain parts we never use."

"They look so innocent. When Harry was two, he had hair like the down of a baby duck."

Now that I'm here in Auntie's house, I hate that I've kept Luz and Harry from her. Then I look over at Bitsy. Her eyes are more heavy-lidded than usual.

"Auntie," I say, rising. "May I use your phone? I'll pay for the call. I'd like to tell the sisters where I am. My cell phone—"

—was lost in the collapse of my house in Dandridge.

While Bitsy eats, I call Sister Isabel, murmur something vague, *I'll be gone awhile. Will you cover my assignments? I'm sorry, but the files and lesson plans were on my desk. When the house came down, they blew away on the wind.*

Sister Janice and Sister Grace crowd around the little phone and say *We love you, Go with God,* and *Stay in touch.*

Do not worry, they tell me.

I climb the stairs to the attic for a few minutes of Call. But the only things that come are quakes like fissures trying to open inside me. I get up and gather our dirty clothes. One of Thomas's socks is stuck in a sleeve. For a moment I wish I had a match.

How can I think that?

Because, of course, it's all coming back. I've come back too, and brought my own demons with me.

Then I hear a truck, a pickup—*the county sheriff's?* I run down the stairs to put my arms around my kids. But it's Uncle Cunny.

He throws his hat on the table. He runs a hand over his hair.

"Another storm's swirling up out in the Atlantic. It's headed for the gulf."

Shookie's folding clothes at the table. I see now that her legs are thick as tree trunks. She wears a pair of bedroom slippers that once were pink and fuzzy. Her steps are short and shuffling.

"God's sake," she says. "All this weather's more than a body can take."

"Put a dollar in the jar on the shelf," Auntie tells me. "For the laundry. Pays for hot water and soap."

If we stay here very long, I'll have to transfer money from our bank to one in Greenfield, or even Jenerette, which is closer. If we stay here long, I'll need to find a job. But it won't be, will it—not long at all. And anyway, that's assuming Auntie will let us stay in this house that's already so full. On the other hand, she and her sister are getting older, and Bitsy's no hand at anything.

When I come down, Auntie leaves the table and turns on the TV. "Lord, Cunny, what are they sayin'?"

He shakes his head. "Already a hurricane, and they're calling it Greta. You can bet your fine china we'll take a hit."

29

Auntie's broiling chickens in the oven. I go outside to study the sky. Bitsy comes too.

I recall how, on Saturdays during those post-fire years, I'd help Auntie with the baking. It was the strangest thing—rolling out pastries, or when I iced a cake, I seemed to stand on higher ground. Uncle loved it. I made coconut cream pies that were whipped and high and perfectly set. For that one, I think, he kissed my cheek.

"How've you been doing, Bitsy?" I say now.

There's this thing about Bitsy: She seems as surprised when she speaks as when she's spoken to. "I guess I been fine." After a couple minutes pass, she says, "Inside, though, I got the depression."

I say, "Oh?"

In a voice as breathy as spring, she says, "You a good mama?"

"I—think so. I hope so."

"I had me a baby girl," she says. "Only you didn't know."

Cicadas are trilling in the oak trees. Through the screen I see Auntie moving around in the kitchen, Shookie coming out of the bathroom, straightening her undies, her slip, and her dress.

"Excuse me?"

"I had me a little bitty baby. She pale, but they say she darken up."

I stare at her wide face, her squinchy eyes and thick lips. Is there something beautiful about Bitsy? Somewhere?

"When?" I said.

"You was here."

"I was?"

"I went to the hospital. You stupid to not notice I's so big."

The hospital? I remember that. Something was wrong with Bitsy's blood. Or blood pressure. Shookie stayed here. She came with a valise and her crocheting—a great ball of cotton with a hooked silver needle sticking through. I never questioned where Bitsy was. I knew for a fact that high blood pressure came to folks who ate too much.

She nods her great head. "I went to the hospital, and they pulled this little gal outa me, an' I heard her cry."

She was right—how stupid I was! How could Bitsy sleep around and not get pregnant? If Shookie couldn't buy her daughter a bra, she sure didn't have her on birth-control pills.

But this is something else. Something more, and it's colored pale pink.

"You had a baby," I say softly. "What happened to it?"

"They didn't let me keep her. Was something bad wrong, they said. But I heard her cry. I called her Felicia."

"That's a pretty name."

And for the first time ever, Bitsy turns a smile on me, the corners of her mouth going up, lips parting.

"You have really nice teeth," I say.

Auntie has her hip to the door, and I hear Miss Shookie talking on and on.

"Bitsy?" I say. "I'm sorry they took your—Felicia."

She shrugs her big shoulders. "I guess she died. Mama wouldn't let me keep her, anyways. She up there now—" She points.

I nod and look up. Clouds have moved in, thick, gray, and forlorn.

"It okay," Bitsy says. "My baby girl, she think I fine. She say I'da made a good mama, change her diaper, comb her hair."

The heat and the cicadas and the world spin around me. Bitsy's words stick.

My baby girl, she think I fine.

30

Wheezer comes home for lunch. We eat cucumber sand-wiches and celery and sweet pickles—Luz's favorite. And potato chips and pecan pie.

Bitsy watches Luz; Luz's eyes are on Auntie; Wheezer studies me.

"Sorry for staring, Clea," he says. "You've grown up, is all. You got real pretty, and you're a fine writer too."

"You read my book?"

At this, Luz looks up. She holds Auntie's book in her lap.

"'Course," Wheezer says. "It was a good read. You were brave to tell the truth."

"In the eye of the beholder."

"It's your truth that counts. I read it twice."

Wheezer's story was greater than mine, although that was one thing being crazy had taught me: Nobody's pain gets dis-counted. Size does not matter. I wonder how Wheezer has dealt with his past.

I shift my eyes to Harry. Auntie has brought him his yellow bowl. He sorts through a few dry Rice Krispies, picks up a couple and puts them in his mouth. I don't know whether to celebrate or keep quiet and let him be.

"In case y'all haven't heard," Wheezer says, draining the last of his fruit jar of tea, "there's another storm brewin'."

Auntie nods, sighing.

Harry has taken a shine to Uncle Cunny Gholar and, for the last couple of hours, followed him around like a puppy. Now Uncle announces that he and Harry should "throw one in the water"—meaning minnows on a hook.

"I believe we can catch us a fish at Duck Creek," he says.

Harry sits up, and his eyes go round.

"After lunch?" Uncle asks him.

Harry nods once.

"Not until he eats a little more," Auntie says.

Wheezer pushes back his chair. "Listen, Clea," he says, "let's take a walk by the river."

"Can I come too?" Luz wants to know.

"Sure," Wheezer says.

She brings her book.

I tell Harry I'll be back in a minute and bestow kisses on the top of his head.

But he has eyes only for Uncle Cunny, who's eating a second piece of pie.

It's one of those smothery afternoons that only this part of Mississippi, with its moist deltas and hot southern sun, can know. The sky, though leaden, still looks blameless. The air is heavy with fragrances—grass and the lily of the valley that grows in deep shade. No leaves rustle in the oaks, where gray moss hangs down. Even the birds have gone to sleep. The river is silent too—not one water frond or cattail is stirring. Oddly, not one bluebottle hovers on the surface.

Wheezer takes up a rock and skims it, perfect, across the still water. Luz knows how to do this; Thomas has taught her. She finds her own flat rock, finds the angle of elbow and wrist, and imitates him.

"I see you're reading the Bible," Wheezer says.

"It belongs to Miss Jerusha. There's nothing else here to read. My books—"

"I have some in my room. You're welcome to look. I'm guessing you're a very high-level reader."

"Very," Luz says, giving her glasses a shove, although they haven't slid down.

We walk for a while, along the bank, toward False River.

Wheezer asks her, "Is this the first time you've read the Bible?"

"From the beginning," she admits. "Although now I'm reading the Old and New Testaments at the same time."

"Ah," he says. "A comparison shopper. You have a very smart daughter, Clea."

"I'm like my mom," Luz says.

"Yes. Like your mom."

This exchange embarrasses me a little. We find a place to sit.

"Tell him, Mom," Luz says. "Tell Mr. Stengle how you got me."

"Why don't you tell him, Luzie?" By now, she knows it backward and forward, and tells it much better than I do.

She likes that. "Mom and Dad were teaching in Mexico when they found me. I was four years old and sitting in the doorway of a plywood coop. Shack. Shed. I was four, and I was having trouble breathing.

"Mom had this grant she'd gotten from the government, and she used it to buy soap and fresh water and underwear. She brought that stuff to us, to the community." Luz grins. "She didn't speak any Spanish, but she handed out bags of dried beans and flour and rice. And she loved on the babies."

Listening, I think, *Those were good days.* On the playa, two other sisters and I had set up a stall where we shaved the kids' heads to rid them of lice and showed them how to brush their teeth. They laughed until they fell on the ground. But not Luz. She had uneven bangs, a serious face, and squinty eyes.

"One day Dad—he wasn't my dad yet—found this donkey cart, and we all piled in."

"There were at least a dozen of you kids," I say.

"They led us up the mountain to an American clinic so doctors could check us out. They gave us chewable vitamins and shots for diphtheria." Luz's face loses its animation.

"I had brothers, two of them. They were fourteen and twelve. They joined the army. I remember Paulo carrying a rifle. He and Rico went off to fight in the mountains, and they died. So I was left all alone. When Mom and Dad found me, I was skin and bone. Starving.

"I was hungry, but Mom says I was more interested in the books she had in her bag, so they borrowed me. It was for just a month."

"How long ago was that month?" Wheezer asks.

"A long time. There was nobody to miss me, anyway. We got me tennis shoes and shorts and tops. We went to an ophthalmologist. He gave me eyeglasses. Spectacles. Cheaters." She grins.

I add, "Luz had asthma; a doctor prescribed a spoonful of syrup once a day and gave us an inhaler for the worst times."

"But they wondered what would happen after they went home," Luz says, taking up the story. "They got my hair cut, had me vaccinated against everything, and loaded me up with books. At four I knew how to read—can you believe that?"

She could. Right away, that had struck a chord in my belly and knotted me up. I didn't care who had taught her, or how she'd learned—I bought her a dictionary, notepads and pencils. A red backpack to hold all her things.

"Mom and Dad flew to the capital," Luz says with a flourish, "and started the adoption papers that would let them keep me for the rest of our lives. Dad had to go home to teach class, but Mom stayed."

I did. I waded through tons of paperwork, then flew to Biloxi on December 24 with Luzie, her tiny carry-on, and her red backpack.

"And that's my story," Luz says. "Well, except that I'm smart. I skipped second grade. I could've jumped fourth, but Mom wouldn't let me. Also, I love mice and spiders and garden snakes. I turn over rocks. Dad teaches biology. He said sometime he should take me to school with him so I could teach his class."

"She sleeps with books spread around her on the bed," I say. "Last year she was president of the school science club, and an elected officer in the astronomers' club at Thomas's college."

"Mom said I could have a membership in Book-of-the-Month Club if I paid for it, so I got a job walking dogs."

To the park and back, I want to say.

Wheezer claps as though it's the best story he's ever heard.

"You're an amazing kid," he says. "And a lucky one."

Luz says, "Why do they call you Wheezer? I don't hear you wheezing." She pulls her inhaler out of her pocket to show him. I've sewn pockets on everything Luzie owns.

"I've pretty much outgrown it. I don't know if they had inhalers when I was a kid."

"You know much about the Bible?" Luz asks him.

"Some," he says.

"Miss Jerusha said you were a chaplain, so I thought—if I had questions, you might answer them."

"I can try, if it's okay with your mom."

"Fine with me," I say. "In fact, Wheezer's the very person to talk to."

"Mom thinks the Bible is a great history book," she says, and I'm suddenly embarrassed by that.

"She's right," Wheezer says.

Luz takes off her sandals and puts her toes in the cool mud.

I feel like I owe an explanation. "There've been so many arguments about which parts we should take literally—and what writings have only metaphoric meaning." I smile at Luz. "I used to wonder why God didn't send somebody down to write a *new* Bible, one that applied to the twenty-first century. And then I realized—maybe He had."

Luz presses her toes deeper in the mud.

I didn't intend to talk so much.

"What I mean is, maybe we have our God eyes closed, you know? There are hundreds of writers turning out thousands of books that tell us how to live better, how to love each other and mend our hurts. What if those are our new Bibles?"

"So many writers, so many points of view." Luz looks skeptical. "Some are a sham, a ruse. Phony baloney."

Wheezer grins again.

"Some *are*." I reach out and rub her back. "But you'll make your own choices and figure things out. Why else would you have been made so smart?"

"I know," she says in that voice that means she's about to quote me. "'Any path to God is a good one.'"

"A sound philosophy," Wheezer says.

I sigh and get up. "I should check on Harry."

"Mom. He's gone fishing."

"I'm sure Wheezer needs to get back to work." I jerk my chin toward the prison.

He rubs a thumb down his jaw and says, "Clea, that's what I want to talk to you about."

My heart lurches.

"Listen," Wheezer says as we pick our way back over the rocks and up the bank. "Down at the Farm, we've got some guys wondering if you'd take a look at their writings."

"You talked about me there?"

Wheezer turns pink. "There are a couple of offenders—"

"*Offenders?*"

"Inmates. We're way overcrowded now, and the hog farm's gone, so there's not much work for them. Crops are in and sold; ground's not ready to be tilled. They hang around the dayroom, lay on their bunks, and that's when they get in trouble—" That grin again. "Start fermenting canned peaches in the shower, hidin' hooch in the walls."

Luz's sandals dangle from her thumbs. She has that fascinated look on her face.

"Clea, you've got this gift—"

Luz waves her arms. "Mom works for the sisterhood. She teaches reading and writing. She'd be perfect!" She's as excited as Wheezer is.

"Hey, then, would you come down and work with a few guys?"

I'm being railroaded.

"We pay a couple of teachers—one in beginning law, and there's this art guy. But some of the inmates work on essays. We got some pretty good writers. You be interested in doing a class?"

"Hold on," I say. "You went from *looking at the writings of one or two* to *working with a class.*"

Wheezer shrugs. "We take what we can get, and we don't get much. I'm always workin' it, Clea. These guys need someone like you."

We've stopped under the weeping willow tree. I remember how its whippy green branches stung my legs—and the love with which Auntie always rocked me, but only after I'd understood my crime.

Maybe Wheezer's afraid I'm thinking too much. "I don't know how long y'all will be here, but if you want to come on a regular basis for a while, I think I can get you a few bucks."

Money. But, God, God. *At Hell's Farm?*

Still, everybody wants to be prized for what they can do. And—what else do I have? "All right."

"Great," he says. "We'll get you down there tomorrow morning." He tells Luz, "Your mom's a great lady. Sometime I'll tell you how I know this personally."

Luz's brows go up. "If Mom's so brilliant, why's she scared all the time?"

31

What, I wonder, *has happened to Finn?*
And Claudie Maytubby and her brothers and sisters?

"Luzie," I say, on the back porch steps. "Will you be all right here for a while? With Auntie and Miss Shookie?"

"And Bitsy," she says. "Sure. Where you going?"

"Just down the road. To see an old friend. I won't be long."

"Mom, I went into Wheezer's room—it's okay, he told me to call him that. He has a copy of your book."

"Luz, we've talked about this before."

"And you always say the same thing!"

"When you're older—"

"There you go again," she says. "I *am* older!"

Is she? Where was I—what did I think—when I was eleven?

"Maybe you're right. But—we'll need to talk about it first."

Her eyes are almost as round as her glasses. "When can we talk?" she says. "Tonight? Tomorrow?"

"In the next day or two. Meanwhile, promise me you won't read it by flashlight after I'm asleep."

She sighs. "Cross my heart. But you won't forget?"

"I won't."

"Anyway, I'm liking the Book of Mark all right. And, Mom. Did you know Abraham was circumcised when he was ninety-nine?"

If I were laughing these days, I'd laugh at that. Maybe Luz won't find *Halo* unsettling at all.

"But," she says, ever curious, "what kinds of things are you going to tell me?"

"I did some bad stuff."

"All kids do things wrong. Base, low, foul. Devilish." She looks especially owlish. "Mom—did you ever just say you were sorry?"

⁂

The houses seem miniature and across Potato Shed Road, beyond the prison field, the line of poplars doesn't seem nearly as far away as it used to. A single row of inmates is out, working the soft ground. They look not to be chained anymore, the way they were when I was a kid—no more clanking and shuffling along in step. Still, a supervisor—a guard in that remembered gray uniform—stands with a baton, and I see over my shoulder that another patrols the tower's outer walkway. A rifle is hard across his chest.

I wonder what move the prisoners must make before someone throws a switch and sets off the siren. I recall hearing that wailing now and then, and shots fired too, but I didn't pay much attention to what they meant.

The lane is narrow and not as long as I recall.

On the Maytubbys' porch, a stick-skinny black woman is smoking a cigarette. By the thickness of her glasses I know it's Eulogenie Maytubby—that and the fact that she has one arm.

I stand at the road, at the very place where Denver Lee once helped his pretty bride out of the yellow car. Here is that patch of hard land where little boys wrestled and naked babies nursed at swollen breasts.

"Excuse me. Eulogenie? I know you don't remember me—"

She exhales and squints against the smoke. Her voice is still tiny, like her teeth used to be. But I hear her clear. "I knows who you are."

"I'm Clea Ryder now."

She takes another drag on her cigarette.

"I wanted to come and see how you're doing. How Claudie is."

"Claudie be dead," she says.

I stand there dumbly. *"I'm sorry?"*

"Bad news, ain't it, if you care to think so."

I can't take this in. Claudie Maytubby shouldn't be dead. *Can't be.*

Eulogenie flicks the filter off the end of the porch, and I shiver in the heat and wait for it to flare up in the dry weeds, but it doesn't.

"Can you tell me—how—how did she die?"

"Kilt in a race riot up to Arkansas. Blown to pieces with a pipe bomb, if you don't know."

Do I remember reading about that?

"What was she doing in Arkansas?" She'd never live that far from her sister.

Her face is bony and pinched. Now her mouth pinches too. "Her and four white folks was meetin' in Little Rock, at one of them adoption places."

"Genie, I'm so sorry for your loss."

"Likely not. You a Shine."

"I mean that. I am." I'm also mortified that at one time I had the hate and audacity to call her *Plain Genie.*

She shrugs. "One minute they was all talkin', and then they

was . . . gone." She cocks her head, and her face crumples in an ugly way.

I move to stand at the foot of the steps. "I—"

She half rises from her chair. Her mouth opens, and I see that she's lost some of her teeth. "Don't you come up!" Her voice is bitter and cracked. "I got me this house an' my welfare check an' a pack of cigarettes, and I don't need you tellin' me you unnerstand. You done enough here!"

"Genie—"

"You was always sayin' to her, *Go on, Claudie Maytubby. Be all you can be.* So she did. She left here to bring home her new baby, an' she never came back—what you think about that?"

"Claudie was adopting—"

"I assign you blame. You got you a husband, and I seen your chirrun. I got these bad eyes and bones all cattywampus; my ovaries never come on. Miss Clea Shine—or whatever yo' name is—who gonna love *me* an' marry *me,* do you think?"

"Claudie's baby—"

"A little Chinese baby boy," Genie says, and she takes off her glasses. "You go on an' get outa here, now. Don't you feel bad, an' don't you worry, Miss Shine. *I bein' all I can be.*"

32

Luz has helped Aunt Jerusha bake a pie—lemon, with meringue stacked like summer clouds. At the table Luz is reading Bitsy a cookbook, adding definitions and synonyms. Bitsy looks fascinated. Luz looks up, tells Bitsy about her books and the computer, how our staircase came loose on Lilac Lane, the ceiling cracking, Harry's blue bed and his rabbit tumbling down.

"Through the hole," she says sadly. "Through the fissure. Abyss."

Until this moment, on this very day, I've never seen Bitsy look so sympathetic. She shakes her head and heaves herself up the stairs with her mama's folded laundry.

Mamas, I think, are a tangled lot—Bitsy, whose baby was taken from her, and Plain Genie with her undeveloped ovaries. Claudie, who'd gone north to bring home a little boy with almond eyes. And my mama. And me.

Miss Shookie'd had Bitsy. It shakes me to think that Jerusha Lovemore never had babies of her own. Just me. And I ran off. What a disappointment I must have been.

Shookie sits now, with her crochet hook and ball of cotton, at the far end of the sofa. She likes TV game shows and spends a lot of time bickering with the emcee and nodding off.

Then a truck door bangs, and I jump from my chair. But they're just back with the fish, Harry holding tight to Uncle's hand. Harry watches him clean them under the tree. I watch from the steps. Light slants in and catches the filleting knife and the silver scales and Uncle's blunt nails. Then, in the kitchen, Auntie lets Harry stand on a chair and keep an eye on his fish while she rolls them in cornmeal and drops them in the sizzling fat. My boy's wearing a big polka-dotted apron against the grease. He helps her roll out dough for hush puppies, lowers them in on a big spoon, and the oniony smell rises up and fills the kitchen.

Uncle Cunny comes behind them, puts his arms around both. I'm surprised Uncle hasn't moved in here too.

As if my mind is not full enough with Harry and the prison and Thomas's infidelity—not to mention coming back here at all—I cannot stop agonizing over Claudie. She never got to bring her boy home.

At dinner, Luz eats her weight in onion-fried potatoes, cole-slaw, and filleted fish. With his small fingers, Harry peels the breading away and pokes at the white meat with his silver spoon. Auntie cuts it up for him with her fork, blows to cool it, and Harry lifts a piece to his mouth. My eyes sting, and I look away.

The conversation is about the mess of branches along the river.

Uncle and Ernie Shiloh will bring their chainsaws. . . .

—The weather is turning; the air is still.

The fish were biting.

Because he's eaten some, Auntie brings Harry Ovaltine and a

straw to drink through. He takes a sip, lays his cheek on his plate, and goes to sleep. Too tired to put his thumb in his mouth.

"My," says Uncle Cunny. "Would you look at that."

I rise from my chair. "I'll just carry him up."

"Let me do it," Wheezer says, and he comes around and lifts my little guy, light as air, and takes him up the two flights of stairs, and I follow. Wheezer lays him on the cot, and I pull off Harry's shoes and socks and his shorts with fish scales still clinging. I tuck him in.

A wind has risen. In the south gable, the glass rattles in its frame.

"The storm?" I say softly, although I think nothing would wake Harry.

Wheezer shakes his head. "It's a ways off yet."

I leave a light burning, and say without meaning to, "So many things in my life are shot to hell."

"Well," Wheezer says, "I'm not one of them."

❈

Once upon a time, I was falling in love.

There used to be a song like that. *"Once upon a time I was falling in love, now I'm only falling apart."* Nicki French or maybe Bonnie Tyler. "Total Eclipse of the Heart," that was it.

I wonder if eclipses bear as much weight, or go down as significantly in history, as tropical storms. In the last fifteen years I've held a lot of hands, seen a lot of scared folks, watched a lot of them die. In that very last second, the light went out. I know some simply gave up. I believe some died from broken hearts.

For a long time, Thomas has been gone from me. But I had no idea how physical it was. And I know the girl—a sulky navel-studded student named Sunny with bee-stung lips and weighted eyelids. What an embarrassment for Thomas, who's been making a fool of himself in front of his friends—*our* friends. I am probably the last to know.

I'm guessing Sunny is not his first affair. Back when we were signing papers that would make Harry ours, I'll bet Thomas was screwing around.

33

Next morning, fog rolls in, spreads its wings, and holds fast in spite of wind gusts that should have driven it away.

Wheezer comes downstairs, helps himself to bacon, and pecks Auntie on the cheek. "You ready?" he asks me.

"Don't worry about the children," Auntie says. "There's plenty to keep them busy here."

I have been shaking since dawn. Hell's Farm is the last place I want to go. What if, while I'm there, they look up my name and call the sheriff? What if my family never sees me again?

I leave the table, thinking I'm sick to my stomach. I kneel over the toilet in Auntie's bathroom, but nothing comes up. I've had only coffee. My legs cramp, and my heart vibrates in my chest.

In my growing-up years, I watched loads of convicts go past this house, being trucked to the pig farms or the far cotton fields. They stood braced between the high backboards, holding their hoes. One guard drove while two others, with heavy clubs in their belts, rode in back. Or the prisoners were marched across the field, feet chained together, hoes in the air, hands shackled at the waist.

I've seen, and I know. And last night, from the attic window, I snuck a long peek.

Hell's Farm is a big brick building that used to be a plantation manor. The only thing left to tell its history are the four white columns and a broken concrete porch. Behind are the outbuildings and the long, low barracks they call cages. When the river rises, that land is first to flood.

On the far side, I recall, is the steep-sided creek. When the river's running, like it is now, the creek swirls with tree limbs and sewage. There's a rickety bridge across the trench, although I've never crossed it, and on the other side is Potter's Field, the county cemetery.

I remember too what the prison looks like close-up because, as a child, I walked its fence and clung to the chain-link. I always wanted Claudie to go down there with me, do a proper job of spying, at least until they ran us off.

Wheezer is on his cell phone with someone—the warden, I think, still setting things up—and it's nearly eleven before we step out into the oddly green morning. He looks at the stacked and rolling sky, says this storm is going to be a big one.

While I've waited, I've removed as much dust from the attic as I could, and washed and dried the sheets and towels. Folding gave my hands something to do. Auntie had the radio on. Greta is now predicted to increase as it crashes onto the Mississippi coast tomorrow morning.

We set out for the Farm.

By the time we arrive at the gate, I am sweating and drawing on my last reserves of breath. There's a bronze plaque that reads: STUART P. HAVELLION STATE PENITENTIARY, ESTABLISHED 1922.

Although I'm sure they recognize Wheezer's face and his name, it's his clipped-on ID badge that seems to be gold. The gate whines open, and we step in. It closes behind us, and the second one rolls.

"Sally port," Wheezer says in explanation. "For deliveries and visitors. A security thing. One door has to close before another one opens."

In a tiled entryway, there are a counter and bored-looking guards, and an office behind. A telephone, an umbrella stand, and a long concrete hall. I sign my name once as a visitor and again for something else, surrender my driver's license, my wristwatch, and the belt to my pants. I keep my wedding ring on. Maybe it will go better with these guys if I look married. I step out of my shoes and through an electronic arch. Even then, I am waved with a metal detector and my shoes inspected, my pockets turned out. I'm required to open my mouth while two different people shine a light down my throat and look under my tongue. And all the time, their faces are impassive.

Wheezer, who holds a briefcase into which nobody's even looked, leads me down the hall, through more steel doors. Men with dim faces sit behind high dark glass and push buttons that get us through.

They rattle and clank behind us, and I clench my fists to ease the shaking.

Wheezer says, "I should have warned you, Clea—there are rules, strict rules, for while you're on prison property. No skirts or panty hose, no makeup, no perfume. Next time you can bring pencils, a notebook, whatever. Carry them in an unzipped bag. Oh, and keep your voice modulated in the classroom and never say anything personal about yourself. If you're answering a question, or giving directions, look the offender in the eye, quick, then away. Got that?"

Offender. A hard word to get used to. But that's why they're here, isn't it—because they've offended. *Me too.* I nod.

To the right, I see the visitors' room—rows of metal stools in front of thick glass, each window with its own black phone on the wall. We climb a set of stairs.

Wheezer looks fit, like he's run up and down these steps a thousand times. He says conversationally, "Farm covers sixteen hundred acres. Even with the barracks, this place was originally intended to take in four hundred. Now we've got eight portable barracks and over two thousand inmates. Highest the count's ever been."

I wish he'd stop talking. In a few minutes I'll be standing in front of convicted felons, and I have no idea what to say.

"Most of 'em work out on the farm," Wheezer says. "In the cotton fields, prison laundry, or the kitchen. We've got more men than jobs—but I told you that."

"Yes." I also wish he wouldn't walk so fast.

"If they earn it, they get time in the yard."

"What do they do to earn it?"

"No pullin' shanks or throwing food, no beating the shit out of each other. Sorry," he says.

"You get a lot of that—fights and things?"

"Enough. 'Specially when a man first comes in. Corrections Department used to make false teeth when they got 'em knocked out. We don't bother anymore. Got a couple hundred in maximum security downstairs."

"Downstairs?"

"Yup. In the cellar. Hell of a thing to dig in the delta, water seeping in. Guess they thought it was cheaper than adding on."

My heart beats double time.

"We got restriction out in a concrete blockhouse—"

"Restriction?"

"Isolation. Guys who had to be cut out of the herd. They spend twenty-three hours out of twenty-four in their cells. Except for the guard that takes them to the showers, they never see another face. Well—their lawyers, but most of those have given up and gone back to divorces and jaywalking cases. Jeez, I'm overwhelming you."

"What does an offender have to do to be put in maximum security?"

"The violent ones. Murderers, rapists. Sometimes they come in here, already bulled up on the bus, struttin' their stuff, and we have to set the dogs on 'em—big honkin' Rottweilers. Nobody gets eaten." Apparently, he's making a joke. "Don't worry, you won't come in contact with the worst."

We turn down a narrow hall, and I see that the rooms on the right are small, the lower walls solid, the top wire mesh—each with a table and two benches bolted to the floor. "Lawyers use those cages to meet with their clients," Wheezer says.

"No privacy anywhere."

"They get plenty in their cells."

To the left, through a window, I see an open room, each table accompanied by four permanent stools.

"Third-floor dayroom," Wheezer says. I guess he's counting the cellar.

Beyond the dayroom is a long row of steel doors—cells, I imagine, two men to a cell, each no more than six feet wide.

Privacy.

"Wheezer, my God, are all prisons like this one?"

Over our heads a guard sits, working buttons in a cage that looks to be reached by a catwalk.

Wheezer lifts a hand, and the guy waves back. "Some are worse; none are better."

So says the chaplain.

All those growing-up years, the rumors I had heard were true. I think of the men in the dark and the damp, two floors down— the ones who've become the worst of the worst. Maybe there are trustees down there, too, with rifles, playing cards and using bullets for poker chips, waiting for an inmate to break a house rule so they can chain him to the wall or gun him down.

Wheezer ushers me into a windowed room. There's a long table, behind which I must sit, and six bolted-down desks three across and two deep—the molded-plastic kind with an arm for writing on.

"All yours," Wheezer says, and opens his briefcase. "I got you some paper from the office and five pencils. Stay in your chair or behind the desk."

Christ.

So I'm to have five. I wait a long time for them to come, for someone to bring them to me. Then here they are—single file, followed by a bull of a guard, who tells them, "Take a seat," and hits my table with the flat of his hand. When my heart is beating again, he says to me, "They think they're mean sonsabitches, teacher, but I'm right outside the door—" He laughs at his joke. There *is* no door. "And I can take 'em down with one hand behind my back." He grins widely at the man up in the cage.

I wonder, *who are the real assholes here?*

Each of the five slides down in his seat, knees apart and hands on the desk, their orange suits making them all alike. But they aren't.

We are a class.

How am I to hand out paper and pencils if I can't move? I think, *Screw that rule,* and pass things around.

The guard misses nothing, and he swings back in, this time

his palm hitting the glass so hard, I think it will break. Nobody looks up.

"I see one pencil lift offa the paper, your ass is mine!" he yodels out like he's calling hogs. "Say, 'Yes, boss!'"

Five mechanical voices: "Yes, boss!" They take up their pencils, hands cramping, heads down, grinning wickedly at one another.

I can't sit in this chair. I want to push both it and the table against the wall, but they're anchored to the floor. I choose a point to the right, farthest from the "boss."

"I'm Miz Ryder." That's what Wheezer has told me to say. And so, with the shuffling of big feet and murmured jibes and counter-jibes, we begin.

I hold out two separately cupped hands. "On the day I taught myself to read, this is what I knew: In one hand I held the solid letters of the alphabet. *B, D, F, G,* and so on. I thought of them as islands.

"In my other hand were the soft ones, the vowels. They were bridges from one solid place to another. Together they were like—the Florida Keys. Land and water. With that map, I could read—and write—any word, any phrase.

"I love that you want to write. There's a profoundness in thinking on paper, maybe remembering the past. You can explore who you are now . . . predict the future. Or," I say with a smile, "in this class, you can make it all up."

They look at their desks, their boots, the linoleum floor. They think I'm a lunatic. Who can blame them? Through a six-inch strip of window, I can just make out the gunmetal sky, a ragged flight of blackbirds.

"I once witnessed some crows," I say, "gathered in a circle in the grass. In the middle there was this one ruffled misfit. Then suddenly all these circled-up crows stopped chattering to each other, and they attacked the one in the middle. They pecked him to death."

One guy has MONDALE stitched to his pocket. He's an older guy, heavy, shiny black with almost no hair. According to my list, his first name is Wesley.

"Mr. Mondale, why do you think they did that?"

He says, "I got an idea, but—you want us to make up shit? Pull sumpin' out our asses?"

They all snicker at this, so I smile too.

"Tell me what you really think."

"Bird was already dyin'. Poor guy was sick with some disease. Bastards couldn't be bothered carryin' him no more."

Wesley, it appears, has an aching heart. "That may be."

Closest to me is Raoul. He's dark—South American, maybe, with a nose that covers half his face. Although he's three feet from the back wall, he keeps glancing over his shoulder. "One in the middle stole a piece of bread." His voice is high-pitched. "He broke a rule. He breaks them all the damn time, always getting a case, called up before the man. Really, it's a wonder he lasted this long."

Everybody laughs.

Wesley shakes his head, runs an enormous hand over his eyes.

There's also this little white guy, Frank. He has big teeth and an oft-broken nose. "Fuck that. Damn crow ain't acceptable here."

"Here being Mississippi."

He thinks that over. "In the South. Wherever."

Is he talking racial? I don't think so. Gangs form in prisons. They've all seen this played out—join or die.

Wesley says, "Bird had shit for brains. Didn't call the man 'boss.'"

This time they almost fall out of their chairs laughing.

The guard bangs into the room, his jaw tight and his chest barreled out.

"Hold on!" I say, and I step up and press my palm to his shirt buttons, the first I've felt the gray twill of those uniforms. I think about how I used to fear them, and of the night I spied on Bitsy in the field. That guard's pants were around his knees and his backside was shining. "Sir. You're disrupting my class. If I need you, I'll call."

There's dead silence in the room, but he goes, the guard goes, and I tell my students, "Okay. I want to begin to know who you are. I want you to write about an hour or a day, in your life, that shows where you came from."

Frank of the big teeth: "We all come from our mamas."

"Well, I jus' come from yours," Wesley says, and Raoul laughs in a high whinny-snicker that makes me want to laugh too.

Raoul says, "I tell you right now, Miz Ryder, we come from ba-a-a-d times. You got a weak heart? The stomach trouble? 'Cause it ain't pretty. I kilt a guy with a butcher knife."

"Goddamn liar," says the fourth man. He's been silent until now. His name, improbably, is Willie G. Willy. "You want everybody to think you're bad, man. You ain't shit. I heard you got busted stealing a roll of carpet off a truck."

"Matched my living room," Raoul said, sulking.

The fifth man, whom they call Horse, has said nothing.

"He my cellie," Willie says, introducing Horse. "He's writing a vampire romance."

I can see Raoul and Wesley want to hoot and whistle, but I put a finger to my lips and nod toward the door. They keep it down.

"Glad to have you in my class, Horse," I say. "I look forward to reading your work. I'm—I'm glad to have all of you."

"We gonna meet again?" Raoul has taken a prissy-ass attitude. "Or you gonna ride off into the sunset like most teachers do?"

"Other teachers come here?"

"Oh, hell," says Raoul. "We learnt to sew. I made an apron."

Wesley grins. "One come to help us get our GED. She didn't last two days."

Willie G. says, "Her two eyes went in different directions. Black Monday, my man, you run her off."

Black Monday is apparently a nickname for Wesley. Willie G. is privy to it. I guess he's earned the right.

"I'm here for a while," I tell them.

"Okay, then," Raoul says.

Frank picks up his pencil. "You want somethin' like—that time we got a riot going? Nightsticks, teargas, shanks poppin' out. Some guys used fingernails, went for the throat." He looks over at Raoul. "Fought like goddamn girls."

"I didn't fight like no girl," Raoul whines. "This Aryan dude broke off a piece of chain in the yard, that's what. Gutted two ol' boys like fish, lined the rest of us up against the wall. Things turned sour quick."

Willie G. says, "My brother got ripped up pretty bad that night. They didn't know we were brothers 'cause we got different last names. We went on awhile. Then one night he sent word down, he had all he could stand, workin' in that laundry wit' *Fold the towels, keep the edges sharp, stand up straight, take a dump.*'"

Incredible stories, and they hurt, and I love them. I hold up a hand, and Wesley and Raoul take up pencils.

Beyond the window, in the far, far distance, I hear a train whistle by, and I am spellbound and saddened. I was born a quarter-mile from here.

They write for twenty minutes. I ask them if anyone would like to read what they've written. No surprise, Willie G. has written about his brother. He calls him Joey. After the chain incident, Joey got himself transferred to a hoeing detail, and one day in the field when they were all watching freight cars go by, he jumped out on the track. He died for the next three thousand yards. Willie G. stood, watching, while his brother's pieces were strung up and down the line.

I tell Willie G. that I've never heard a tribute written with so much love. I wait for them to hoot or make faces. But they don't.

Big Wesley Mondale, who has almost no hair on top of his head, writes about his beard. It grows too fast and so thick that they make him shave twice a day. He says they oughta let him keep a razor in his cell, and not one of those pink girlie tricks, either. He pumps iron in the rec yard and does five hundred push-ups every day in his cell. Back home in Hattiesburg, he has a sister who's eleven.

The same age as Luz.

He hasn't seen her since she learned to walk.

While I listen to these stories, my ignorance weighs a thousand pounds.

I ask Horse if he'd like to read.

Horse is a study. He looks like a killer. He wears a wedding ring. I can tell that he bites and tears at his nails. His arms and face are barked with ravines and scars in the shape of scimitars. His long body curves over his desk, and his singleness—his aloneness—is so palpable, I could scoop up a handful. I wonder what kind of woman ever wanted him, or if one will again. He says, "Ain't nobody wants to hear this stuff."

"We do," I say.

He tucks his long chin in. I note the knobs of his Uriah Heep fingers; long, thin feet that must require special-made shoes. He reminds me of a tree bent by centuries of wind.

Raoul says, helpfully, "Horse, here, ran a laundry and"—in his chair, Raoul makes a girly move with his hips—"*sexino* in Texas."

Sexino?

"One-armed bandits, video porn, girls in the back," Raoul explains. "He was just passin' through, seein' his mama, somebody asks for his license. Horse jumps outa his car and beats the dude up. But the dude's dead now, and the judge says on account of Horse boxed in the army, he's gettin' life."

"That's the shits," Wesley commiserates.

They read. They've written about convenience stores and cops and sex, grinding poverty and family, too much meth and not enough corn bread. *Songs of the South,* I think.

Although they could keep paper in their cells, they want me to have their stories. I collect the pencils. Horse hands in his work without reading it aloud. The guard marches them out. Beyond the door, Raoul picks up a grin and walks with a bounce. *A front,* I think, *a cover for who he really is.*

Clea Shine is in the jail—and this is what it's like. *Good God.*

I'm supposed to leave quickly now, find my own way out, but, as I walk, I look over Horse's story. It's about three guards who beat a sex offender senseless. One of his eyeballs is wrenched out of its socket; his arm is broken; twelve tiny bones in his foot are crushed. He spends eight months in the infirmary.

On my way out, an old guy with a mop and bucket of water is swabbing the entryway. He moves closer than is smart and murmurs, "Miss, some of us ol'-timers, we wanna tell you—we knew your mama."

"*What?*" I must be falling down stairs. I am floating in space.

"Sometime Clarice here. Trustee slip her in."

The foyer stretches ahead, distorting so that the door is unreachable. In this long, long space, I am exposed.

Wheezer comes up and puts a hand on my shoulder, takes an umbrella from the stand. We go out into rain that's lightened to a fine mist.

God, God, something has stripped off my careful mosaic and uncovered Clea Shine.

I don't know if Wheezer heard.

34

We stand under the prison's overhang while I blink against the mist and try to clear my head. The air is fresh but oddly not cooler. After the real storm has come and gone, the humidity will be insufferable.

Wheezer says, "Listen. Thanks for doing this, Clea. It was a lot to lay on you, but I'm not above begging."

"You're welcome"—I look up at him—"Francis? I don't know what to call you."

There's a roughness to him that neither shaving nor scrubbing nor being a chaplain can erase. He could dress in the finest clothes and scour his skin till there was nothing left, and he'd still be the boy I found under the house.

"Call me Wheezer," he says, grinning. "You're the only one who ever did—you and Finn. Hey, you're making a difference here. We'd like you to come back tomorrow, if you can swing it—the warden, your students, me."

"I was only with them half a day. How—"

"You could start around nine, be finished by noon. Maybe Friday too, if that suits you."

Three days in a row. Wheezer was right about himself—he'll

do what he needs to, stand up for his cause. Did I, at this end of my journey, emerge nearly as strong?

But I have not yet come to the end of my story.

"Wheezer," I say, "why are you here? Why didn't you run? You must have terrible memories of this place."

He takes his time answering. "No better or worse than yours. I heard about the way your mom was, and all."

Here is someone to talk to, not like Thomas, who ate and slept in our house but lived somewhere else. We seldom spoke. He's never even asked me about the raised lines on my arms or my feet or my belly.

"Sometimes it all catches up with me," I say. "Like a ball of yarn that wants to unravel, you know? Other times, they're more feelings than thoughts, and I have to find the right words to express them."

"You did pretty good in your book."

"Fictionalized," I tell him.

"Don't underestimate yourself. You're great with words. I read the reviews."

"Wheezer. Your life here was far worse than mine."

"Yours *was* bad, Clea. You didn't deserve it. No kid does."

"The Oatys kept you under their house, for God's sake. I've thought about you and wondered what kind of kid—adult— does it take to survive that?"

The rain has stopped. We walk to the sally port and wait while we're buzzed through. Wheezer makes little puffing noises with his lips. "Surviving is a basic thing. Getting by. Staying alive in whatever way we can. It doesn't mean we make right choices or drive fine cars or have good jobs. It means we found a way not to die. I survived."

"I know about that," I say. I push my sleeve up, turn my arm over, and show him a dozen short lines and scimitars. "Some-times Luz touches them, but she never asks."

"She will."

"I know. And I guess—I'll tell her the truth."

"You're that kind of mom."

"So—"

"Those two Oatys were my uncles, the old geezer my grandpa."

"My God."

Wheezer lifts his shoulders, like a kid. "My mom was their sis-ter. My dad and the two uncles ran a meth lab back in the woods, but my daddy wasn't very good at it. Blew up stuff, killed himself and my mom too. After that the two Oatys brought me here. But the old man threw a ringtailed fit, said he was gonna die for sure with this skinny-assed kid around. So they—they put me under the house. I was there two, maybe three, weeks when you came along."

My throat aches. "You were a strange sight, that's for sure."

"I guess so. I sure was glad to see you. But then you went away, and I thought you weren't coming back. I thought maybe I dreamed you."

"I went to get Finn," I say. "And then Auntie. After that, every-thing got big and noisy."

"Yes. I thank you for speaking up."

"Just words," I say. "What happened when Pilcher took you away? Where'd you go?"

"That was just the beginning. I ran off every chance I got. No-body wanted this wormy little runt, sickly looking, no color in my skin. By the time I was twelve, I drank every damn thing I could get my hands on."

I know about drunks. As part of the sisterhood, I can't count the number I've plucked from the gutter. And bathed. And given a meal. I don't do it to be Christlike or out of any sense of charity. Unlike some of the sisters who can give of themselves till there's nothing left, I think something different. These folks who live in the gutter, on the edge of life, are only people filled with hurt. When I first left here, I did that too. But the alcoholics. I know those broken blood vessels and anguished eyes. "It still deals you trouble."

"Every day of my life," he says, "like a patch of poison ivy. One minute I can work it through, and ten minutes later I'd kill for a drink. It's just gonna be like that."

I ache for him. "How long has it been?"

"This time? One hundred and eighty-two days. Hell, we hold AA meetings twice a day, right here at the Oasis of Love Bingo Hall and Prison Camp Center."

"Not just for canasta and funerals anymore?"

"Well, those too," he says, grinning. "Those righteous ladies hightail it outa there before we drunks show up." He looks along the lane to where my mother's house stood. "Luz said you work with an oblate."

"An interdenominational order."

"Good for you. How'd you get from here to God?"

It feels good to talk. "How did you?"

He barks out a laugh. "Struck by lightning. One night at a meeting, I was standin' in the back with a cup of coffee in my hand, and—there it was. I guess somebody'd made the right kind of speech. I nearly fell over myself, confessing my sins. Folks picked me up and took me in."

"Finally, the right kind of people."

"Yup. Went on to a little podunk college, seminary."

"Same here," I tell him. I like looking this man in the eye. It feels clean.

He puts an arm around me and gives me a squeeze. "I'm glad you came back. So I could say thank you. Now you need to go see Finn."

"Finn! He's still here?" And my gaze automatically shifts to the river, to the great oak trees.

He points across the field. "Past the poplars, where the creek runs through. He's got a place in a clearing."

"He became a recluse—"

"I take groceries sometimes, or a new pair of boots."

"Whatever happened to his daddy? Is he still here at the Farm?"

"Ask Finn."

"I will. In fact, I'm going now."

"I didn't mean this minute—"

"I'll follow the creek, Wheezer. I'll be fine."

"Shit," he says, and thrusts the umbrella at me. "Take the right fork into the woods! You couldn't miss it in good daylight, but—"

"I'll be fine. Tell the kids I'll be home directly."

I'm amazed to be walking away from the prison. Apparently, it isn't my time yet.

And I need a few minutes of solitude. I intended to come to Call while I walked, but the woods are dripping and messy, the road muddy, and night is coming on.

I wonder what it would have been like if Finn and I had stayed friends. If we'd ended up together, say.

35

I'd always thought love was a waste of time, but there it was. It hurts to remember. I was, literally and figuratively, right off the boat.

I did not fall on my knees in the presence of Professor Thomas Ryder, but his shyness and his intelligence thrilled me—the way he looked at me over his glasses, as if, finally, he'd found something worth looking at. He taught biology at a private university in Dandridge. I was in my twenties, he in his late thirties. I think that's why I liked him—he'd lived long enough to know who he was. With a funny little grin, he told me his students razzed him because he and I walked the campus hand in hand. Said he felt like a kid.

And he looked like one—that gray hair tumbled and falling over his forehead, his shirt untucked in back. More often than not, he wore mismatched socks. He was long and lean, and even after showering and splashing on aftershave, Thomas still smelled of formaldehyde and other science-lab things.

Sometimes he wore bedroom slippers to class, and at home he could never find his books or his papers or his pen. He misplaced the mail, his coffee cup, his bookmark, and, sometimes in the park, his old dog Ruff. When Ruff died, we took a shovel and buried him on a quiet piece of shoreline. Thomas was more bereft than any man I'd ever known. Just like me, he had unlit corners. How could I possibly not care for him?

Thomas had these funny eyebrows too—not long or particularly thick, but they seemed to run every which way and were so tangled that when he combed his hair, he combed them too.

The only family that was left to care about him was a pair of elderly aunts in nursing homes in Florida. Most nights, he came to the door of the efficiency apartment where I lived, and together we went out and walked along the beach. When it rained, we stayed in. Conversation usually ended up in the bedroom.

Thomas's hands were large and square, his fingers blunt. They found corners of me I didn't know existed, and whether he was on top of or under me, he lifted and thrilled me. Then we lay on our backs, exhausted and caught up in the damp sheets. Thomas slept while I lay, wondering how in the world we had found each other.

Saturday nights, we sat in the broken-down chairs of coffee shops while we drank Arabica roast and discussed the world's problems and how we would solve them. We dissected books and movies and the six-o'clock news. We rearranged the country's politics. Thomas was a good man with a quick mind.

He made love beautifully, with strong, slow hands and his hair falling over his forehead.

"I was wondering, Clea," he said one night when we were drinking coffee, "if you would just *consider* marrying me."

I watched customers pick up their coffees in cardboard containers and juggle apricot cake in waxed-paper squares. "Thomas—"

"You're the one woman I want to spend my life with," he said. "Think about it, will you? At least—don't say no."

But being with Thomas was like some grand rehearsal—I kept waiting for the show to start.

"I have to," I said.

There was a hopeful hitch to his untidy brows, and he leaned forward and laced his fingers on the table. "Have to what—"

"Say no," I said.

But then I learned something about myself.

Sister Margaret Redemptor had sent me to teach in a backwater community where the district needed someone to work with remedial reading students. The kids sat on the floor in what I had learned to call Indian-style. Now they called it crisscross applesauce.

However far behind they had fallen, these kids' ears were screwed on, waiting for words that would come out of my mouth. I'd brought along a copy of Dr. Seuss's *Horton Hears a Who*. I settled in to tell the story and was amazed at the rise and ring of my own voice.

Then I got down on the floor and showed them page one, and the printing of words and how, together, they made a sentence. They went to their tables and fisted their pencils. I distributed paper, and on the sad green chalkboard I drew a capital A.

"Look!" I said. "Both sides of this letter seem to be falling in!"

Their mouths came open.

I asked, "What do you think is holding them up?"

And so it went, unorthodox and lovely.

Thomas said those same things about me. I doubted the lovely part, but I allowed the rest. I liked his company, his funny habits, and the adoring look in his eyes.

On Tuesdays, he sometimes drove me to Fong's, where the sisters met, and ate kung pao chicken and read a magazine until it was time to go home. Then we'd curl up on the sofa and fool around, end up in his bed.

Thomas had a small patch of gray hair on his chest, and while I twined my fingers in it, I laid my ear to his ribs. I loved to hear his strong heart beat.

He had fallen in love with me, and I couldn't get over that.

He asked me again to marry him, and I said yes.

36

I wonder what made Finn move so far back in the woods. But, then, he'd lived in a tree. Maybe he never grew fit for society.

I realize, now, I haven't eaten all day. And, Lord, I wish I had a flashlight. A million years ago this creek was just a dent in the land, but now it's racketing and foamy. On the back side of the Farm's big house, tree branches and debris crash into the False River, then churn south into the Pearl and on to the blue-water Gulf of Mexico. Payback for what nasty weather it's shoving our way.

I am soaked to the skin from the wet scrub, and before long I see what must be Finn's place. If it is, he grows a few straggly vegetables, keeps a goat tied in the yard, and owns a snapping hellhound of a dog. A few pieces of old farm equipment lay in the yard like fossils, shiny with rain.

It's the woods that disturb me, the trees and vines leaving only the smallest clearing. I wonder if Finn uses a hatchet—and how often—to cut the kudzu back, trim the brush. The place looks bleak, like someday the undergrowth might just take it over, take it back, and Finn along with it.

The ribby white dog plants its feet and bares its teeth, growls rising from its belly, coming up through its throat.

"Good dog," I murmur, and stand stiller than still. But I've folded the umbrella and hold its point at the ready. "Good boy, good dog."

The hair stands up on the back of its neck. The goat watches me from the end of its rope.

"Finn?" I call out, risking a bite, rabies shots, bleeding to death in this back of beyond. "Finn, are you here?"

The dog steps off to the side, but the barking is incessant and loud enough to be heard in False River, and he *snap snaps* with his teeth.

Who was it, Auntie or Shookie—someone told me Finn lived in a shack. Whoever said it was right. The house is faced with beige stucco that's chipping away in chunks—sills, sashes, and door frame rotting, and the whole thing no bigger than one small room. By the door a barrel is half full of rainwater, and there's another in the side yard for burning trash. I step up to the door and knock, then knock again, then try turning the knob. Hammer with my fist and call out, "It's Clea Ryder. Clea *Shine.* Finn?"

There's a small window in front and one in the back, and both are covered inside with yellowed newspaper, tears mended with tape, some of which doesn't stick anymore. I cup my hands to the glass but must stay watchful of the dog, and anyway, it's impossible to see inside.

The dog flinches and turns on its tail, snapping at fleas. I wonder if I made a mistake in direction, trying to clear the mind-clutter while I walked. Maybe I didn't follow the creek far enough, or I have come the wrong way after all. One thing's sure—this little house is locked up tight, and if it weren't for the animals—

which someone must surely be feeding—I'd have thought no one lived here.

I take the same trail back.

The prison yard lights are on now, illuminating the asphalt road. From here I can make out the shape of Auntie's tall house, where a car has just pulled into the drive. I see a man getting out, a shape in the dark—not a neighbor or the sheriff but one I know well.

He steps onto Auntie's front porch, which no one ever uses. The door opens, a slant of yellow lighting up the red salvia that's planted there, in tins. He disappears inside. Thomas Ryder.

37

I'd like to think this is a bad dream, Thomas being here. I knew he would find us—asshole—but I wasn't ready. I might never have been. I could have stayed here and played house with my children until I was hauled away, and never seen him again. In my mind I am angry, but I ache over what has happened behind us and what must come next.

On the prison road, I stand in the mist as long as I can. There are puddles on the asphalt and puddles in my heart. Wind sings through my head but clears nothing away.

I am the woman who shared private thoughts with inmates today. Then:

Sometime Clarice here—

—Trustee slip her in.

I am the woman whose two children are right now preparing to eat supper in the house on Potato Shed Road. And with them is Thomas. God, I hope he's hugging them, holding them to his heart so they know their father loves them. Yet—he doesn't deserve them. He's a liar and a cheat, and no one invited him.

What if he's come to make trouble, wants to fight me, take them back to the coast? But he won't. For a long time, Thomas has been off somewhere in his head, hasn't known any of us existed.

I climb the back porch steps, ease the screen door open. For the first time the house feels cold inside.

Luz is forking up long strands of saucy spaghetti and has her hair tied in one of Bitsy's do-rags. She looks up from her plate. "Mom. Dad's here! I made the sauce—and the meatballs and—"

"Terrific," I say. I've never been able to get Luz near the kitchen.

It's Uncle Cunny who's taking Thomas's wet coat, pulling up a chair for him. Right now Thomas looks cold and wet, and so hunched over, he reminds me of Horse.

I stand in the kitchen and have no substance.

Auntie looks at me. "Sit yourself down, child, unless you want dry clothes first. We're eating early tonight, in case the edge of the storm pushes in. Oftentimes, the electrics go out."

I sit. Auntie's eyes shift from me to Thomas and back again.

Shookie sighs loudly.

Confusion crashes, but Auntie irons it away. She asks for Thomas's plate, and it's passed around. So there've been introductions. No one else is acting like this is unusual. They cannot see the weight crushing me. But Thomas feels it; I see it in his eyes.

"We'll talk after supper," I say smoothly. "Luzie, this looks really good."

"You have to put Parmesan cheese on it," she says, handing me the shaker.

Shookie's forking in some pasta, but she's in a bad mood, says her knees are killing her, thinks she needs to see a pediatric over Slidell way.

Until this moment, I've been mostly numb, but now I am angry. Uncle forks salad onto my plate and catches my eyes with his dark ones. Even he cannot save me. "How'd class go today, Clea?" he asks.

"It was *gloria*, thank you for asking, Uncle Cunny." *In excelsis Deo*, in fact—if it weren't for Thomas.

"Well, watch out, 'em boys'll shine you on," Shookie says, addressing me with the tines of her fork. "They gonna tell you what you want to hear. You think they gonna write you fine stories, that it? Won't tell you shit that's real—where they come from, not about they mamas nor they papas, or how they raised them up."

It's a long speech. Uncle says, "Shookie?"

But she's wagging that burgundy head and rubbing her knees under the table. "Only the good Lord seen what they done to get theirselfs locked up. White girl, you never gonna hear the whole of it," she says.

White girl. There it is, poured out of her mouth.

I think, *After all these years*.

No one eats.

"You got ev'thing," she says. "They got nothin'—come there afraid, and getting the livin' hell beat out of 'em. Teeth knocked out, fingers busted. Get back from sick bay, they stuff's all tossed, they lawyer's gone, and now they don't know ear from asshole."

Luz's mouth is almost as round as her glasses.

Bitsy says, "Mama—"

Wheezer sets down his water glass and lays a hand on Shookie's back. But she's not done by a mile.

"They got to choose up sides, doncha know, old guys figuring who takes the new one, gonna charge him to breathe, bend him over a barrel, tha's what."

I shiver and glance at Luz and Harry. I'd thought that same thing.

"Tell you right now," Shookie says. "What pain they brought

with 'em ain't nothin', compared to what they goin' through. No matter what big or little thing they done, they got to sound hard, with their talk about killin' and rapin'. Time passes, they turn mean, that's what."

I don't remember the last time I looked in Shookie's eyes, saw their ragged-edged corneas, making her soul look old. God help her, that she knows all this.

Auntie once told me they'd lived in Greenfield. When she left the circus, she came down here to be with her sister. So—*Shookie was in False River because someone she loved was locked up in Hell's Farm.* I come around the table and squat next to her.

She looks at her plate. "They're wonderin' how they wound up within a million miles of that place. They talk about who all done 'em wrong. They get to be arrogant sonsabitches, coverin' they asses day and night. White child, there ain't no such thing as livin' in prison, it's all dyin'. All dyin'."

She takes a mouthful of cold tea and lets it wash down. "Runnin' wild with nightmares, missin' they kin, backbones curled up and shakin' under the sheets."

Wheezer pushes back his chair, lays his other hand on Shookie's arm, like maybe he thinks she's falling, falling.

"I ain't done talkin'," Shookie says. "They get what they want outa you, 'cause they shine you on. You watch out—ain't no man goin' without very long. If he be down on his luck and in need of thangs, he find a way—postage stamps, say. A ice-cream bar on a hot day."

She says softly, "Then one day, your man leanin' back, makin' out like life is all right, but he say one wrong thing, get on somebody's bad side, and he go down in a heap on the floor, kilt. The prison, they send you bones in a wood box. You stand in a field and bury it on your own."

"Oh, Miss Shookie."

"Mama," says Bitsy, struggling out of her chair. "I'll fetch your pills. Then we'll get you on up to bed."

Auntie's elbows are on the table; her head's in her hands.

Shookie rises, unsteady, from her chair. I wonder how much longer her legs and thick ankles will be able to navigate the stairs. "You remember this, Clea—the troot's plastered over so thick they can't find it."

At the foot of the table, Thomas doesn't know where to look.

I take the bottle Bitsy brings and shake out two tablets. Shookie swallows. She looks cornered and old.

"Oh, girl," she says, as Bitsy leads her from the table. "You gullible as hell, you give yourself away to them mens. They'll shine you on 'cause they hearts is dried up and gone to dust, like old cake. Don't believe nothin'. And that's all."

"That's all," whispers Harry.

In two seconds I am around the table and holding my boy and wondering if anyone else heard.

"Harry talked!" Luz cries. "Miss Shookie made Harry talk."

This is a household of secrets.

Holy hell.

✻

Light as rain, black as mud, Uncle rises and brings himself a cup of coffee, pours it gently up, and sips from the saucer. "Hurricane coming, category two."

✻

If it weren't dark I'd take Harry outside, tell him and Luz about growing up here—show them how I used to climb out the window, how Finn swung like a monkey from the tree.

If I can talk to felons, I can talk to my kids.

I think about my first writing class this morning. I didn't offer much. Five men out of—how many? Two thousand?—left their shoebox cells for an hour and twenty minutes. If they never write anything but fiction, class is a diversion for them, a place to go.

Auntie puts sheets and an old quilt in my arms. "On the sofa," she says, not looking at me. "Bed down your man."

I hate this. I don't want to see Thomas or hear him or be any-where near him.

News comes that the storm is stalled in the gulf. It's picking up size and speed, of course. Maybe, I say, Greta will turn eastward to Alabama and the Florida panhandle.

Uncle says, *Fat chance.*

38

Politely, Thomas thanks Auntie for the supper. She tells him he should be thanking his daughter, and he does, bending over Luz, planting a kiss on top of her head.

Auntie asks of him, "Where you stayin' at, Mr. Thomas? You got a place for the night?"

He stands, awkward, I with the blanket in my arms. "I'm at the Covey Motel, just this side of Greenfield."

"A long ways for you to be comin' and goin', storm heading this way and all."

"It's not so bad," Thomas says.

Ever since Shookie said her piece at supper, he has not taken his eyes from me. I'd like to ball up my fists and blacken them both. He comes into the parlor, sits on the edge of the sofa.

"Mind you, the Covey's a pure rat trap," Auntie calls from the kitchen, and I know what is coming. I shake my head firmly, but she pays me no mind.

I put the bedding on the sofa, sit on the floor with Harry, and finger some things I gathered in the kitchen and brought to the carpet. Because Auntie's insisted, he's temporarily given up his spoon for a washing. "This is a fork, Harry, and a knife, remember? Pop bottle. A can of soup. Can you say 'soup,' love?"

These are things Harry knows, of course, but I'm so afraid that if he doesn't speak, he might forget.

I settle back against the chair leg. As a kid, I sat here, against Uncle's bony knee, reciting my times tables and planning my escape. To Mama's house.

I take a pen and draw a face with a crown, on my index finger. I tell Harry, "Once upon a time there was a king who wore only fine clothes. He dressed in his very best ones when he paraded through the streets, so the people could see him. They cheered and cheered." I draw a face on my other index finger. "One day, a tailor came to town."

In the kitchen, I hear dishes rattling. Uncle Cunny is drying. Wheezer has gone upstairs.

I tell Thomas, "It's his favorite story, 'The Emperor's New Clothes,'" and I watch, with some pleasure, his embarrassment at not knowing.

"Clea—"

"Luzie, why don't you take Harry to brush his teeth, put his pajamas on him? I'll be up shortly to finish the story."

"Wait! That reminds me," Thomas says. He rises and heads for the back door. "I have a couple of things in the car. For the kids."

He goes out and comes back with an armful.

"Books!" Luz cries. "Oh, Dad, you saved my Greek history! And the atlas too!" She hugs him around the waist. Her *Modern History of Greece* is a wreck. But it's been carefully dried, and the curled pages unstuck.

From under his other arm, Thomas pulls Harry's rabbit, white with dust, the stuffing still wet and lumpy. I wish I had been the one to save it. My breath catches in an almost-sob. The whole day has been more than this white child can bear.

Auntie gives me the arched brows. "Mr. Thomas, you go on in to the Covey now and fetch your things. We'll put you up on the sofa till the bad weather's past."

"Auntie," I argue, "your house is already over-the-top full."

"I won't have it any other way. Family should pull together in hard times. 'Parently you forgot that. Besides, Cunny's going down to Greenfield early, to bring plywood for windows, and I'm riding in with him."

Uncle finishes the wiping up, drying his hands.

"You and Francis will be up at the prison," Auntie says to me. "That way, Mr. Thomas can stay with his children."

I cannot fathom whose side Auntie and Uncle are on, and why no one's on mine, but then scold myself for thinking they should feel torn at all. I haven't told them what's happened, and no man can judge what he does not yet know. The real battle between Thomas and me has not even begun. In the morning, if he had a mind to, Thomas could take the kids and run. I, myself, have a history of running.

When Luz and Harry have gone upstairs, I say between my teeth, "Thomas, you and the kids be here when I get back at noon."

I cannot tell what he's thinking. In this household, everyone seems happy but Shookie and me. But then, Miss Shookie has never been happy. Now I know two strong reasons why. She loved an offender, who lived the life men must live in prison, and then he died. Perhaps just as bad, there was a white child abiding under her sister's wing.

I have a niggling concern about Auntie and Uncle's trip to

Greenfield tomorrow. They're going for lumber. Is it possible they'll stop by the sheriff's office?

Surely they would not.

But somebody will.

Who?

Anymore, I don't know. I'm so tired of this worry, this fear I've carried, living in its shadow. I'm sick of lies and cover-ups. This may be the hardest decision I've ever made, but when the storm is over, I'm going to face up to it. Turn myself in.

Wheezer bounds down the stairs. "Damnation, you all. I got the radio on, and it looks like, tomorrow, Greta's going to be a bad one."

39

Our third morning here, Luz wakes me early. Around the gables, the wind has picked up, but it's not yet raining.

"Mom."

I open my eyes. She's standing at the foot of the bed. "*Mm?*"

She points to the window in the far gable. "What happened to the house next door?"

My heart lurches. I long to roll over, go back to sleep. Pretend I didn't hear. There's no point asking her what she means.

"A lot."

"You can tell there used to be a house. There's some steps and pipes and stuff. I asked Aunt Jerusha, but she said I should ask you. Mom? Is that what your book is about?"

"That," I say, blinking sleep from my eyes, "is what the book is about."

"You said we'd talk. You could tell me in chapters."

Smart Marie-Luz. Maybe, chapter by chapter, I can mend some damage. Pay it back. With this prison class, have I already begun?

I let out a puff of breath. "All right. Yes. I'll be gone a couple of hours. You and Harry stay here with Dad. Then, when I get back, we'll talk. Okay?"

I touch her hair, dark and fuzzy, unbraided. I look over at Harry. For the first time, last night, he slept well, the misshapen rabbit under his arm.

⁂

Thomas is up, rumpled and stumbling through the kitchen to the bathroom.

I step out into the wind. Even as I stand there, a new and lower layer of gray clouds moves in. Out over the river, gulls dip and rise in jerky circles, trying to find a slipstream to ride. Luz informs me that this is not a good sign.

"They always fly ahead of a storm," Uncle agrees grimly. He's arrived for breakfast and to pick up Auntie. "Been years since I've seen them this far inland. Even worse, they're still headed north."

Inside, Auntie's got waffles ready and the radio playing.

"Hurricane's predicted to hit the coast about five o'clock," she says.

It's not yet eight. Uncle butters a waffle. "Means things will get pretty ugly here tonight."

Wheezer thumps down the stairs and says to me, "Plenty of time to get you back before the storm. Just let me grab a bite."

I forgo breakfast and follow Auntie to her room. Close the door. Perch on her candlewick spread. She lays out a dress for the trip to Greenfield and finds serviceable black shoes.

I am already on a fine edge about the weather, about Thomas.

"Aunt Jerusha," I say, "I recall that you came to False River to be with your sister. Miss Shookie'd come here to be with her man. There's one more thing I need to know. Tell me, please, about my mother."

Auntie dabs sweet-smelling lotion into the palm of her hand,

rubs her raw knuckles and ashy elbows. She looks neither surprised nor distressed.

"In the 1930s, Clarice was almighty sick of frostbite, 'cause
she hitchhiked down from . . . Minnesota, I think it was."

"My mother?"

"Your grandmother. Your mama was Clarice the Second.
You're the third."

I hold my breath.

"She raised up a clapboard house on this side of the Pearl—
the house where your mama was born." Auntie sighs like something's taken too much space in her for too long a time.

She sits beside me on the bed, holds her stockings in her
hands. "That was back in the years when the rain wouldn't come,
and the pecans failed. The sun beat down, oh, yes, Lord. My papa
told me he could hear the earth groanin', watch them cracks
widening. My fam'ly was in Greenfield then, along the Pearl.

"Even in the delta, corn died a foot tall, weighted down with
dust. Every day was an unswallowable thing. I was just being
born about then.

"Folks here and in Alabama, and clear to Kansas, they loaded
up and headed for California. They heard they was money in the
strawberry fields. Some were bound for Hollywood. Shookie,
she'd already fallen in love."

I did some quick figuring, caught myself wanting to stroke my
face.

She looks at her hands. "Men, passin' through, knocked on
your grandma's door. She bedded 'em down on her porch or her
sofa, some upstairs—Clea, you asked to hear this. Before that
first winter, your granny grew round as a melon."

She paused. "Nobody claimed to be father to that child."

"The baby was my mother."

"That's right."

"Go on."

Auntie purses her lips, remembering. "That baby girl, *also* named Clarice, grew up comely and with a taste for gin."

My thoughts are tumbling. I interrupt. "Why didn't you tell me about Miss Shookie before?"

"Shookie's business."

"All right. Yes."

"She had already come here to live. She said your mama was a hellion, paid no mind to the law. When your grandma died, Clarice had her buried in Potter's Field, across the creek. Where old prisoners go. Then she went home and fashioned a bar in the parlor and turned the place into a juke joint. That's when I came to False River."

"From Izzie Thorne's."

"Tha's right. Ollie Green used to go and sit in your mama's parlor, try to save her soul. But she backtalked him awful."

Like me, I think.

"She was a handful, a grown woman puttin' the Reverend in his place. I remember him saying, 'Jerusha, the lights were on, and the corks were poppin', and I couldn't change a thing.'"

I watch Auntie's face.

"Gents would park in her dooryard and pay their dues. But you know how that was."

I do. I did. In my mother, men found a beautiful face and an itch to be taken. Her hair was like silk; her breasts and thighs were north of voluptuous.

"Times were still hard," Auntie says. "But—oh, my—piano music flowed out of that house. It wasn't long before *she* birthed *you.* On the kitchen table."

"So as not to ruin the silk sheets on the bed," I said.

"You came into the world the color of a sweet peach, squalling and damp as a three-day rain."

I half smile. I love that someone has a sweet memory of me.

"Shortly, she brought you here in a basket; you know that too."

"Yes. So she could get on with swilling gin and jitterbugging till dawn. And you're sure you never knew my daddy."

"I never did."

"He could've been traveling through, or a guard or a convict released from the prison. A parolee. Anybody."

"Yes. I don't think Clarice even knew, how she *could* have known."

"All right."

"So then here you were, this third Clarice—long-legged and willful. We called you Clea. Me and Cunny, we wanted so bad for you to stay clear of that house."

But I couldn't. How I wish I had.

She says softly, "And then one day, you leveled that place to a bed of ash."

It's the first time I've heard anyone say it out loud.

I can tell that Auntie likes Thomas, which feels like a betrayal. He's sitting at the table with Harry in his lap, and he's holding a waffle that Harry is buttering but not eating. Shookie pours coffee for herself and Thomas.

She and Bitsy are down early too, in case there's something to see. In the event I throw dinner plates or slam Thomas against the wall. Miss Shookie, after all, needs fuel for the fires of her gossip. Meanwhile, there's no sign, no aura around her—nothing to signify regret at her outburst last night.

We are a full kitchen.

Auntie says, "Luz, think you and Bitsy can make us a spice cake this morning? Recipe's right here, pans under the sink. Use waxed paper to line them. Shookie can show you how to beat the frosting."

Luz is excited. From the doorway, she watches as I get ready to leave. I'm wearing black pants and the short-sleeved white blouse I arrived here in. I've cleaned the mud from my sandals, but this afternoon I must buy plain tennis shoes so my toes don't show when I go to the Farm. With some embarrassment, Wheezer has asked if I'll wear socks with my sandals. I've used the least-scented soap in Auntie's bathroom. I have my folder of the inmates' stories, and notebooks and pencils from the trunk of the Honda, which we are taking today, before the storm.

"Mom," Luz whispers from her place next to me. "I've also been thinking—do you think I could learn about Call?"

"Marie-Luz." I stroke her hair. It's pulled back in four barrettes we found on the floor of the car. I kiss her cheek. "All things are possible."

40

Raoul comes in with a bounce. He and Willie G, big Wesley, little Frank, and Horse take the same seats.

"You read our stuff?" Raoul asks. I bet, when he was in school, he chewed gum and cut up. He glances over his shoulder at the back wall that's right there, and grins wide and brilliant and toothy at me. Two of the many sides of Raoul Sanchez.

"I did, and they were wonderful. I've written on each one— what I especially liked, what I suggested. Today we're going to expand the way we think about ourselves."

They've settled quickly and are so quiet. Maybe they're already wearying of this. "Let's talk about the masks we wear."

I wait for some dumb burglary comment, but no one says anything.

"Every day, each one of us is many people. We love, fear, hate. It's like changing hats. We put on a different mask to deal with each specific thing."

"Or person?" says Willie G.

I recall Wheezer's warning. Am I getting too personal? How the hell do you teach a decent writing class without getting up close?

"That's right." I come around and set my butt against the table. "Think about the time before you came here. You were sons, brothers, fathers, lovers. Maybe you had a job, went to school, made plans. You were sick or well, religious, patriotic. For all those things—" I look up and out at the strip of dark sky. "For each of those things, you wore a different mask. You wore one when you heard 'The Star-Spangled Banner,' another when somebody gave you a rash of trouble. Imagine they were real masks you put on and took off. Each one showed who you were in that moment."

Raoul snorts. "Willie's got him a hangover mask. Musta been something he drank."

"Shut up," Willie G. says. "I'll put a permanent mask on you, flavor of the month. So now we're in here—"

"Yes," I say. "Especially in here. You still wear masks, and you change them constantly."

They are silent. I know this is true. I was a master at covering up. I witness the shifts in their horsing around, see it in their writing. Shookie was on the mark—they shine one another on. Today I'm giving them a tool with which to do it.

"How d'you know anything about us?" Frank says. "How you know we do this?"

"Because we all wear them. We're human and complex. We can't help it. I doubt that anyone ever achieved singleness—great leaders, maybe. Zen masters. Jesus Christ."

"They wasn't human," Willie G. says, and at the looks on the faces of his prison brothers, he amends, "I mean—they had special powers."

"Did they?"

Willie G. says lightly, "You think we're human, Miz Ryder? You sure we ain't monsters?"

I shake my head slowly. "You're not monsters."

"Shit," Frank says. "Some days I'm so fuckin' many people, I can't count 'em. An' Horse, here—he was a man of business. He wore one mask when he dealt with customers—"

"And another when he talked to vendors or his banker," I say, helping him along. "But Horse was other things too. Today I want you to write a short paragraph for each of four masks you wear—or wore."

"When we was outside?"

"Or inside, yes." I hand them paper and pencils. "And you're to name each mask—each persona you take on."

"What you mean, *name* it?" Wesley says.

"Well . . . when I hear someone sing 'America the Beautiful,' my eyes tear up. My heart beats like crazy. I'm so red, white, and blue, if I were to look in a mirror, I'd see stars where my eyes are, stripes for the rest. An eagle poised above my head. Hokey, maybe, but that's part of who I am. And I'd call that mask . . . Summer."

"For the Fourth of July," Raoul says, like he's figured out the theory of relativity.

I smile. "Maybe. But I could have called it Hot Dogs or Freedom or Mary Lou. It was mine to choose. *You* are to identify *your* masks and name them."

"Four of them goddamn things," Wesley says.

"Yes."

Their fingers cramp, and they begin to write. I think I hear thunder, but it could be cell doors rolling shut. Beyond the little window, lightning flashes.

I walk among the short aisles, look over their shoulders, put my finger on a page. "Strong word," I say. "Great start. I like that—keep going."

I read a little here and there. Only Horse hunkers down, covering his paper with his arm.

Willie G. writes that he wants to go home. He misses his sisters, his dead brother, his mom and her cooking. He calls that mask William. He wears another entirely when he thinks of an old love. Still another is the man who rode here on the bus, guilty, watchful, stripped of dignity. He calls that man Done.

Wesley calls one of his Ax.

Sweet Jesus.

"Hey, this jus' between us?" Wesley asks. "Or does the man read it too?" The guards, warden, the district attorney.

"Only me," I say.

He writes that, just now, a cold sausage patty is in his pocket. He stole it from the kitchen where he does the heavy cleaning. He sleeps afternoons. Every night at ten o'clock, he dresses and goes back to scrub the grills, the vent hoods. He mops the floor. Sometimes there's an extra pork chop that he cabbages onto. He's always hungry. Mama's growing boy. Maybe he chows down later on this contraband, or trades two chops and four stamps for a cup of hooch—if he brings the container. He calls it Good Times.

And on it goes.

They write for an hour, and I don't interrupt. When Horse and Frank put down their pencils, I call time. I can't afford to let them get restless.

They spend another hour reading and listening and mumbling about more ways to say things, but they lack yesterday's enthusiasm, more like they're watching me, waiting for answers to which no one's asked a question. I bob my head and smile, but I feel them sliding from me. As if they're slipping into a dark hole.

Have I done something wrong? Have they heard about my mother, that she came here and serviced the guards, *and would I?*

I move on. "Sometimes I'm asked which of these masks is the real me. The real you."

They wait.

"And I always answer—we're every one. It takes these four—and four times four more—to make up who we are."

They don't ask me if that's bad or good.

"It is what it is. You're complex people, and that gives you a lot to write about."

I drop my notebook and pen on the table. Frank jumps as though I've fired a shot. "Okay, gentlemen, what's going on? What's on your minds? You're way too quiet."

I walk the floor.

Raoul shifts in his seat.

Willie G. stretches out an orange leg, inspects his state-issue boot.

Wesley says, "This your last day, teacher."

Is he threatening me? Or is it something else? It's my plan to be back unless I'm in a cell myself. If I say that, Wheezer will think it too personal.

I recall Miss Shookie saying, "They get what they need." *Ain't no man goin' without very long. If he be down on his luck and in need of thangs, he find a way . . . a ice-cream bar on a hot day.*

A prayer is in order: *Lord, keep me on my toes.*

Frank with the big teeth says, "We know what's comin'. We been through it before. Only this time it's big."

"What is it—that's coming?"

"Storm," Raoul says. "Bad one, we got a feelin'. You around, you'll see what kinda masks we wear then. Hurricane come, it's the same ol' *'Yes, boss, no, boss,'* but we're all chained together 'cause they can't take a chance. Can't have the place fallin' down and us offenders running wild. We know this much: 'Round here, you sure as hell gotta know how to swim."

"The Farm is going to flood," I say.

"Lookit you," big Wesley says. His voice is so much deeper than the others'. "You a baby. You don't know shit."

I give him a long, sad look. "Wesley," I say, "I know shit."

His brows rise fractionally.

Frank scrunches up his face. "Ol' Greta's gonna go bad for me. I ain't as big as some of these guys. They don't take care of me, I'm done for."

"Keep talking," I tell them. "In fact, on another piece of paper—" I hand them out quickly. "Write it down, all of it. Tell me what you expect with this hurricane."

They seem better about this, up and anxious. They write and write. But the guard has stepped inside the door, and they won't read.

I don't blame them.

Our time is up.

41

Wheezer has chosen to stay awhile at the prison. I walk home.

Uncle and Auntie are not back yet. Miss Shookie is parked in front of the TV, studying the weather, watching the swirling blues and reds of the satellite hurricane as it plows into the Mississippi coast. Incredibly, she has Thomas spreading mayonnaise on bread, making her a baloney-and-cheese sandwich, pouring her a glass of iced tea. He and Harry have, in fact, laid plates and knives and forks around, expecting God knows how many of us for lunch.

More thunder rolls, heavy bellies of sound.

Shookie has given Harry a half-dozen sets of bright-colored beads to play with. He is wrapping them around his rabbit and himself. I say hopefully, "Harry, did you think to tell Miss Shookie *thank you?*"

Harry looks at me. He looks at her. He says nothing but holds his brightly Mardi-Gras'd rabbit to his chest.

Luz is talking enough for both of them, supervising Bitsy as she ices the cake. I have never seen Bitsy do anything like this.

Luz has already told her father about the collapse of our house, our night in the hot motel room, another in the car. A shame, because I would have liked to comment that with all their fancy computers and weather watching, no one predicted that such a little storm might have such a great impact on Lilac Lane. But they didn't know, either, that our house was unfinished, bolts loose, floors still buckled. Maybe I also wanted to wield a few innuendos about the vicious power of Thomas's love life.

Not in front of the kids. A line spoken, I assume, between separating parents the world over.

"I'm running in to the Family Dollar," I say, and add stiffly, "If they get back with the plywood, Thomas, you'll help nail it up?"

Thomas says, *Of course.*

It looks the same, just older—floors cracked, the register updated. The merchandise is the same kind of stuff, plus cell phones and earbuds, twelve kinds of shampoo. I throw my plastic bags into the car and drive to the far end of our road, park, and get out. I head back into the woods, once more toward Finn's place. Today, it's easier to find in this strange half-light. Somehow, the clearing even looks smaller than it did yesterday. Why isn't Finn out here with an ax, defending his space?

"Finn?"

I knock on the door.

"Finn!"

"Go away," he growls—*someone* growls—from inside the house. The dog barks.

"It's me, Clea. Finn, is that you?"

"Aw, Christ."

"Can I come in?"

No answer. I try the knob. The door opens. The dog snarls.

With the windows covered, it's very dark inside. I can hear the wind humming through the trees and the high tangled kudzu and under the windowsill.

When I step into the house, I feel as though I'm bridging a great gap. Two parts of my life are coming together.

Sister Anne Benefactor would say, *It is what it is.*

"Crissake, Clea, get on outa here and leave me alone."

"I—wanted to see you. It's been a long time."

I hear Finn breathing in the near dark, but there's light from the doorway, not much to see by. He heaves a great sigh and turns toward me. "You've always been pigheaded. Why couldn't you leave it alone?"

My eyes are on Finn, on the pink and puckered far side of his face.

"Well," he says. "Shit."

I take a step closer, lifting a hand that's separated from my body. "Oh, Finn."

"Clea, don't you for one second get weepy. I got me this cabin, and a good dog, and I grow radishes and poke salad, and you can just go back the way you came and act like you never—"

"Shut up," I say. "Unless you're going to tell me what happened."

"I didn't ask you here. I don't like folks snooping around."

"But—"

"My daddy passed on, down at the prison."

I lick my top lip. "I'm sorry."

"Guess I shoulda stayed in the tree."

Bad joke. "Tell me the goddamned truth, here and now."

There's a narrow bed, and crates with things stacked in them. A table, one chair. "I burnt down your mama's house," he says.

"You did not."

"You asked for the truth; what you want me to say?"

My throat has closed up. My breath whistles.

"You didn't set that fire, Clea. Shit, you were just a kid."

"Like you weren't."

"I came in that night—"

"You came *in*?"

He looks at me with his one good eye. The other's half closed and empty, the skin tight and terrible from his forehead, slanting back to his ear. Scars pull his mouth up and back on the left.

"I went there a lot," he says.

I am stunned. "You went to see her—"

"Yes."

"Oh, God, Finn."

"I was a normal kid. Then." His right shoulder shrugs. "She—showed me things."

"I—"

"She smoked all the time. I told her those things were bad for her, but she didn't listen. She didn't listen to anybody. I was upstairs, puttin' my pants on, and when I came down she was sitting in the middle of the floor. You were asleep on the porch, holding the damn thing. Anyway, I picked it up, took the last couple puffs."

"No."

"Yes. Then I dropped it on the floor in the front room, by the curtain, and I watched it take off, and I went to the porch and pulled you outa there."

"Where did you take me?"

"Down by the river."

I am without breath or blood, a cardboard flatness of myself.

His voice comes through a tunnel. "I tried to go back for her, but the ceiling came down, and the smoke . . . I couldn't get through. I could see she was already gone. Then I ran off."

I try shaking my head, but nothing happens. No part of me works, not one muscle or sinew or joint.

He comes to me in two strides, takes me by the shoulders and propels me out into the yard, where the air has turned green. The trees blow and bend hard. "I want you outa here, girl. And I'm askin' you polite—"

I smack him with my open hand.

"—I don't want you to come back."

I pound him with both fists, angry fists, blood clouding my eyes, filling my ears, passing through me and around, red and more red.

"Goddamn you!" I yell into his face, the good side, because he keeps the bad turned away. "I've lived my whole life in guilt, and *you can't come along now and make me innocent*!"

"I didn't *come along*, girl. I've always been here."

My legs want to give out.

He catches me with his hands, same hands, I remember them. And that one green eye. He says, "After the way she treated you, I knew they wouldn't take you to jail."

"You sonofabitch!"

"Clea," he says. "You are innocent. You are."

42

I feel crooked—put together wrong—as though my joints are no longer reliable and might carry me in any direction. Auntie and Uncle are home. I barely remember driving here from the prison end of the road. I know the sky looks bad, and the wind is bad, the grass beaten down, Auntie's salvia broken off. The parlor windows are boarded up. Two tall clay pots have fallen over and shattered against the house, and a plastic cup and other things roll around on the lawn.

It has been a summer of storms.

But there's something more, off center, and, coming in through the screen door, I feel it and see it—even with the blocked-out light. It's an alteration of things, like a room whose furniture has been turned around. It's on Thomas's face too—an honored, almost noble, look. Where has Thomas come by nobility? I try to make sense of it, but I've been through too much today.

Harry is wearing a new striped pullover and red tennis shoes—Auntie must have brought them from Greenfield.

Luz claps her hands. A bracelet dangles on her wrist. *Charms*, I think. *Silver charms.* Wheezer is here, having been called from the Farm, his blond hair tumbling, face grinning, grinning. There is cake on the table, and sandwiches cut in quarters and paper napkins set out. Auntie is still in her pearls and serviceable shoes and holding a piece of paper that she hands to me.

I unfold it.

And read. "Auntie!" I take her in my arms. "A marriage license! You and Uncle Cunny! Oh, my Lord!"

I put my arms around them both, and the three of us hold on as we have not in a very long while.

"'Bout time you got around to it," Miss Shookie says.

Bitsy helps herself to a deviled egg.

Auntie offers an embarrassed smile. "At our age," she says. "We had blood tests last week, didn't tell a soul."

Uncle looks proud, and his handsome face and brown eyes send pure adoration Auntie's way. *What other junk dealer,* I ask myself, *wears pin-striped suits and a white shirt and tie?* He makes the deals—his partner, Ernie Shiloh, drives the truck.

"Ernie's on his way," Uncle says.

His pencil-thin mustache is still so trimmed and refined. I wonder how long he's loved my Aunt Jerusha. *Forever.* And he does not need to cover his feelings anymore.

"Got a judge to waive the waiting time because of Greta," Uncle says, grinning.

A friend, no doubt. Everybody knows the poker-playing, guitar-picking, how-can-I-help-you Cunny Gholar. "Now that we have the license, Francis, we'd be pleased if you'd conduct the service."

Even Bitsy smiles. Luz hugs me, all grins, all happy. Everyone's *happy*.

I am rarely speechless. "Oh, my word. Oh, Auntie. Uncle Cunny, I'm so pleased for you."

Ernie Shiloh comes in, roaring, "Well, if it weren't me marryin' you, Jerusha gal, it best be Cunny." There's more hugging and hand-shaking.

With her mouth full, Miss Shookie says, "Now maybe Cunny'll park his ass in a pew at First and Last Holy Word."

"Not on your wrinkled old life," Uncle says. "Francis, you'll do the honors?"

"Yes!" Wheezer says, running upstairs for his Bible. He comes down and lines us all up, Miss Shookie standing as Auntie's matron of honor, and Ernie as the best man. Blessing of all blessings—Harry stands with Uncle too. *Gloria*. My boy's spoon is in his right pocket, a ring in the left, and his cheeks are pink, the corners of his lips trying not to smile.

I flinch only slightly when Thomas touches my arm.

Now I know where the salvia has gone. Luz plucks a handful from a glass of water, shakes the pretty red flowers over the sink, and folds Auntie's hand around the damp stems.

"One for yourself, child," Auntie says. "I got to have a flower girl."

I wonder if wedding synonyms crowd Luz's head. Her dark Spanish eyes are lit up. I imagine it was Auntie who gave her the silver bracelet—she's brought them presents for this special day—and it was she who wound Luz's braids around her head, the way she used to wind mine.

I want to shout that I love them all, but that would mean Thomas too, and he's on the outside, not deserving to be in. Still, he is here today, and privy to this priceless thing.

Wheezer asks if he can lead us in prayer. I hold Luz's hand and bow my head.

"Amen," Wheezer says when he's done, still grinning. "Dearly beloved, we are gathered here in the sight of God to join Jerusha Lovemore and Cunny Gholar in holy matrimony...."

I cannot think of anything more holy.

The late lunch that Bitsy and Luz have prepared is wonderful. Never has baloney with mustard tasted so good. Thomas raves about his daughter's cake. She is joyful, while Bitsy's at the table with her head down, shy. Uncle kisses both their cheeks and tells them it's the best wedding cake he's ever had.

Halfway through lunch, Uncle rises from his chair and leads his bride to the bedroom off the kitchen, where his brown suitcase stands in the middle of the floor. The door closes, and we all look at one another and begin to clear the dishes up. Shortly we hear thumping against the wall, on the floor—then laughter, stuff falling and crashing, other loud bumps, and Auntie squeals.

Oh, my Lord!

Luz says, "Mom."

"Oh, lawz," Miss Shookie says.

I usher the children up from the table and we, all of us, stumble out of the house and into the yard. My hair whips my face. There are no lawn chairs because everything's battened down and locked away. Wheezer's admiring Harry's new tennis shoes.

But Luz, true to her soul, is not done asking. "Commotion, disturbance, fuss. Mom. What *was* that?"

Thomas puts an arm across Luz's shoulders. He says sadly, "Honey, that's what love sounds like."

※

Even as Thomas is once again begging, "Clea, we have to make time to talk," the rain comes. Fat drops splatter the lawn, the leaves and hanging moss of the trees, and our faces, and we all hurry inside, into the dark and windowless parlor.

Uncle comes out of the bedroom, straightening his tie and asking for another slice of that dandy spice cake. Auntie is beside herself with embarrassment and has changed into a housedress. She rummages for candles. I bought some too, at the Family Dollar. Auntie gets down the matches.

The prelude to the storm is an angry one. Things are out there, banging against the house. Miss Shookie turns on the TV, and we watch as bleary cameras focus, through rainy car windows, at a deserted and roiling coastline. Water covers the road. Wood planks and debris fly end over end, and someone shouts, *Find shelter; take cover!*

Greta has increased to a level-four hurricane. Thomas wonders out loud how bad it will get here. Says he doesn't think hurricanes actually travel upriver. Uncle says, *Yessir, they sure do.* He tells us that some of his northern kin recalled the 1950s, when Hurricane Hazel rumbled down the Saint Lawrence as far inland as Lake Ontario.

Greta is predicted to do the same.

"We'll be fine," Auntie says, smiling at Harry.

Wheezer's Bible is still in his hand.

Cunny looks at the clock on the wall. Ten minutes to five. He says, "Jerusha, honey, we'll fill every pitcher and jar with water. This is gonna spawn hellacious tornadoes. Dark as it'll soon be, we won't be able to tell one from the other."

43

The rain pounds steadily, frazzling our nerves, forcing us to wait and watch and walk the floor. There are eight or ten candles, a box of matches, and a flashlight, glasses of tea we haven't touched. Around ten o'clock, the electricity blinks out. We bunch together with two fat candles lit in the parlor, melted onto saucers and sending up thin black ribbons of smoke. In the bathroom, a taper burns in a coffee cup. By the light of a flame, I check my watch. Almost midnight, the wind outside rising in bedlam. We hear the shutters rip off the east side of the house.

"Cunny," Auntie says, hands pressed flat in her lap. "There's a lockbox under my bed. Insurance policies, the deed to the house. I think we should bring it here."

Uncle goes with her. He holds her hand. It's hard to think of them as husband and wife. Wheezer takes the flashlight.

"Clea," Thomas says, "could I see you in the kitchen for a minute?"

Luz clings to me and to Harry and the chair in which the three of us are piled. She has fetched her books. They're under her feet. Harry noisily sucks his thumb. It was only a few days ago that I bundled him in the woolly and we ran from our home on Lilac Lane to the college, to the motel, to here. My poor children. And poor Auntie and Uncle. What a rotten honeymoon.

"Thomas, it's not a good time—"

"There is no good time."

I sigh. "All right. Luzie, sit here and keep your arms around Harry. Dad and I will be just there, by the stove."

The problem is, everyone can hear. Thomas urges me into the bathroom, where I insist that we leave the door open.

"Clea—"

I sit on the lid of the toilet seat. He pushes back the shower curtain and balances on the tub.

"What is it? Say what you need to say."

"I—I'm sorry."

"You're *sorry*?"

"I know this is only a small part of it, but, Clea—you didn't love me when you married me. We both know I was always on the fringe. But I—I wanted to be first. No, hear me out. Please. I was always second, or third, or fourth, after your work and the kids and the house."

"I never ignored you!"

"It sure as hell felt like it," he says. "You never really wanted me or needed me. Look, I know what I did was wrong, but—"

I stare at the floor and wonder—who teaches a woman how to love a man? On that day of instruction, why was I passed over?

"How many girls, Thomas?"

"Clea—"

"How many?"

"Three."

"Sweet Christ. I was giving my *life* in penance."

"Yes, you were. That's another part of the problem."

"I didn't pass myself around like you did in your office, and God knows where else! I would never do that!"

"But you do pass yourself around. You're so perfect. And all I've ever been is—*old*. Jeez, it takes two people to make a marriage—or break it. Can't some of this be your fault? Can you own half our problems?"

"Thomas, if you're caught with a student, you're going to lose your tenure—"

"Clea!"

"I'm—"

"You're what?" he says, and then softly, "Clea, why can't you ever just say '*I'm sorry*'?"

"I have to get back to the kids," I say.

He nods.

Luz comes to where I'm washing the last coffee cup.

"Mommy?" says Luz, who never says *Mommy*.

I put my arms around her. "I was born on the kitchen table in the house that once stood next door." I begin as though I'm reading from a book. And maybe I am. Lightning claws at the sky. "Right away my mother brought me here. In a wicker laundry basket." I smile down onto my daughter's face, as if the basket is a funny thing.

Luz waits.

"And I stayed."

"Your mom didn't want you?" And now I remember where Luz comes from.

"I guess—she had better things to do. Unlike me." I cradle her face. "There's nothing more important to me than being your mom."

"And Harry's."

"Yes."

"What was your mom like?"

"Well, she liked to dance. She was tall and willowy, and she had these pretty legs and red, red lips. Her name was Clarice Shine."

"Clarice," Luz says. "Like you."

"Yes. But I never wanted to be called anything but Clea."

"Clea *Gloria*," says my daughter.

"She did things that were not very nice. She entertained men."

"Mom. I did read the back cover of your book."

"Aha. Well. Here's what we'll do—we'll read it together, a few pages at a time."

Luz thinks that over. "That would be good."

"And we can stop anytime, if either of us needs to."

"That sounds okay. Satisfactory. More than adequate. Can I go upstairs and get the book?"

"If you hurry."

And she does. I stand at the kitchen table and watch. She has four volumes stacked in the middle of the living room floor—the two Thomas brought, Auntie's Bible, and my *Halo*. I wonder, now, at the title I gave it. I should have called it *Prison Annex*. Or *Surviving Mother 101*.

Outside, the wind howls. It blew like this the night I left here and caught the last bus from Greenfield. Blew me right out of that bus and onto a street, where I squatted on a corner. A few days later I was hunched under a cardboard box. I stole food and coins, and I knew about pain. I found an old razor blade and sliced my palm, watched the red blood flow, and waited for relief.

And then somebody found me and led me away. I didn't know what town I was in. I had lost my books and my suitcase. They sat me in a clinic, asked me if I was pregnant or HIV-positive.

When they touched me, I flinched. A lady gave me soap and told me to shower and asked me if I had finished high school.

People moved me around. They gave me a bunk to sleep on and fed me three times a day, although my stomach hurt, and I had diarrhea almost all the time. I washed dishes and made beds in a house, and one day someone put a book in my hands. I smelled the spine, opened the cover. I got a library card. I signed my name to a paper and found myself six hours a day in a college classroom. I wrote things down and read books and took tests. I walked home to the basement room in the big house where I lived. From time to time I went to the little sink and took scissors and opened an inch of skin, then another. I watched my blood run down the drain, taking with it the words that told who I was and who I'd been, and I was glad to let them go. I sliced the tops off my knuckles, and on one occasion I drew a deep line on my belly with a paring knife, then another on the bottom of my foot. With each cut flowed more meaning, until it began to feel extremely purifying. I cut myself once for the Maytubby twins and all they had suffered, and once for Finn, who missed his daddy, and another time, deeply, for the white ringmaster at Auntie's chicken circus. My secret was both liberation and punishment. I sometimes asked out loud, "Mama, are you happy now?"

My therapist was Janet. She found me bound to a bed in a psychiatric ward. Even tied down, I clung to those bed rails as if I might blow away. Later, she had me set free and moved into a room with other girls.

Janet got me a job in a bakery, selling éclairs, and every day she walked with me, down the street and around a corner. In that little shop I spoke to no one. I lined caramel-nut twists on huge metal trays and swirled frosting on cupcakes.

Every evening I sat with Janet, who asked me things like, "Why do you think you kept going back? To your mother's house—why did you do that?"

"I thought one day, she'd change, be somebody else."

"Could that ever have happened?"

No. What a waste. What a waste of a child's identity and energy and love.

"Yes," said Janet.

From the bakery I brought her a slice of my thirteen-egg-white angel food cake.

"Do you remember a time when you didn't hurt?" Janet asked.

No. Like an underline to the truth about waste.

"Anger creates chaos," Janet said.

"Yes."

"What does it sound like—in your head?"

"Like a million monkeys all chattering at once."

She'd smiled. "You have a way with words," she said. "Sustaining resentment takes a lot of work. You must have been *very* tired."

"Yes."

Finally, I told Janet about the fire, all that I remembered.

Damn Finn. Damn him to hell for poking a hole in my memories.

The next day I'd gone back to the bakery and eaten a chocolate donut and licked the sticky icing from my fingers. Then I went for a walk. I discovered that the houses in that town were old and grand, the downtown buildings tall and glassy, and the parkway along the water green and in bloom. The cemetery, it turned out, was two hundred years old and shady, and birds sang here.

Janet helped me enroll in more college classes, and while I occasionally cut myself before an exam, I went on seeing her and wearing Band-Aids while making cinnamon buns. Fall and winter went by and then rewound in spring and summer. On and on, again and again.

Sometimes I spoke of the men who had come to Mama's house—guards in gray uniforms that frightened me.

"Here's what happened," Janet said. "Not only did your mother not give you the love you needed—deserved and rightly expected—she gave it to someone else."

Back in the bakery, I rolled and sugared and fried peach, apple, and blackberry pies. We sold out every morning. The boss gave me a raise.

After second- and third- and fourth-year classes, Janet said things like, "Clea, you're not responsible for your mother. Nothing she did was ever your fault."

I'd always thought I was insufficient, never enough for Clarice Shine. Now, from what Auntie had told me, Mama was never enough for her mother, either.

"Can they still arrest me?" I'd asked Janet one day.

"I don't know," she said, and I thought no less of her.

※

"Clea?" Auntie says, and I realize she's said it several times.

A growling has begun, and rises in its fierceness, like animals wild and let loose in the yard.

Uncle jumps to his feet. "It's the river!" he says. He cracks open the back door. He and Wheezer hold tight to the screen, but the wind rips it as though it was a paper kite, and they grip the door frame. Uncle has a flashlight that doesn't shine far but doesn't need to. The river covers the yard, lashed and frenzied into foam. As though it were an angry ocean, it laps the middle step, and murky water and trash are blown into the kitchen, and Bitsy screams.

Uncle leans on the door but cannot turn the bolt or fight the tide. "Everybody upstairs!" he says. He shoves the flashlight at Thomas while he sloshes through to Auntie's room, rips pillowcases from the bed, and begins to empty things from the refrigerator. Luz and I reach into the pantry for bread and cans, and I remember a can opener. We climb up the stairs, lugging plastic jugs and Auntie's lockbox to the upstairs hall. Getting Shookie up, urging Bitsy, who is screaming. We all sit on the top steps and listen while the river grinds and strips the porch steps away and rips off the front door.

When the first window blows out, and the plywood goes, Thomas grabs Harry and Luz, wraps them in a blanket from Wheezer's bed, and takes them to sit on the bottommost steps that lead to the attic.

I think Uncle helps Shookie and the shrieking, always-shrieking Bitsy. I wish someone would slap her.

It is impossible for me to rise from the seventh step. Below, the windows explode one by one, and chairs, tipped and broken, wash out through the doors. Someone has lit a candle upstairs, and calls my name, but I think about others along the lane—how they're surviving. I hear Wheezer, again, saying, *Surviving is just staying alive.* I worry about the inmates at the Farm who are surely manacled and maybe now drowning. I say a prayer for Frank.

And I think of Finn across the field, claiming I'm innocent, and Thomas, right here, telling me I'm guilty.

I feel the house shake and the steps twist under me.

"Get up! Get off the stairs!" Thomas shouts, reaching for my hand, and he drags me up. Behind me, board by board, the steps pop apart and fly off in the night, leaving great gaping holes between the downstairs and where we hunker now—what the devil is holding us up?

The wind feels like a giant, whipping and beating. I see Thomas hold the kids close as glass whistles along the hall. Auntie clutches her face. Uncle calls for the flashlight and presses a handkerchief to her cheek. Someone brings more blankets, and that's when the roar starts—a freight train passing over and around, for certain, and I'm shoving Harry under a bed, pulling Luz in with me. Thomas is here too, flat on his belly on the floor beside us, hands over his head. I don't know where the others are. I'm afraid to move too close to the wall.

Overhead, something snaps—something finite and heavy—the cracking of a huge collarbone, or a skull maybe. Probably the attic roof is gone, and I wait for the trembling floor to tip and send us into a slide, down into the river that's by now flowed across the field and is surely a mile wide.

The wind blows from directions that are legion. More boards pop loose. Water is sucked into the sky.

"Jesus Christ," Thomas says, and he's pulling us out. "We've gotta go up!"

"It's a tornado, Thomas! We have to go down!"

"There *is* no down. Clea, get the kids *up*!"

Harry's slung over his shoulder, and he half carries Luz, and I see the attic staircase with its wall blown away, and someone has gone down in the upstairs hall. I see Wheezer take Luz up. On the topless attic floor, they crouch and are lashed by the rain and soaked to the bone. But, right here, Shookie is screaming.

It's Bitsy, lying outside her bedroom door. I am on my knees in the hall, feeling for a pulse in her neck, calling her name, Uncle calling mine, and then he is here too, groping in the dark. Broken timber is piled on her, on the steps that, a minute ago, went up. Now there are almost no steps at all.

"God, God," Uncle says, and someone is keening. Maybe that's me. "We have to carry her up. Thomas, sir!" But there's nowhere to set so much as a foot, and Thomas pushes rubble out into the night. The strangest things scream away on the wind.

We press against the inside wall. I scramble back into the room, where I drag a sheet from the bed.

"She's gone," Uncle says. "Her neck's broken."

The floor rattles. The three of us do our best to turn Bitsy and wrap her in the sodden sheet. We bump going up, one step at a time. Some risers and planks are missing. *Please, God, don't let her fall through*. My own heart is breaking.

Three more steps.

One. Two more. Then I lie down on the attic floor, hold my children, and huddle under what's left of the roof. Thomas comes and wraps his arms around us.

From here, if it were daylight, I'd be looking out on the land where I was born. I might conjure up Mama, watch through a window while she danced in her high heels. Her feather boa was pink and pretty in the afternoon sun.

Harry has found the blue woolly.

It's cold in the attic, and the wind is still fierce. Harry looks to me, his thumb in his mouth. How can I tell my boy that life is not only a series of devastations? How do I say that to a four-year-old? How can I tell him there's more when I've spent all my life looking for higher ground? And here it is, three stories up, on Potato Shed Road.

Through a window, in a flash of forked light, I think I see Finn in his tree house. Then the oak sweeps away in the flood and is gone.

We hear the familiar whine of nails bending, things breaking.

We hold on, and after a while, the wind subsides. Luz has her inhaler; she breathes out and takes a puff. It's the first time she's used it since we've been here.

I think about something Thomas said. I can hate, all right, and feel sad or excited. I know pain over things lost, but he was right—I can't remember many times when I told anyone I was sorry. Even as a child, with my incessant verbiage, it was probably the one thing I said least.

Nor have I wept much. Now Bitsy is dead. Instead of a wet bedsheet, I wish she were wrapped in fine linen. I lay down by her body, fling my arm across her belly, and cry as though I have never cried. On this night of the storm, I can't stop.

"I'm sorry," I tell her. "I'm sorry, I'm *sorry!*"

On her hands and knees, Auntie comes to me. She sits by me, pats me.

"I'm sorry," I say.

"The worst is all behind you, Clea June."

"But—"

"Sometimes an apology is all you can do."

I cry for Bitsy. I tell her I ache for the misery I dealt her. I weep, too, for Claudie and Genie and Denver Lee. For their mama, for Miss Poole, and for the prisoners at the Farm. I sob for Finn and his daddy, for Miss Izzie Thorne. I cry for my babies, and for Shookie, whose child is cold and dead.

The rain has slacked off, but the night isn't over. Lightning and rolling thunder slam in, dirge after dirge. And the river hasn't crested; the water's still rising. Up here, someone must stay awake and on watch. We scrounge up quilts and things to lay our heads on and take turns drifting in and out of sleep.

Toward dawn, we hear the crack of a rifle, and then another, and Wheezer rolls over and stifles a terrible sound. I think, somehow, he might have been shot, but he is on his knees, hands clasped in prayer. An offender has run, and now has been found and is probably dead.

I too have been found. I'm sad for the child I was. All through the night, I have cried myself sick.

A brilliant new sun is coming up. Uncle's digging into the pillowcases, passing out broken crackers and cheese and quartering apples with his pocketknife. Thomas is rationing half-cups of water.

I lie on my side and stare out where the river used to run, and see, through cracks in the floor, the water that has made us an island. Every piece of junk in Mississippi bobs on its surface.

The False River—about which there has never been anything false—has been fed by a stormy and outraged Pearl, and now trees and chunks of Auntie's home, and others', move around us in a tidal swirl. Across the way, the field looks like a rice paddy. The stems that poke through are actually treetops.

Below us float front doors and porch posts, furniture I don't recognize, wooden pillars, a pickup truck that's upside down. Auntie's Kia is in the driveway; my car and Uncle's truck are gone. Finn's tree has sailed away, downriver.

I hiccup. "Auntie," I say, from where I lay on the floor. "If something happens to me, will you tell my kids I loved them? Will you look after them?"

Auntie is tired and thin-lipped. Her night has been long; her own eyes are red-rimmed. "I will not," she says. "Now, you get yourself up, Clea Ryder, and take care of your own."

44

We wait through the long morning. From here we can look in three directions but are unable to see along the lane to the south, afraid to move around much on our rickety perch. Uncle has ventured halfway down the stairs to the second floor, but the house shakes so badly, he has given it up.

"If we had rope," Wheezer says, "you could lower me over the side."

Auntie says, "If wishes were horses, beggars would ride."

Wheezer grins. "If frogs had wings, they wouldn't bump their asses."

What we do see is dark water, risen around us, on out past the poplar line to the east. To the north, it's covered the ground floor of the big house at Hell's Farm and has washed away most of the outbuildings there. It looks like a lot of people are crowded onto the prison roof. I wonder whether I'm looking at the warden and his staff and maybe the guards up there, or if they've tried to save offenders too. I think of the weight of waist and ankle chains, and wonder how many have drowned.

Harry's rabbit has ridden out the night hanging from Thomas's pants pocket. So Harry has that, and his spoon, and his woolly, and his parents and Auntie and Uncle, who love him. He has Shookie, who has spoiled him but who is now curled on the floor, pillows under her head, mourning a very private loss.

"Mom," Luz says. "Last night, you missed Call."

"I did." I've missed several.

"Tell me what it's like," she says.

I reach for a box of Raisin Bran and offer her some, put a pair of raisins on Harry's tongue. The storm has taken everything from the attic. We have only wet quilts and what things we hauled up from the kitchen.

"Call is about forgetting who you are, Luzie."

"Jeez. Why would you do that?"

"Well, when a person has had a traumatic life, when he's gotten lost in all the bad things that happened to him, it's critical for that person—for every person—to know that he's still important."

"That he matters?"

"Yes. He has worth. That's what I want you and Harry to know. How important you are to me, to your dad, to this world. Okay?"

"Okay."

"Then, after a while— and this usually doesn't happen till you're grown up—"

"You think I'm different from most kids, huh?"

"I know you are. You're wonderful and brilliant and loving and beautiful."

"Cut the *beautiful*, Mom."

"You will be. That's a whole other thing. . . ."

"So *after a while* . . ." she says.

"Yes. Some folks discover an even deeper truth. A very precious truth."

"I'll be twelve in two weeks," Luz says, of whatever I'm about to say. "I'm ready."

I can't help but smile at this amazing daughter. "I'm so blessed to have you."

Harry opens his mouth for more raisins.

"Mom. Okay. You said a 'precious truth.'"

"We learn that we are *more* than our bodies, and our minds and our thoughts. If we subtract the body and the thinking, then *being* is what we have left."

I'm a fine one to talk about subtracting.

"Wow," Luz says. "Without thinking, I bet it gets kind of quiet, huh?"

"Very quiet. Nothing is left but awareness."

"But—my heart will keep beating. My lungs will work. And my kidneys and liver and gallbladder—"

"Exactly. Without your help. You don't have to do anything to just *be*. That's why people stay aware of their breathing when they meditate. Because breathing has no form."

"That's what you guys—the sisters—do at Call? You breathe, and you just *are*?"

"We say a prayer. Then we try."

I might add, *We are very kind to ourselves,* but that's something I keep forgetting. Poor Clea Ryder, child and adult. Been a long, long time since I put my arms around her.

Luz says, "But what if—you know—something's burning on the stove? Or your kid starts crying, or you have to sneeze?"

"That's the thing. You can't push life away. It won't let you."

"Then how do you get quiet so you *can* just be?"

"Well—first you turn off the stove, you make sure the baby's napping or taken care of, then you put your arms around all that you have, all that's around you—embrace all the sounds and the smells—"

"*Embrace*. Snuggle, enfold, wrap up."

"Right. You embrace the circumstances of your life. You sit down in the middle of all that, disconnect from it for a minute, or two minutes, and *just be*."

"What happens to the things around you—like atomic particles and your husband's birthday and stuff?"

"It'll still be there when you're through being. But for a few seconds, or a few minutes, you don't think about anything. And if you have to sneeze, you just sneeze, and then come back to that quiet place."

"Can we practice?"

"We can. Tonight, when I go to Call, you do it with me."

"Why is it called *going to Call,* when you don't really go anywhere?"

"Because when life is hectic, we feel *called* to a saving stillness."

"Mom. I used to think, when you went to Call—you were going somewhere. Away from me."

"Oh, Luzie, no. I take all the wonderful things you are, all the love I feel for you and Harry, and I breathe it in and out at my center, and it makes me a better mom."

I wish it had made me a better wife. Such a lot yet to learn.

"And—I never stop hearing your voice, no matter what I'm doing."

"But you didn't hear the storm that day. At our house."

"No. To tell you the truth, Luzie, I wasn't being quiet inside. I was doing lesson plans and daydreaming."

"You were mad at Dad."

Yes. For some time, I had been "mad at Dad."

"That's all there is to it?" she says. "It's like—meditating?"

"There's more, of course. But that's basically it. And that's enough for one night."

"Give me a hint about the rest," she says. "Like—coming attractions."

"Well, the best things are coming *right now,* and you don't even have to worry about how they'll get here."

"I kinda like this, Mom."

"I'm glad, baby girl. I wish I were better at it. But I'll keep working on it."

"I love you, Mom. I'm sure glad you came by me that day."

"Luz! You *remember* the place where we found you, where Dad and I fell in love with you?"

"It was getting dark in my chicken coop," she says.

"You were so little."

"You wouldn't have seen me if you hadn't struck a match."

45

Time passes by. We spread quilts to dry. Overhead, the sky is the brightest blue I have ever seen, and the air is cool. Uncle says he can see from here to Wednesday.

Where the floor feels the most solid, he has peered over the edge, Thomas holding his ankles. Uncle thinks, under the water, the kitchen walls are intact. But the table and chairs, and the parlor, are gone.

"Water's down some," he says. "But it'll be a while."

"Will someone come and rescue us?" Luz asks.

"You bet," Uncle says. "If nothing else, they'll come because the prison's down the road."

Wheezer hasn't taken his eyes off what's left of the Farm. I know that's where he longs to be. *His people,* I think, *need his presence and his prayers.* Today is Saturday—normally, visitors line up at the gate, waiting to be buzzed in, jockeying for a parking place in the grass. This day, no visitors will come. No visitors will ever come.

Two more shots ring out. I cover my ears, and Luz cries a little.

Before long, we hear the putt of a motor, and Ernie Shiloh arrives in his boat, piloting it downriver, dodging branches, loaded with supplies and rope. He's been handing out bottles of water and sandwiches up and down the way. He's taken on passengers, bundled and shivering, one holding what looks like a broken arm—the young couple who live in the old Oaty place, others.

"Hey, up there!" he yells. "How y'all makin' out?"

"We need down, Uncle Ernie!" Luz calls out.

"Well, ain't that the by-God truth," he says.

His weathered face, once white but now summer-red with the sun, is the best thing we have seen in a long time. "Jerusha, you doin' all right, hon? Ain't nobody sick or hurt?"

Auntie bites at her bottom lip. "We've lost one young woman," Uncle calls down, meaning Bitsy, whose body is wrapped in a blanket.

Ernie shakes his head. "I'm real sorry, Jerusha, Miss Shookie. If we can get your girl down, we'll make room here, and I'll ferry her to town. The funeral home's upstairs is high and dry."

"River's dropping pretty fast," Uncle says. "Come around the other side, Ernie, and tell us what you see. Can you get a ladder up?"

Ernie motors around the house, shaking his head. There's no good place to anchor a ladder. His report is what we know or suspect—the parlor is gone, but the corner timbers seem strong, kitchen's intact, first-floor stairs missing; the second-floor steps to the attic look rickety but might be usable, although part of that wall's been ripped away.

The first order of business is Bitsy. None of us is hurt except Auntie, where she caught a shard of glass in her cheek. It looks to be an inch long, and it's not deep. The bleeding has stopped.

Ernie tosses up a pair of ropes, and Uncle and Wheezer and Thomas truss Bitsy like a Christmas turkey. I watch, dry-eyed, as they strain and lower her over the side. Ernie rolls her onto her back in the bottom of his boat, and people move their feet, and he says with some embarrassment that it might be wise to leave the ropes on her till he's transported her safely. Then he'll come back, double-check the stairs, and help us all down.

Wheezer asks, "While you're this far, Mr. Shiloh, could you carry me to the Farm?"

"Damn mess up there, boy," Ernie says. "Fence down in some places. Y'all hear the shots? If the electrics were working, the siren'd be going off right and left."

"Lord. Convicts are out, running wild," says Shookie, mopping her face with her sleeve.

But Wheezer's mind is set, and he lowers himself over the lip of the attic floor, shinnies down a two-by-four and drops into Ernie's boat, nearly tipping it.

"Be back shortly," Ernie says.

"We're fine," we say, all but Harry, and watch him putt away. He motors on toward the Farm and clear through a space where the high fence used to be. Nobody stops them. Rolls of razor wire are out in the river. Finally, a guard comes and helps Wheezer climb in through an upstairs window. Then Ernie comes back, past our house, just him and the lost and wounded, and Bitsy.

My cousin, Bitsy.

Just past noon, the water has receded enough that we can see the muddy floor in the kitchen below.

And the damnedest thing happens.

We hear Ernie's boat coming down what is probably the middle of the swollen river, but this time it's crammed with people and high, wobbling stacks of cardboard boxes. A long ladder is strapped on top.

He ties the boat up to what was once the front door, and a half-dozen ladies look up and smile. And smile . . .

Sister Isabel!

Sister Grace!

And shy Camille—three in all.

Luz's mouth goes from merely open to wide. Her whole body is quivering. I am stunned and breathless and unable to move.

Here is a fortress that will stand against even Millicent Poole and her demons.

Sister Isabel sees me, holds up her arms, and cries out, "Sister Clea Gloria!"

I nearly fall over the side in my anguish to touch them, to hold them, to know I'm not dreaming. They are really, really here. They're wearing pants and men's workshirts rolled to the elbow and rubber boots—and in the bottom of the boat are more boots!

"We've been passing out food and blankets along your road!" Grace cries.

Isabel says, "And water—don't forget water; we have gallons—and there's more! Sister, trucks are coming into Greenfield this morning. Praise God, I didn't think we would ever get here!"

I wonder about towns along the coast. Camille clasps her hands and tilts her head back so that the sun shines on her face. "Red Cross, the Salvation Army—so many helpers."

But False River has the Sisters of Mercy.

Ernie has decided the old front-porch slab is the best place to anchor a ladder, and he raises it up, and while the sisters wobble in the boat, trying to steady it, he climbs up, steps in through the blown window, tests the bedroom floor, and comes to the foot of the stairs, where the wall is missing.

He calls down, "Hand me up the hammer and bag of nails, ladies!"

My darling Sister Isabel launches herself up the ladder. Ernie works awhile on the stairs, testing each until he and Isabel come up them, one by careful one, and they are in our arms. Or perhaps we are in theirs. I cannot let go of Isabel, nor she me, and then she gathers up Harry and Luz, whom she knows and who love her, and there are introductions all around.

We take the pillowcases with what is left of our food, our water, and quilts, and are led down, careful to keep to the inside wall, crossing what was Shookie's bedroom, and I am swinging my leg onto the ladder, looking down into faces I adore, and sadness sweeps over me:

I should have loved Thomas as much as I love them. As much as I love Luz and Harry. At least that much.

We step into the boat and put on rubber boots. There are small ones for Harry.

Auntie's floor was constructed on three concrete blocks, and, incredibly, the blocks have held. "Prob'ly with the weight of the house," Ernie says.

So we step up to where the parlor floor still is, under sodden carpet and six inches of mud and slime. Then we are all in the house, and there are more introductions, Uncle saying, "I will never remember your names, young ladies."

Camille blushes and tucks a stray wisp under the scrap of scarf that holds her blond hair.

Auntie says, "Ernie, if you can drive this boat of yours back to the shed, there are rakes and shovels. I think we need those first."

"Can do," Ernie says. "Then I gotta get this baby back in the river. Won't be much longer—y'all will be on dry land. Muddy, for sure, but you can move around. Gents, help me unload these boxes." There are sleeping bags and rolls of plastic.

"Ernie," I ask, "are you taking some of this to the prison?"

"No, ma'am, I'm not. Their help should be on the way."

We pile things on the kitchen counter, on the stove, and in the sink, and begin opening cupboards. There are still a few dishes and cans in the back. Thomas finds an old ottoman that has lodged itself against the house. He drags it up and shakes out a plastic bag that he lays over. A place, he says, for Miss Shookie to sit.

He helps her to it, like a queen to her throne. I look away.

Shookie worries about her knitting. She cries a little; she works her hands.

I hunker down so I can see her eyes, swollen almost shut, and take her face in my palms. "I'm so sorry about Bitsy. For all your pain."

I also regret that I've always found Shookie to be a disagreeable old woman. Sister Benefactor always said *Compassion begins at home.* First, I suppose, one must realize they are home.

Is acceptance in the Bible? Of course it is.

Marie-Luz will read and absorb those verses, the way she knows the Dewey decimals. For now, she's watching me. She comes and puts an arm around Shookie. "I'm going to bring you a nice cup of water," she says.

I say, "Later, Luz and I will go upstairs and find a nice dress for Bitsy to be buried in."

The water level goes down more. Before long, Ernie is back in his big-wheeled truck. He tells us that whole concrete slabs were lifted in town, and dropped across roads, making them impassable. Just here, along the lane, he saw a La-Z-Boy reclining up in a tree. In the field across the street where no cows ever grazed, several are dead and bloated, legs sticking straight up. In Greenfield, he says, trailer houses were whipped off their foundations, and cars were flung around like toy trucks.

Thomas's car is behind the church. Ernie doesn't know if it'll run, but he'll bring his truck and tow it home, if Thomas wants. Ernie hasn't seen the others. Thomas asks where the nearest garage is, and Ernie tells him maybe up in Worley's Bend, north of here. He can take it there.

"If it'll wait a day or so, I'll ride along, if you don't mind. See what can be done with it. Pay for your time. And gas, of course."

Ernie's agreeable.

When we take a break and pass around a cup of water, I murmur, "Thanks for bringing Harry's rabbit. And the books. You didn't have to."

"I did have to," he says. "They're my kids too."

"Be some time 'fore y'all have electrics," Ernie is saying as he gets into his truck. "Generators was all bought up last storm, but I'll try to find y'all some candles, maybe a kerosene lamp."

Auntie has kept our matches dry.

I run out and catch Ernie.

"Please take me to Finn's. I'm sure you can get through."

"Can't do it," he says. "I'd have to run up alongside Devil's Creek, and I'd never find the road. They're tellin' folks to stay away from the Farm."

Auntie won't even think about leaving. "This is to be *your* house someday," she tells me. She spreads her hands, and her smile is sad. "It's always been so. When we pass on, Cunny and I are leaving it to you. Not much to look at right now—"

Oh, how I love this land, and the river—and this old house, with its parlor and rocking chair, where I've weathered more storms than memory can count.

"Looks like we'll have to rebuild the whole thing," Auntie says.

We shovel and eat canned pears and cold Campbell's soup

and fancy biscuits from a tin that survived. We rake at the rubbish and sweep the ceilings. Uncle builds a fire on some bedsprings that washed into our yard, and sets the coffee pot on top. We drink from cracked cups. Then we work some more.

Auntie has a wheelbarrow, and we dump the muck across the road in the field that's still underwater. There, these great leafy globs of vegetation will rot in the sun and go back to the earth.

Far up in the yard—almost to Mama's—Uncle Cunny digs a hole for a toilet. Perhaps I will start thinking of that as my land.

"Let me help you there," Thomas says. He gathers broken pieces of cinder block to get our backsides off the ground. They cut an opening that's splintered and fit for no bottom, then file it down and lay it across, and we use two branches to string a curtain around. This is our latrine. For wiping, we'll use an old catalog that's right now drying in the sun. Ernie says he'll see if he can scrounge up a bag of lime.

When the mud is mostly gone from the kitchen counter and stovetop, and the parlor rug's up and the floor is scraped clean, we use lumber that's landed here to fix the holes in the walls in case more rain comes. This being August, that's sure to happen. Best we can, we spread a blue plastic tarp on the roof. The Sisters of Mercy have cleaned and scraped and fetched and dragged and come up with sawhorses and wood for a table.

There was a first-aid box in Auntie's bathroom, and Sister Anne has tended to Auntie's cheek. Thomas's glasses are broken, and I bind the corner with adhesive tape. He looks the way I remember Plain Genie. I ask Ernie about her.

"Fair, I guess," he says. "Her kitchen's tore up. I left her some supplies. She don't talk much."

I know. But she's alive.

That night, we climb up the ladder and arrange ourselves on

the second floor, which Uncle and Ernie have deemed to be safe. In case of looters, we haul our usables up with us. There's a gentle breeze.

I sit on the pallet I've laid for Luz and Harry and me, and take Luz gently through Call. I, myself, embrace all that I'm grateful for. I've used a lot of mental energy in the last twenty-four hours, looking back at who I used to be. But not as much as I spent, years ago, alternately loving and hating my mother.

Mamas, through their strengths and weaknesses, pass everything on. They teach daughters, who teach *their* daughters, and so it goes, one set of hurts coming down to another. Then I look up at the stars and tilt my head and remember something my therapist once told me, to see the other side of that coin.

There is no such thing as always doing our best. How utterly exhausting that would be. We just do what we do. And maybe it's enough.

I know where my mother did her best—and with whom. Just doing what she did was not enough for her child. Only I can break that chain, fix the past and the present. It pains me to think that Thomas is right.

I'll begin now.

I snuggle next to Luz and stroke her hair. "I'm so sorry it's sometimes hard for you to breathe."

She smiles a little and closes her eyes.

The night is quiet, no crickets chirruping. Then—and maybe it's just my girl's labored breathing, but I think I hear music, honky-tonk in slow motion, ragtime on the wind. That once-fast plunking music has now become a slow, hurting waltz.

✶

The gulls are gone; we're left with one unholy mess, no electricity, no running water. We slog up and down Potato Shed Road, seeing who needs what—candles, matches, drinking water, canned peaches. Things that will keep without refrigerators, and packaged tightly too, so as not to draw rats. Everything is draped in wet leaves and weed. Cars are on porches. Dogs are dead; we are quick to bury those. We build cook fires in yards, open tin cans, whisper blessings and encouragement, and set to untangling a fisherman's net from somebody's door.

On Auntie's property, it's hard to find anything dry enough to burn, but Thomas and Uncle Cunny drag broken junk from the house—some of it ours. We burn what's useless and save the nails. Sister Grace has been given a hammer and a plastic bag, and was put onto yanking nails from any drifting thing she can find. Sister Camille hums softly as she works—something Auntie used to sing, but I can't remember its name or the words.

Up and down the road, people we know, and do not know, look broken in the eyes, hauling branches and bits of flotsam to their bonfires. Some houses defy logic, their underpinnings washed out and whipped off to who knows where. First floors are gone, while the second floors are left standing. Who'd ever have thought the Pearl, and our placid False River, could have done so much damage?

Genie Maytubby has lost part of her back wall, and her stove and furniture washed away.

Ernie comes around three times a day in his big-wheeled truck. In spite of sheriff's orders, he's been past the Farm and over to Finn's. He reports that the goat is gone, and so is the shack, the dog. He's checked Devil's Creek.

"Likely drowned," Ernie says.

I pinch my lips together.

"Or," Auntie tells me, "he doesn't want to be found. Clea, baby, you leave that boy be."

46

Then Wheezer comes home, and somehow it's Monday. I insist on holding class. He walks me down. His clothes are caked with mud, and I wonder, *When was the last time he ate?* He looks a little like he did the first time I saw him.

Because the fence and gate are twisted and inoperable, guards are posted around the Farm's perimeter.

Most of the low buildings have been knocked off their blocks and tipped into the river. Two went over the bank of Devil's Creek, which will have to be searched for bodies and dredged for debris before there's more flooding.

I wait for Wheezer to toll the count.

He says, "Seventy-four dead, six of those shot. Eighteen more missing."

"My God."

"We're keeping the eighteen under our hats, though they're long gone by now."

"What's happened to the big house?"

"Beaten to hell. Foundation's all cracked. Northwest corner broke off and went in the river. Took the kitchen and the infirmary with it. We dug six guys out with our hands. One was our doc, Clea. Here on his own time. Jesus Lord, if I ever wanted a drink, it was then. Now."

He sucks a deep breath and puffs out some air. "Corrections Department will send buses for the rest. Takes time when other prisons are full too, and have to shift things around. State sent us army rations, but we can't let 'em open their own damn tins— meanwhile, they're eating and sleeping on the ground. And we've got a makeshift infirmary set up here in the yard.

"We've cleared out the big stuff that washed up—refrigerator, sofa, broken umbrellas, anything these guys could use to hurt themselves or each other, piled it up across the road. Might have Jerusha look, see if some of her belongings are there—"

There is most of one fence left. Where it's lying over, the space has been patched with wire and, because there are no safe buildings, everything's been moved out into the open. This means there are no classrooms, no cages, no tables left. Raoul, Wesley, Frank, and Willie G. sit in bandy-legged chairs in one corner of the yard. The best chair faces them. It is for me.

Someone says, "Ma'am?"

I look up at a new man, dark skin, orange stripes, and he's barefoot, with his pants legs rolled up.

He says, "Chaplain said I could join up."

"Of course. Here—take my chair."

"No, ma'am." He folds himself down on the still-wet ground. "Name's Roland Maytubby."

Maytubby? "Are you any relation to the Maytubbys down the road?"

"Yes'm, they my kin. Genie's my sister."

Lord, Lord. "Does she know you're all right?"

"Yes, ma'am. She came to the fence, and I talked to her 'fore they caught me and dragged me away."

"I—I used to play with your sister. Claudie."

"Yes, ma'am."

No judgment, no expectation on his face. Just waiting. The guard who brought him is stone-faced and beak-nosed.

I lean toward them with knees together, pencils and paper on my lap, and elbows on my thighs, palms pressed as if I am praying. "All right. I read your stories from Friday—" Has it been only that long? "I admire you guys for knowing who you are, in the middle of—this."

Even if they don't have a clue, I think. *Even if they made up everything, and they're shining me on.*

I spread my hands. "After I read them, I put them in the trunk of my car for safekeeping. Now nobody knows where my car is."

"Then we glad you din' have to drive here," Raoul says, trying for humor. Nobody laughs. "Hey, we got no bunks, no soap, no coffee, but we got a teacher, right—you ain't washed away."

"I didn't wash away."

"When you find our papers," Wesley says, "go on and keep 'em. We got nowhere to put anything, no cells, no footlockers."

"Everything's gone," Frank says, looking at me. *Frank, who was so afraid he'd be chained and go under.*

"You survived," I tell him. "Where is Horse?"

"Upstairs hall come down on him," Willie G. says, his face turned away, speaking to no one. "He's—in the infirmary."

"Can I see him?"

"You got clout with Mr. Stengle."

I pass out paper that I've scrabbled for, and stubs of pencils that Uncle sharpened with his pocketknife, and a couple of old pens.

"Today, let's write fiction. We'll make up a character, show him in a setting, but not here"—I wave my hand, and that brings the guard. I shoo him away. "Start with your character doing something physical."

Their opportunity to say something lewd slides away.

"We're looking at his movement, muscles stretching, the lengths of bones, the way people stand up or sit down."

"These private, for sure?" Willie G. asks.

"They are private."

"Other ones was too," Frank says. "Now they floatin' somewhere in Alabama."

Wesley says, "Teacher not responsible for no hurricane! Nobody knows you there, anyways."

They all nod and tilt their heads and think. And they write. Roland too. In twenty minutes, they hand me papers that are barely legible and full of pencil-point holes from writing on their knees.

Raoul wants to share. He's written about Miss Betty Inez, dancing on the stage of the Ivory Club in Juárez. While he reads of her tassels and fringes and gyrations, Frank and Wesley rear back in their chairs and hoot and slap their thighs, and Frank's dragged up by the guard, whose baton is now drawn.

I settle things down.

Our time is up, and the guard takes them away. They're not allowed to carry their chairs. Maybe this corner of the yard is now the visiting room.

As always, I read while I walk. Wesley has written about a man washing sand from collard greens in his kitchen, setting the leaves to cook with ham hocks and red-pepper flakes. At the end, there's a message for me.

Now on, teacher, you call me Black Monday.

P.S. Monday, for short.

Willie G.'s character has crossed a line, and is hunted by dogs with ears flattened and drooling lips and snapping teeth. The dogs draw back on their haunches, then leap across a river. Through the woods on the far side, the man flounders on.

Willie's writing himself, of course. What if he's telling me he's going to run?

I ask for Francis and wait while someone fetches him. "Wheezer, I want to see Horse; can you fix it? In the infirmary. Please."

We make our way through the broken brick and cinder block, legless cots and twisted tables, urinals, battered kitchen pots. A dozen army cots are set up, and two men with batons are in attendance, while two inmates work over the injured guys. There are splinted legs and arms, one man groaning, one crying into his wrapped hand. Horse lies on the farthest cot, curled on his side, almost unrecognizable under bandages made from torn sheet. Blood has seeped through.

"Horse," I say, and get down on my knees, my mouth so close I can smell his scabbing, his congealing blood. His bones look brittle, his skin stretched tight. He's so fragile. I wonder—if I touch him—would he break. . . .

"Teacher," he says, sounding smaller than Luz, as small as Harry. "Hold my hand?"

"Ain't allowed," says the guard.

I take Horse's hand.

He does not break.

47

Another shot.

God help him, I hope Willie G. has not run. When Wheezer comes tonight, I'll ask him to intervene. Poor Willie, he'll know I've betrayed his confidence. Then they'll pen him up. Chain him down. Put him under suicide watch.

Bitsy is buried at eleven o'clock. The funeral-home car can now make its way through town, through the mud and the junk, to the cemetery in back of First and Last Holy Word Church. Shookie has chosen a white casket with painted roses. I think I won't go to the service. I can't.

"Of course you will," Sister Isabel says. "We'll support you. We'll hold you in our arms."

Miss Minnie Roosevelt, who once came to our back-porch concert, and who grew old without marrying, is going to sing "Amazing Grace."

Ernie, in his best Levi's and steel-toed boots, and with his truck's windshield scrubbed for the occasion, has brought an orange. He peels it and pockets the bits, divides it into sections for Luz and Harry. They scarf it up. I close my eyes in relief.

We clean ourselves the best we can and climb aboard the

truck. Harry sits in front with Ernie and Shookie. He's wearing a pair of overalls that drifted by Saturday, on the flood. I said *Thank you*. Then I washed them and dried them, and they fit him fine.

It's a short drive to town. The church, on the far end of Main, looks like it could use some repair, and I wonder how much of that is because of the storm. Ollie Green, in a blue suit, meets us there. I look around the cemetery, at all the newly heaped earth, graves that were dug in the last couple of days. A dozen stick markers have sprouted like weeds, with names painted on.

Miz Millicent is here, in a faded housedress and a black wig that's too big. The hair is too thick; the bangs hang in her eyes. Wheezer has come too, and Genie Maytubby, who stands off a ways with a girl in a very short skirt—and the nice folks from the Oatys', her arm in a cast. In the farthest corner of the cemetery, the new preacher is conducting another funeral—three weeping people around a plain wooden box.

Our Bitsy has the best.

The service is short. Minnie sings in a wobbly voice, and she moves us to tears. "'. . . Once was lost but now am found. Was blind, but now I see.'"

"Ashes to ashes and dust to dust . . . in the sure and certain hope . . ."

After the prayer, we move apart for the requisite visiting. When Reverend Ollie, with Millicent Poole at his heels, asks me how long I'll be staying, I have no answer.

He says, "You doin' a fine thing at the Farm, Sister Clea, and those men need you. You're a holy woman."

Millie Poole steps up. "Ollie Green, you're a fool. None of them Shines was no way holy."

"Now, now," says the Reverend.

Losing Bitsy and the house and all that we own has taught me that every connection is valuable—but this one is plain hard. It has plagued me since I was old enough to be Millicent Poole's victim. Now she's grown old and feeble and pencil-mark thin. I'm surprised she has come. Her eyes are gone to slits, her mouth permanently pulled up in a nasty smirk, and she keeps turned away, like I'm something that's catching.

I walk over to Genie and touch her one arm. "I'm so glad you're here. How's your place? Can we help?"

"Denver Lee's comin'," she says, tight and pulled in, and clinging to the girl. "He be he'pin' me."

The time for tiptoeing is past. "I'd like to walk down, if you don't mind. We can talk, you and I."

She looks at me with those dark, angry eyes, through those thick, thick glasses.

"Please," I say.

"My kitchen's tore up. And I ain't got nothing to say."

"That's okay. We'll make a fire in the yard, a pot of coffee. I want to tell you I'm sorry for the way I treated you when we were kids. It was arrogant of me, and very wrong."

Her face says nothing.

"Genie—when we were going to school, you and me and Claudie, I recall that reading didn't come easy for you. *No—hear me out.*" I rush on. "That's what I do now—I teach adults to read."

"You think I's worthless 'cause I can't cipher?"

"No! Genie, you have more worth than I, more than all of us put together. I just thought—while we're sitting, and having coffee—I mean, if you *couldn't,* and if you *wanted* to read, I could teach you. I'd like that."

Her chin is up. "I never had good eyes."

The girl has a tattoo of a parrot on her neck. She squeezes Genie's arm.

I nod. I'll write big looping letters, and somewhere we'll find a magnifying glass, maybe get her eyes checked.

"I know. Oh, please, please, Genie, don't think I'm being up-pity—I just wanted to do something for you. I don't mean to sound full of myself, it's just something I can offer. As a friend. If you'll let me. If—if Claudie was here, and she couldn't read well, I'd sit down with her and show her that the whole world lies on a single page. It's just—I didn't want this chance to pass you by."

Lord, Lord, I'm talking too much.

"I'll think on it," she says.

The pretty girl smiles and puts her arm around Genie.

"This be Chloe," Genie says. "She Claudie's girl."

I feel my eyes go wide. Claudie's girl? *Claudie's girl?*

The new baby, the orphaned Chinese boy, was to be a little brother for her. I can't tear my eyes away. Chloe is tall and sweet-faced, drawn on and pierced through in a dozen places. She has both her arms. I love her at once.

I cannot help laughing.

"I'll bring the coffee," I say. "And my daughter, Luz."

There is to be no feast after Bitsy's funeral; there's no one to bring food.

Thomas says, "Let's walk back, Clea, just you and me. Luz will look after Harry. I think she's hoping we'll work things out."

There is a rifle shot, then. I hear it but feel it first, in my feet. It travels upward, splitting me like an earthquake. Thomas puts an arm around me. He looks more tired than I've ever seen him. His eyebrows are in disarray, his glasses taped. I want to smooth down his hair.

"Clea. That girl, the one in my office—"

"Sunny." I move away.

"Yes. It's bad enough that I did it. I'm so sorry you saw. Did the kids see . . ."

"No."

"I've known for a long time how sick that was, and how sad. I was just so damned empty. You had the kids, and your work—"

"You had your work too. You are—were—a respected teacher. Do they know, the others, the rest of the staff?"

Thomas shakes his head, but it's not a *no*. He has that yet to deal with. "I made a fool of myself. Jeez, I really thought I needed her—them. For a while, they made me feel young. I was—scared," Thomas says.

"Of what?"

"I don't know—maybe getting old."

This poor cemetery. So many stones have fallen over or broken, graves sunken in.

"Did it work?" I ask. "With the girls? Did they make you feel young?"

He sighs. "I couldn't keep up. They made me older."

We walk awhile.

"We lived in the same house, but we've been apart for a long time," I say. "Even while we were finishing the paperwork on Harry."

"Yes," he says.

The air is so clear here, washed by the storm.

"Thomas—do you remember that little coffee shop near the beach, where we used to go?"

I do."

"You'd bring Ruff, and we'd drink lattes and give him blueberry muffin."

He laughs a little. "Sometimes we'd walk down and watch the

waves come in. I loved that sound. I can't ask you to forgive me. Too damn many transgressions. God, I regret it all."

I pinch my lips together. I know transgressions.

"The more time went by, the more separated I felt from you. I realized there are parts of you I don't know—like this one." He spread his hands, meaning *Here, False River*. "You kept to yourself, right from the start."

"Yes."

"I'm embarrassed to admit, until I saw it on our marriage license, I didn't even know your real name was Clarice."

"Not something I like to share. Or remember. But—you're a professor of biology, Thomas. You dissect things. I'd think you'd be curious. You never asked me anything."

He shakes his head. His gray hair flops. "In the lab I know what I'm going to find."

So it is *then*—for the first time ever—I tell Thomas my story. I begin with the day I was born and give him the long version. I tell him about Uncle Cunny teaching me under the willow, about school, and Claudie. I talk about my mama and the fire. I do not tell him about Finn's confession.

"Sometimes," he says, "you were like two different people. Closed off to me, but then you'd go and pick up somebody off the street."

"Closed to you because you knew me—open to them because they didn't."

"But we're talking now. Maybe that's an omen."

"Of—"

"I don't know. We'll figure things out, together?" he says. "When you and the kids left, I begged the sisters to tell me where you were."

"Which one caved?"

"Sister Anne. Clea, there's something else too. When your book first came out, I read it and liked it well enough—but I didn't see how it could possibly be true."

"Your own life was sad. No family—"

"I'm really sorry."

There's a lot of sorry going around.

"Me too," I say. "But being sorry isn't enough—for us. For this."

"I know. First things first —" He gestures timidly, as though he's afraid of pricking my balloon. "You realize Havellion is a prison only for men."

"It's one of those absurd things I haven't been able to reconcile. All this time I couldn't come back because I was sure I'd be arrested. I was afraid of the prison."

Maybe I was afraid I might have to say sorry.

"You have to get that weight off your shoulders," Thomas says. "Here's what we'll do—we'll have Mr. Shiloh drive us to— where's the courthouse, the county seat?"

"Greenfield. Oh, Thomas, what if the file's still open, and I'm arrested and charged with her murder!"

"Enough," Thomas says. "You need to hear it; you need to know."

48

Before we go home, Ernie's going to carry us to town. Uncle sounds chipper, but there's a lump in his throat. "It'll only take half an hour."

Or thirty years.

Shookie comes too.

At the sheriff's office, Ernie waits outside with Luz and Harry. Harry's cross-legged in the dirt, drawing pictures with a stick. Uncle has given him an old army canteen, and Harry keeps it half filled with water and strapped over his shoulder and across his chest. He wore it to the funeral; he's wearing it now. He's in ready mode with his survival gear.

Luz's face is full of questions. I sit on a folding chair in the sheriff's office, looking out at her. Auntie and Shookie sit still as stone, their purses in their laps. Thomas's hands rest lightly on my shoulders.

I hold my breath.

The sheriff, who was probably a toddler at the time of the fire, says, "Yes, ma'am, there is a file on that case. Right here in my cabinet. I know it well."

"You're not old enough to remember," I say.

He grins some. "Older than I look, ma'am, and I do recall it. And I've had a phone call or two since you got here. Before the storm."

"Who called you?" I say.

"'Fraid I can't say."

Thomas says, "What can you tell us?"

"Three people dead. Victims were one adult female, two males identified as guards from the Farm."

I pinch my lips and breathe in and out.

"Pardon me for saying this, ma'am, her being your ma—but she's a legend around here. Too damned many people hated Clarice Shine. Every lady in town and half the men—she knew everybody's secrets. One of the dead guards' wives had divorced him. The other had no kin, far as we could find out. Way I see it, we're never gonna know who started that fire. Coulda been Clarice herself. State agreed. Case was closed a long time ago."

Closed.

All my life, I have nurtured and babied and raised up this fear, twisted it every which way I could think of. I've kept it watchful and fast and sure-footed. And all that time, it was my own true self that made me so afraid. My guilt, my sorrow, and Millie Poole's curse.

Just now I'd like to strangle her.

I can't stop shaking.

Work needs to be done in my head and in my heart. How the *hell* do you shuck off a curse?

When we step outside, Uncle looks at the sky, blue and clear, and says, "Don't you spend time being sorry about your subtracting, baby girl. You were torn in half and bleeding. You stayed alive."

Auntie tilts her head and admits, "We had a plan. Girl, you

were stubborn and a pain in the ass. But if they went and claimed you did it, we were gonna go to the sheriff—Cunny, Ernie, Shookie, and me—and say we each started the fire our own selves."

I stare at the gravel in the street. The broken sidewalk. I understand why Harry is silent, how his words fail him.

Uncle smiles. "We woulda confused the hell out of things. Listen," he says, "on our way home, let's stop by Millie Poole's, see how she's getting on."

"Confuse her too," Ernie Shiloh says.

"Not me," says Auntie. "I had enough for one day. Take me and Shookie home."

49

Smoke rises in wisps all up and down the river, burning trash, fires for cooking. The rest of us get out at Millicent Poole's. Ernie takes Auntie and Miss Shookie on home.

Right here, where Miz Millicent's garden used to be, is where I caught Auntie's gray goose. Now it's hard dirt and bramble. She looks small and lost in her wig, sifting through waterweed with a stick, poking at what's left of her place—two walls gone, some roof flown away, rooms gutted. She's living in a tiny corner of her house. Ernie and Uncle hang a piece of plastic where one bedroom wall used to be, so she can sleep there, dry. They find her stove by the river, and drag it up, cleaning connections, checking cords, hooking it up.

" 'Lectricity comes on, Miz Millie," Ernie tells her, "I'll come back to see how this ol' stove's makin' out."

She nods.

In the side yard, Reverend Ollie snaps twigs and feeds them into the fire. Even Thomas pitches in.

Miz Millicent wheezes. "I hear you're down 'ere, teaching 'em boys to write their *memoirs*." She makes it sound illegal. Pornographic. I see by Luz's face that she has heard.

"Something like that. Miz Millicent—"

"I remember you, gal. Full of the devil with your backtalk. Always in need of a good whippin', you ask me. Now you got that boy, demon's took him too, snatched the talkin' right out of his head."

I inhale. "Miz Millie, you have any recollection of being a little girl yourself?"

She looks sideways. "What's that got to do with anything?"

"You were a child once. Born in innocence. As a baby, you weren't set upon by demons, nor the devil."

"We ain't talkin' about me."

"Well, maybe we should."

"What makes you think you know so much?"

"Because I was just a child, Miz Millie. Innocent like you. My mama didn't want me. Every little child wants its mama."

"I don't—recall mine," Millicent says, and I think—*or you don't want to.*

"I was lost. But it was my mother—a real person—who lost me. I wasn't touched by demons. Nor were you."

Miz Millie's eyes cast around and light on Luz. "So now you workin' at the Farm."

"Yes."

The storm has taken its toll on more than Miz Millicent's land. Strands of wig hair cling to her ears and her wattled neck. She turns watery eyes on me. "Don't think for a minute those sons-abitches gonna let you inside their shaved heads."

She sounds like Shookie. I use Ernie's hammer and pull nails from a length of wood. "They're a lot of men who made bad choices, Miz Millicent. No demons involved. They chose where they are."

She makes a snorting sound. Suddenly she looks hurt and afraid.

"Truth is, they've got things to say, Miz Millicent, like all of us. You got things too, I bet. Sometime, I'd be happy to listen."

"That place down there, Clarice's lot, it's full of demons—"

"Well, then, I'll work on sweeping them out. 'Cause it's my place now. Might be nice if you'd come down and say one last prayer—"

The hollows and planes of her face work themselves into something else. "Reckon I could, but—don't you be stupid, girl. Them men down there ain't gonna tell you nothin'—not what they done, or about folks they let down."

Something new is in the wind. She lifts her rake and combs leaves from the prongs.

"I don't care what they write," I say carefully. "As long as they do it."

Her eyes narrow. "Tellin' lies, that's what."

I put down my hammer. "They're doing all right. I don't mind that they shine me on."

Nearby, Luz is listening too.

"Girl, don't go gettin' attached," she says, and shakes her head once. "They'll steal your heart and cheat you past Wednesday."

"I'm sorry?"

She's wearing a flannel shirt, sleeves too long and rolled up. Her eyes are jittery. "Where's Ollie Green—"

"Miz Millie—did you have a man—some family, a true love—down at the Farm?"

"Don't you speak to me about love," she says. *"Where's that Reverend?"*

"You had a man in the prison, I *know* you did—"

"I'm just a bedeviled ol' woman. Get on about your business. Leave me be."

The smoke burns my nose. "Miz Millie, let's sit here on the porch step. Come on, now."

I lead her gently. She rocks back and forth and hugs her elbows. "Goddamn thing is hot," she says, and pulls off her wig. Wisps of red hair are stuck to her scalp. I sit on one side of her, Luz on the other. "I need Ollie to take me for my shot."

"Your shot?"

She lifts her chin, the way Genie did. Maybe it's something about living on Potato Shed Road. "My methadone shot."

I remember her opium den with its smoke rolling out on the porch. No wonder that goose was happy, tramping in her gardens, eating her grapes. I can't say I haven't wondered what's become of her habit. "Miz Millie, that's great. You're going to a treatment center. How long have you been on methadone?"

"Ten year, on and off," she says stiffly. "Some good times, some bad. Ollie helps me."

Luz is watching Miz Millie's face.

I say, "We're glad to hear it, aren't we, Luz?"

Luz takes an old hand in her dusky one. She says, "How can I help, Miss Millie? What can I do?"

My daughter. My Luz.

"You're the smart one that reads," Millicent Poole says.

"Yes," Luz says. "How did you know that?"

"I hear everything. You ain't her girl, her own bred child."

"I'm adopted," Luz says. "So is my brother, Harry. I love my mom, and yes, I do read. Would you—would you like me to read to you sometime?"

Miz Millicent stares at Luz. She has been taken by the shakes. Ollie Green sees and come to her. "Millie, it's time we take a little drive," he says. "My car's down the road. I'll fetch it now."

I lay my hand lightly on her rounded back. She has the spine of a bird. "You had someone at the Farm. Is he still there?"

She exhales like it's the first time ever. Like she's letting out toxins. "He was a black man. A fine man. I gave up every-thing—my mama and daddy—to be with him."

I nod.

She's shaking harder but lets Luz stroke her. "Before he went there, he had a true heart. One month in a cell, he was as fulla hisself as the day is long. That's what prison does, you know. Said it weren't that he didn't love me—his mind was wild with bad dreams, had to watch his back every minute, an' he didn't need to worry about me too."

Incredibly, I hurt for Millie Poole. "How long ago was that?"

"Thirty year. I coulda packed up and moved home, I guess, but—"

"You didn't want to—"

"Didn't want my family sayin' 'I tol' you so.' Truth was, all my heart was gone."

"You went on loving him—"

She begins to cry. "I used to send money, make sure he got things, you know? Till he had no more use for me. 'Fore long, he had ladies—pen-pal letters and more presents than a man knew what to do with."

"But you used to go see him?"

Her fists are balled tight. Life depends on her rocking. "That first year, every Sunday. He got put on a field gang, a hoe squad. Monday through Friday, they'd march past on the road, chained at the feet. They'd come back around sunset, sun-blistered and stinkin'; you could smell them from here. Gal, you seen 'em."

I had. Many times.

"Oh, when he said he was done with me, I argued. But he said he had to let me go. It weren't the way of life at the Farm to be faithful."

"Is he still there?"

Ollie Green pulls up in his car. Luz and I help her up. Miz Millicent's face is tight and trench-dug.

"What does it matter?"

She's shaking. I reach for a blanket in the Reverend's car, cover her shoulders. Close her door and say through the window, "Miz Millie—I'm just wondering—what was his name?"

"His name is William. An upstanding name."

"Yes, it is."

"William Garnett. Willy. We was married when he'd been inside one week and four days—even though we knew he was never comin' out again."

An odd little chirp rises up in my throat.

I set off running.

Jesus Christ.

Jesus Christ.

Wheezer has kept an eye on our man. All week, in class, I've talked about nothing but writing. I'm worried sick.

Miz Millicent, after a shot of methadone and much cajoling on our part, has partially agreed to my plan. But she's reserved the right to back out at any second.

On Saturday morning, Luz and I show up with a broken compact of makeup, an eyebrow pencil and a brush, a cotton summer dress we've borrowed from the nice lady who lives at the Oatys'.

We've scrounged up a tub, and we hang sheets and heat water and pour in bubble soap.

Luz says, "Mom. We're a spa!"

Luzie and I hold up towels while our "client" takes off her clothes and sets herself down, making whimpering and somewhat prayerful sounds. I wonder how long it's been since she sat in a tub. With our eyes averted, we soap her up, scrub her with a soft brush, and rinse her skin gently. Then we wrap her in towels and pat her dry and sit her in a chair, apply cheap moisturizer that I found at the dollar store.

"You smell wonderful," I say. "Like a real southern lady."

I apply powder to her cheeks and chin.

She wails and moans.

"You'll be fine," Luz says. "Miss Millicent, you're already the belle of the ball."

"I don't know, I don't know."

She weeps, and we cover her tears with more makeup, and she cries again.

I work conditioner into her scalp.

"I need my wig," she says. "I got to wear a hat."

"No, ma'am," I tell her. "You're pretty as a picture." I comb her hair back with my fingers and catch it up in a black ribbon that used to be Ernie Shiloh's string tie.

"Lookit me," she says, miserably. "Demons came on me, that's what. The devil took me. Pulled out my hair, wizened my face. You cain't fix that."

"Those weren't demons, Miz Millie. That was time. And worry. And love, not used up." I open the top button of her dress and apply makeup to her throat. Along the road, yesterday, I found a long string of cheap pearls. I've cleaned the mud from them, and polished them, and I hang them around her neck. I touch lipstick to her pruny mouth. Millicent Poole looks like a whole other person.

Also, today, the sisters are leaving. Last night, there was a great deal of hugging and kissing. Right about now, they're probably piling into Ernie's truck.

"Oh," Miz Millicent wails. "I changed my mind. I ain't goin'."

"What a shame to waste such beauty," I say.

"You are lovely," Luz tells her. "Stunning. Winsome."

Ernie chugs along the lane as Luz and I stand there, applying lotion to Millie Poole's thin wrists and arms.

The sisters wave.

I lift a hand in deepest thanks and say, "Raise your head, Miz Millie. Love is passing by."

⋇

I was wrong about visiting day. A sagging chain fence has been erected down the middle of the prison yard. Offenders line up on one side, company on the other. In the corner of the yard, the five chairs are still standing. Wheezer has commandeered that space for us, and it's a good thing. Miz Millicent is trembling so hard, I don't think she could stand. And it's not because she needs a shot.

I hold her hand and squeeze tight while her man walks over. I can see that he is as scared as she is.

My belly is caving, my heart bursting. What must the two of them be feeling?

"Miz Millicent Poole," I say grandly. "Mr. Willie G.Willy. William, it's nice to see you on a Saturday."

"Miz Ryder," he says, without looking this way. "Millie. Oh, Millie—"

They each take a seat.

And that is enough.

50

There is nothing left, now, but to face my mother's house—rather, the land it once stood on. And there's not much there.

I'm standing in the twilight, in the grass that has lifted from the flattening of the hurricane. I'm alone. Alone. A soft wind sighs through the oaks along the river that is now sleeping. Calm. Calm, a lullaby.

I have given this house—and by extension, my mama—all the chances they deserved, and I have given the land all the angst I can spare.

I say to the bits of foundation and pipe, to the back steps that lay rotting on their side, "I'm not sorry. I'm not. It would be wrong to say I am."

Thomas and I walk the lane one last time. I tell him, "I grew up on Potato Shed Road. Every day I saw the prison, the wire winking in the light. I thought I knew our neighbors. But I didn't. I was a child, as self-centered as a child must be, and I never made the connections."

Thomas says, "Before, I didn't believe in miracles—"

"And now?"

"I do. Clea, I will never cheat on you again. I love you. Will you come home with me? I was thinking we could find a good therapist."

I love you. He's waiting for me to say it back.

"Thomas, I can deal with only one thing at a time. Go home, will you, and clean up Lilac Lane?

"Luz and Harry and I are going to stay another month so I can meet with my class, help Auntie and Uncle get back on their feet. Then I'd like to take the kids to Belize City, enroll them in school. Luz can speak her native language. Harry'll have lots of kids to play with—most of them living tougher lives than his. I'll work at the Sisters of Mercy clinic."

"But—"

"For a year, Thomas. We all need this. Then—the kids want to come back to the river. There are plenty of people to help me clear the land, maybe build a cottage. There's already talk of building a boys' reformatory where the Farm was."

"And," Thomas says. "You and me?"

"We'll see," I tell him. "Just wait, and we'll see."

Maybe I'll come back and write another book.

51

I have rented two rooms, plain-scrubbed, near the canal. The kids and I love it. They've drawn autumn leaves and fat turkeys, and we've cut them out and taped them to the walls. We've sent twenty postcards home to False River, and Luz writes long, descriptive letters to her dad. Luz, who's turned twelve, is captivated with the work at the clinic, where, after school, she labors harder than anybody. She helps me watch Harry, who attends all-day kindergarten and plays ball with the other boys in a street blocked off behind the market.

Luz has discovered that books in the stall around that corner cost only a few cents.

Auntie received a letter from Izzie Thorne, and she forwarded it to me. Miss Izzie is in Africa, just now, disbursing money she raised to dig water wells. I have no doubt she'll get the job done.

November comes, and Thomas flies to Belize. He joins us in a little café for a Thanksgiving dinner of wild rabbit and fried calabaza. The kids lift glasses of cold *horchata*—boiled rice water with milk and vanilla and sugar.

Mostly he and they wander the marketplaces, among the cheap cameras and painted Mayan plates and strings of green chilies. I want never to keep my children from him—I envy them knowing their father at all.

I knew only my mother, and what a mess that was. In the last year of her life, I struck a lot of matches.

It was I, of course, who set the fire the night she died. I took the cigarette from her mouth, went out to the porch, and touched it to the floor by the cot where I lay. I watched a circle of wood blacken and grow larger and begin to smolder, saw the flame ignite. I had no thought for Mama or anyone else. If I burned up, it would be the end of all our troubles.

Perhaps Finn was there; maybe he saved me, dragged me down to the river. Somebody did. And maybe, last summer, when I saw him in the woods, he thought by confessing, he could save me again.

In the mornings, the four of us walk to the cathedral where Luz and I sit in Call with other sisters. Today my knees are bare, my denim skirt short. Luz has chosen one just like it. Her hair is wrapped in a triangle of cloth. Harry leans comfortably over her lap.

When we all say *Amen,* he hooks his chubby arm around her neck, pulls her down, and whispers in her ear. Thomas and I watch. A moment passes. Harry does it again.

Luz whispers back.

Harry smiles up at us. Timid. Like a baby emerging from an unfolding womb. A newborn lamb with a voice.

Thomas puts an arm around my shoulders.

"Gloria," I say.

We. Shall. Not. Be. Moved.

In Appreciation

In the making of this book, I want to thank the people of southern Mississippi. I am truly sorry for your many natural devastations. It's easy to see why you keep returning.

Eternal blessings on Robert, Barbara, and Annette who looked up and saw me standing there.

And now (drum roll, please): to the incomparable Danny Baror, for believing in my voice; and to Kate Miciak, who is my dear friend as well as my bright-and-shining editor, thank you from all the corners of my heart. Kate, you are surrounded by the most wonderful crew.

As ever, Kathryn, *gracias* for reading and questioning me. Hugs and kisses to the Dead Writers, who lent their eyes and ears, and blessings for all time on other friends who listened and listened.

And of course to Gary and all my family—I love you, I love you.

About the Author

CAROLYN WALL is an editor and lecturer. As an artist in residence, she has taught creative writing to more than four thousand children. She is the author of the award-winning debut *Sweeping Up Glass*. Wall lives in Oklahoma, where she is at work on her third novel.

About the Type

This book was set in Albertina, a typeface created by Dutch calligrapher and designer Chris Brand. His original drawings, based on calligraphic principles, were modified considerably to conform to the technological limitations of typesetting in the early 1960s. The development of digital technology later allowed Frank E. Blokland of the Dutch Type Library to restore the typeface to its creator's original intentions.